Praise for *The Art of Confidence* DISCARDED BY THE
URBANA FREE LIBRARY

"Using a notorious art forgery case in New York City as a
starting point, Wendy Lee spins her own fascinating take
on how such a thing might come about. Told from multiple
viewpoints—including the forger, the gallery owner who
commissions the forgery, and the man who buys the
painting—*The Art of Confidence* gives us a glimpse into
each of their worlds, all full of intrigue and sadness."
—B. A. Shapiro, *New York Times* bestselling author of
*The Muralist* and *The Art Forger*

"With a cast of characters including a Taiwanese businessman, a young college dropout, a failed Chinese artist, and a
desperate gallery owner, this enthralling novel examines the
lengths we will go to, to fight for what's ours. Each setting,
from Ridgewood, Queens, to Taipei, Taiwan, is convincingly
rendered; each character is as genuine as an authenticated
painting. Art's creation and existence causes a ripple effect,
reinforcing how closely we are all connected, and how
much we depend upon these ties."
—Allison Amend, author of *Enchanted Islands* and
*A Nearly Perfect Copy*

"*The Art of Confidence* is a gripping read, a swirling tale that
weaves together the schemes and struggles of people touched by
the murky, malleable question of value in art. No one is blame-
less, no one left unchanged when one woman manipulates the
vicissitudes of the art world for her own good. Wendy Lee gives
us an original, clear-eyed look behind the gallery windows and
behind the studio walls, and you will be completely engaged."
—Robin Black, author of *Life Drawing*

By Wendy Lee

*The Art of Confidence*

*Across a Green Ocean*

Published by Kensington Publishing Corp.

# THE
# ART OF
# CONFIDENCE

Wendy Lee

KENSINGTON BOOKS
www.kensingtonbooks.com

KENSINGTON BOOKS are published by

Kensington Publishing Corp.
119 West 40th Street
New York, NY 10018

All Kensington titles, imprints, and distributed lines are available at special quantity discounts for bulk purchases for sales promotion, premiums, fund-raising, educational, or institutional use.

Special book excerpts or customized printings can also be created to fit specific needs. For details, write or phone the office of the Kensington Sales Manager: Kensington Publishing Corp., 119 West 40th Street, New York, NY 10018. Attn. Sales Department. Phone: 1-800-221-2647.

Kensington and the K logo Reg. U.S. Pat. & TM Off.

eISBN-13: 978-1-61773-490-8
eISBN-10: 1-61773-490-X
First Kensington Electronic Edition: December 2016

ISBN-13: 978-1-61773-489-2
ISBN-10: 1-61773-489-6
First Kensington Trade Paperback Printing: December 2016

10 9 8 7 6 5 4 3 2 1

Printed in the United States of America

*For Neil*

# Chapter 1

I'll start off by saying I had nothing to lose.

Although, I have to admit, I didn't have much to gain by what I did, especially in terms of the money. I still had to give lessons at the senior center and make those lousy copies of Impressionist paintings for tourists to buy.

I suppose I did it because I wanted something to show for the thirty years—longer than I had lived in my homeland—that I had been here in America. Something that was properly appreciated, even if someone else got all the credit.

Thankfully, my wife was not around to see what I had done. I don't think she would have approved of my actions, though not for the right reason. "You'd probably make more money collecting plastic bottles," she would have said. I don't think she would have really wanted me to be one of those Chinese people shuffling down the street in their canvas shoes, backs bent nearly double underneath clear sacks of plastic picked out of other people's trash, like hermit crabs with iridescent shells spat up from some otherworldly sea. I'm still a few years and ounces of pride away from that.

Although I don't know how much pride there is in what I do to earn a living. Every week, at the Chinese Baptist Church senior center in Flushing, Queens, I take people in their sixties and seventies through the paces of drawing an apple, a teacup, a potted plant. It feels like they have already moved into another plane of time, where seconds are minutes. I'm sure my hour-long lesson feels like an entire week. A man guides his brush of yellow paint across canvas with the speed of a midsummer's day, while a woman piles pigment onto her palette as though building a monument.

There's a widow who has her eye on me, despite being at least fifteen years my senior. "Master Liu," she'll quaver, "how can we make the apple look like it's not floating in midair?"

Perspective, I tell her. If everything else—the shadow on the tabletop, the wall in the background—looks as it should, then so does the object in the middle, even if it is flawed.

The widow, who is about as misshapen as the apple she has painted, steps back to look at her work. I wonder what she sees. A round sphere? The perfect apple in her mind's eye?

It's in these times that I miss my wife the most. Especially in light of the widow's subtle flirting, although come to think of it, the age difference is the least objectionable aspect. After all, I am fifteen years older than my wife; when we met, I must have seemed like a geriatric. I didn't have a tragic story about a divorce or a dead first wife or even children. I was just a painter, and for many years my bedfellow had been mediocrity.

I wish I could have told my wife about the first time I met the gallery owner. It was on a perfect summer day, when the tourists were out in force, streaming past my stall on the sidewalk just south of the Metropolitan Museum of Art on Fifth Avenue, chattering in a thousand different languages. Occasionally a school group would straggle past, the uniformed children energetically swatting each other with their notebooks.

Then I saw the woman standing to the side, appraising my

display of knockoffs of Monet, Pissarro, and Sisley. I knew she wasn't a tourist. For one thing, she was by herself. She wasn't one of those women determined to expose her family to art and culture, followed by a hulking bear of a husband and teenaged children in Converse sneakers who'd rather be in Times Square (although they could meet some of my immigrant street-art brethren there, as well).

No, she was a local, probably in her late fifties or early sixties, although well-preserved in the way city women over a certain age are. I could see all the signs: a glossy shoulder-length bob, too-red lipstick that matched the shade of her manicured nails, possibly a face-lift. So as to better look at my work, she had put on reader glasses with geometric frames. I am sure the word she would have used to describe them, as I had overheard women of that age group describe colorful jewelry at the craft fairs where I sometimes sold my work, was "funky."

She looked at me over the rims of her own funky glasses and asked, "Do you paint these yourself?"

"Yes, Madame," I said, getting up from my camp stool.

"They're very good."

I looked at my paintings as if with a new eye. They were all eight inches by twelve inches, so that I could fit a maximum of twenty paintings onto the wire scaffolding that enclosed my small patch of territory on the sidewalk. One entire panel was devoted to Monet, this being the artist most people recognized from being reproduced on mugs, tote bags, and mouse pads. I had copies of his greatest hits: the bridge at Giverny, the Houses of Parliament at sunset, the garden at Argenteuil, the water lilies, the haystacks. The trick in repeating these paintings and not getting bored was to look at them as something else. For instance, whenever I painted the haystacks, I thought of corn muffins. I was much more interested in them this way, not to mention hungry.

"How much do you sell them for?" the woman asked.

I made a mental calculation. I hadn't thought she looked like someone interested in buying a painting—usually those people were tourists who had just gotten out of the museum, spied a copy of a painting they had seen in real life, and wanted to take home a souvenir—but perhaps I had been mistaken. Maybe she wanted a little picture to adorn an office wall, or to hang in her bathroom over the toilet.

"For you, Madame, only fifty dollars," I said grandly.

"Fifty?" She frowned. "For fifty I would expect something larger. I really need something larger."

My perception of her changed. Maybe she was an interior decorator, looking for a painting for a client's wall or a doctor's waiting room. This could mean several hundred dollars.

"I have larger paintings in my studio," I said.

Her eyebrows lifted slightly at this, as if she was surprised to hear that I had a studio. True, it was only my garage, but that was where I kept and did my real work, not out here on the street.

"I also work on commission," I added.

"Perhaps," she said, "I could come visit your studio? You see, I don't really know what kind of painting I want yet. But it has to be big. Imposing. You know what I mean."

I didn't, and readjusted my impression of her yet again. So she wasn't working for a client. Could it be that she was a true art appreciator who wanted a painting for herself, not at another's direction or simply to fill a physical space? This could be interesting indeed.

"Of course," I replied. I wrote my address on the back of a blank receipt slip and handed it to her. "This is the location of my studio and my contact information. You are free to come by any time you like."

"Queens?" The slightest curl of her lip. Obviously someone who lived in Manhattan.

"It is close to the seven train. My name is Liu. I am at your service." I bowed like the old-fashioned mandarin I must have appeared to her, despite the fact that I was wearing paint-spattered work clothes.

"I'll call you if I'm interested." She handed me a business card, although it had been clear by her words that she would contact me and not vice versa.

After enough time had passed for her to walk a block or so away, I looked at what she had pressed in my hand. A piece of plain white cardstock that bore the words *Caroline Lowry, Owner, The Lowry Gallery*. The address was in Chelsea. I flipped the card over to its blank side and back again, half-expecting the words to have disappeared like invisible ink. But no, Caroline Lowry stayed put. Could it be that finally, after thirty years, just when I was ready to give up, a gallery was interested in my work?

I should have known that no real gallery owner would have been convinced of my talent from seeing a few knockoff paintings sold on the street, but at that point in time I could have believed anything. As I said before, I had nothing to lose.

Because I had no wife around for me to tell what had happened that day, I called up my oldest friend in New York, Wang Muping. We had met at the Art Students League on West Fifty-seventh Street in the early 1980s after both of us had just arrived in America as naïve, impressionable twenty-year-olds. We were the only Chinese students in our class; he with long hair and I with a buzz cut, but everyone, even the teacher, had trouble telling us apart. Wang still had long hair, with a few hoary streaks now, and wore a checkered scarf draped around his neck in an attempt to look hip, but in certain lights it just made him look like an old lady.

I asked him to meet me in one of our old hangouts, a diner not far from the art school, where we'd been so poor that we could only order soup and cream-cheese sandwiches. Now, although we weren't that much better off, we could at least order the lunch special.

I should say that I was not much better off, but Wang had made a name for himself in certain circles by parodying certain elements of Chinese brush painting. For example, in a recent show he had exhibited a series of *shanshui* paintings, or mountain-sky landscapes, except the tiny figures typically posed alongside the rivers or atop hills were of couples in pornographic positions. Wang was represented by a sleek gallery downtown, whom he'd tried to get interested in me, as well, many years ago, but my work was deemed too traditional. Now Wang lived in a high-rise that only he considered to be in Soho but was actually on the Chinatown border.

"What do you think of this?" I asked, showing him the business card. "Have you ever heard of it?"

"The Lowry Gallery? It's above Fourteenth Street," he said, pronouncing "Fourteenth Street" in the same way Caroline Lowry had pronounced "Queens." He tapped the address, in the midtwenties and so far west it might as well be in the Hudson River. "Maybe you should go visit, see who is exhibited there. Have you checked out the website?"

"There isn't one."

Wang *tsked*. "So, either this owner is old-fashioned, or she thinks putting anything online will result in her bank account getting hacked. Either way, it's not good."

It was just like Wang to put down any positive news that came my way. Such as when he heard a year ago that I was getting married for the first time in my life, he said, "Too bad, because I was just going to introduce you to my cousin's old classmate who just arrived from Shanghai. She's so impressionable that she'll sleep with you if you so much as offer to show her around." I suspect Wang ended up sleeping with her himself, so as to not waste the opportunity.

"But you still think I should stop by?" I persisted. "What if the gallery owner is there? I don't want to look like a stalker."

"There is no way that anyone would mistake you for a stalker," Wang said in a way that made it a dubious compliment. Then he checked his phone. "It's only three o'clock. You should go now. I'll go with you. I can take a look first and if this owner is not there, we can both go in and pretend we're buyers. You know, like those wealthy Asian buyers from Taiwan or Hong Kong."

I doubted we were dressed like it, especially Wang and his old-lady scarf, but I agreed.

The Lowry Gallery was not one of the relatively newer galleries in the area but located on the ground floor of a town house, one of the few left on a street of midcentury buildings and apartment blocks. Wang strode casually by, looked into the front window, then crossed the street and returned to where I was hovering in the bushes like a dog unable to take a shit. Rather than two has-been artists in their early fifties (well, Wang was not yet a has-been, while I had never even *been*), I felt like we were two schoolboys about to play a prank.

"What did you see?" I asked.

"There was a young woman inside, sitting at a desk. The receptionist, I think."

"The owner could be in the back."

"True. In any case, I'm going in." Wang walked through the door with such purpose that I could only follow him.

The gallery was larger than I expected for something on the bottom floor of an apartment building, the space separated by several white dividers. By the entrance was a desk, behind which sat a young woman whose long brown hair was pulled back in a ponytail. She was not the long-legged, fashion model–type of receptionist such as the one who graced Wang's downtown gallery—I had heard those girls called "gallerinas"—but a plain, dour-faced girl who looked like she would prefer to be anywhere else.

"Can I help you?" the gallerina asked.

"Er." Wang gestured helplessly. Then, speaking with an accent that I had never heard before, even from all the tourists who passed by my stall, he said, "We are just looking?"

"Sure. Take your time."

Wang pulled me by the arm to look at the painting that faced the front window. It was obviously the centerpiece, a huge canvas with colors radiating out from what appeared to be a silkscreened image of Mickey Mouse. It reminded me of a tie-dyed T-shirt, not unlike the kind you could find at a souvenir shop. But I barely noticed the effect, only the price tag.

Wang made a disgruntled noise. "They are selling this piece of derivative crap for ten thousand dollars?"

Ten thousand dollars was a lot of money. Maybe not to all artists, possibly not even to Wang, but for me it would mean being able to pay rent, the opportunity to give up my job at the senior center, to paint what I wanted, at least for a while, which I had never been able to do before.

"Did you have a question?" the gallerina called.

"Not yet," Wang responded. He turned to me. "You don't do this kind of work."

"No, I'm 'too traditional,'" I murmured. My positive thoughts were beginning to drive themselves, lemming-like, off the cliff of my mind. Why was Caroline Lowry interested in my work if it wasn't the kind that she showed?

Wang approached the gallerina with what I knew well from our art-school days was his attempt to turn on the charm, although it was painful to watch at his age. "Young lady, is your boss around?"

"She stepped out for the afternoon," the gallerina replied. "Do you want to leave a message?"

"Can you tell her that Mr. Liu and his agent stopped by?

That is Mr. Liu." Wang pointed to me. "She will know who he is." He displayed the business card that I had neglected to take back from him.

It seemed to mean something to the gallerina, for her eyes widened slightly. I could see they were a pleasant hazel, like a puddle of water that you look at more carefully and see an entire ecosystem within. "I definitely will," she told us.

"What was that all about?" I demanded when Wang and I had stepped outside, and I had swiped the business card back from him. "And what's this about being my agent?"

"This gallery owner doesn't give many people her card," Wang replied. "She's very selective. And for some reason, she's selected you."

"She hasn't done anything yet."

"But she will once her assistant has passed on the message that you stopped by to see her. You can thank me later."

I shook my head, determined that even if Caroline Lowry did get in touch with me, I was never going to tell Wang. Least of all to give him the satisfaction that he was right.

When I returned home, I felt anew the loss of my wife. Our apartment on the first floor of a frame house in Elmhurst, Queens, appeared not to have been touched for hours, not even by sunlight, as I had not bothered to open the curtains when I had gotten up that morning and now it was too dark to do so. Before Jin had come into my life, I had lived like a long-established bachelor, with ingrained habits that came from years of either living alone or not caring what other people whom you lived with thought of you.

While an art student I had lived with a bunch of classmates, including Wang, in a tenement in Chinatown. Then, when I'd needed more space, I'd moved to various apartments throughout Queens, always paying cash and even once agreeing to paint a portrait of my landlady's daughter and future son-in-law as a wedding present in lieu of rent. About ten years ago I'd found my current apartment in a two-family house, owned by an absentee landlord from New Jersey, and agreed to rake leaves, shovel snow, and generally keep an eye on the place in return for the use of the garage in the back as a studio. The upstairs tenants continually shifted from groups of immigrant men who spoke Spanish, families who spoke Tibetan, and students who spoke Korean. They never stayed long enough for me to get to know them, and often the only way I was aware they were there was due to cooking smells seeping through the windows or foreign pop music thumping through the floor.

After she moved in, Jin was especially annoyed by the music and thought nothing of climbing up on a chair and slamming the bottom of her slipper against the ceiling. "It's rude," she would say, and I would remind her that our upstairs neighbors could probably hear us arguing, which couldn't be that pleasant for them.

Our courtship was based on argument. Unlike me, Jin was a recent immigrant from Guangzhou, in the south of China. Because her first language was Cantonese, and mine was Fujianese—the language of my home province, Fujian Province, across the straits from the island of Taiwan—we either spoke to each other in Mandarin Chinese or, less fluently, in English. Although she had studied it in school, Jin's English was not so proficient. She often made mistakes that I patiently corrected, that people were "hospitable" rather than "hospital," they smoked like a "fiend" and not a "fink," and so on. Whenever I did that, she would say, "You know what I mean, don't be such a sticker," to which I would say, "You mean, don't be such a stickler," and on and on it would go.

Our very first argument, though, occurred when we met. I was teaching a live-drawing class for a continuing education course—the organizations that employed me then were considerably more prestigious than the ones now—that met at night next to a foreign language business class. Both classes had a break at the same time, and several of us, including myself, went outside to smoke.

"What class are you taking?" I heard a voice ask as I took my first, much-needed drag (a habit that, with Jin's convincing, I quit soon thereafter).

I turned to see a young Chinese woman leaning against the wall, watching me. Underneath the sodium lights I couldn't tell how old she was, but she appeared young, perhaps twenty-five or so. Like many of the young Asian women whom I saw on the 7 train, she wore a mishmash of fashion that indelibly marked her as a recent immigrant: tight jeans decorated with rhine-stones, an animal-print top, a fake leather jacket. Her handbag bore a conspicuous logo, and her long hair had reddish-blond streaks. All these so-called embellishments could not distract from the fact that she was very pretty. I had no idea why she was talking to me, a man seemingly old enough to be her father. But, after fortifying myself with a lungful of nicotine, I replied, "The drawing class."

"A class just on how to draw?"

"Well, it's live drawing."

"What does that mean?"

"We use live models."

It took a while for this to sink in. "That's naughty!" she exclaimed.

"Actually," I said, "it's the best way to see what's really going on underneath the skin, the musculature and bones, and the way the tendons…" I trailed off when it became obvious that she could not get past the idea of being in the presence of a naked stranger.

"Is it a fun class?" she asked.

"I hope so. I'm the teacher." This did not seem to impress her as much as make her think that I was a pervert for teaching such a class. "What class are you taking?"

"Marketing. I want to become a 'marketing manager.' " She spoke as if the job title were in a foreign language, or a euphemism for something much less respectable.

"What do you do now?"

"I'm a hairdresser."

*That explains the hair,* I thought.

"I work at a salon in Elmhurst, on Forty-fifth Avenue and Seventy-fourth Street."

"That's two blocks from where I live," I remarked.

"Then you should go get your hair cut there," she said. "Or I could get rid of your gray and make you look younger."

I ran a hand over the back of my head—still full, thankfully—but yes, beginning to be shot through with silver. Was this an insult, or a come-on? I had a hard time believing a woman her age could be interested in me in that way. Perhaps she was just trying to drum up business, per the marketing class she was taking.

"I'll think about it," I told her. "In the meantime, maybe you should rethink your marketing strategy of making people feel old."

"Learning marketing is much more useful than learning how to draw a naked person," she retorted.

"If you learn how to sell something to a person, all you know is how they spend their money. If you learn how a person's body works, then you can see into their very soul."

"Tell me," she said through half-lidded eyes, "how much money do you make, as an artist? No, as a teacher of artists?"

"Why does that matter?"

"Of course it matters. It's why we're here."

I wondered if she meant the other people in her class, or the both of us, or immigrants in general. The last galled me a bit, because I had been in this country for almost thirty years at that point, longer than I had lived anywhere else, while she was obviously fresh off the boat.

"You and I are here for different reasons," I told her.

"So you think you're better than me? Because you're a teacher and I'm a student?"

*Because you are young and I am old,* I thought. *Because you are beautiful, and I am someone whose own mother said looked like a monkey when I was born.* "That's not what I meant."

She had turned away from me now, fumbling in her purse for something.

"I'll tell you what," I said. "After the break, why don't you come sit in on my class? Then you'll be able to see for yourself what I mean."

She still wouldn't look at me, so I shrugged, stubbed out my cigarette, and went back inside the building. As my students re-assembled, I looked at them with new eyes. Because this was a night class through continuing education, most of the students were middle-aged and looking for relief from their day jobs. A live-drawing class wouldn't help them make more money, but at least it provided some kind of escape. Was it really useful for them, though? Did it give them, as I had told my companion during my smoking break, insight into human nature, into the soul itself?

Just as I was about to call class back into session, I saw a movement at the back of the room. The woman I had been talking to had slipped through the door. She didn't have an easel or a pad of drawing paper, and there were no extras for her to use, but with determination she found a chair, took out a pad of yellow legal paper and a pen, and tore off the top page, on which she had been taking notes. I watched her as that night's model came to the front of the room, and saw that she did not avert her eyes, but unwaveringly regarded the subject in front of her. In turn, I looked at the model as if I were seeing him for the first time, the striation in the thigh muscle, the corded back of the neck. I guessed he did some kind of manual labor. Every crease and wrinkle mapped something about this person's life, indicating at least how hard he worked.

I moved among the students, observing their drawing. Some of them became self-conscious as I neared, pausing to erase something or darken a line. When I paused behind Jin, she acted like she wasn't aware of my presence. I saw that, unlike a beginner who might try to first draw the face or a specific part of the body, she had just sketched a few quick, abstract lines to represent its general shape. I noticed that up close, her fingers were long and graceful, the nails unvarnished and cut short, the opposite of what I would expect from someone with her sense of style. Of course, I thought. She was a hairdresser; she used her hands.

When the class was over, she departed before I could say anything to her. All she left on her desk was her sketch on the lined yellow legal page. I folded it up and put it in my pocket, taking it as the equivalent of someone giving you their phone number in a bar. Except I didn't need to know her phone number; I knew where she worked.

The next day I walked the two blocks from my apartment to the Number One Modern Beauty Parlor, where I got a haircut and convinced Jin to go to dinner with me after her shift, on our first real date. I learned that she was actually thirty-two and had come over from China five years before. She lived with her sister and her sister's family in Sunset Park, Brooklyn, which made for quite a commute, so perhaps it wasn't surprising that after we had been dating for three months—if you could call what we did dating; since I didn't have the money, we usually ate out in Flushing, in one of the steamy cafeterias or food courts—she suggested she move in with me.

"What are you doing with your life?" Wang said when I told him. Then he congratulated me on finding someone who was willing to be with me, not to mention someone that much younger than me. I might have thought he was envious, but especially after he had been picked up by his downtown gallery, he had any number of female hangers-on, from college students to middle-aged women who were looking to collect artists in the way their husbands were looking to collect art. I could tell, though, that he didn't believe the relationship between Jin and me was real, or would last.

It was difficult for me to believe, as well, even after Jin had moved her small amount of belongings from the bedroom she shared with her two nieces in Sunset Park into my apartment. Most of what she owned appeared to be clothes, fashion magazines, and the occasional stuffed animal or knickknack. That was most definitely not enough to make the apartment homey enough for her, so every day after I came home from teaching a class, or selling paintings at a craft fair or sidewalk stall, I would spot something new, as if this were a game she had devised for me. One day it would be a yellow paper lantern over the bare bulb that lit the living room; another day a set of red ceramic bowls in the cupboard; a third day a jade bamboo plant adorning the windowsill. She thought it was funny that although I was an artist, I barely lived with anything that had a color.

This, of course, was not true of my studio. There I had paintings of all colors—well, shades within the same family, at least. But Jin didn't like to go in there. She complained that the garage smelled of turpentine and musty canvas. After that one time she sat in on my class, she did not attempt to draw again. "That's what *you* do," she said. "I have to find out what *I* should do." The marketing class she had taken when I'd met her had turned out to be a bust, and she was no closer to leaving the salon than before. I knew that she enjoyed working there, chitchatting with coworkers and customers about things she could never talk about with me, but was disappointed that at her age she was only a hairdresser. And shacking up with me, an unsuccessful painter, wasn't going to help matters any.

Caroline Lowry did call me the day after Wang and I had spied at her gallery, and set up a time the following week to visit me at my studio. In the meantime, I agonized over which work to present, what to wear, what kind of refreshments I would have on hand. You would think that I was a teenage girl getting ready for a first date.

The third thing was the easiest to figure out. At first I considered wine, but I couldn't afford anything expensive, and our meeting was in the afternoon, so it seemed inappropriate. Naturally, I decided to play up my foreignness. I bought some gunpowder tea and dusted off an old tea set a student had given me as a present. As for my outfit, Caroline had already seen me in the paint-spattered clothes I wore for tourists. So instead I brought out my best costume, one I only wore when I was giving talks to groups of old white ladies—the Tang suit, with its long-sleeved jacket of black brocade and frog closures.

As for my work, I displayed a couple of half-finished canvases that depicted traditional Chinese landscapes in an Impressionist style. Actually, I only painted variations on a single landscape—a gently sloping mountain—that existed solely in my mind. When some people asked me what it represented, I told them that was where I was born, although the truth was, I had grown up in the dingy alleyways of Xiamen, the island city in the south of Fujian Province. Now Xiamen is a popular tourist destination for the newly rich Chinese. But when I was a child, its beaches were littered with cigarette butts like they were one giant ashtray, and I spent most of my time either chasing or being chased by stray dogs past crumbling buildings that still bore traces of the island's colonial history.

At one point in my childhood, my parents took me on a trip to the province's interior, and we rode a cable car to a mountain's peak. I kept my eyes fearfully squeezed shut as my mother implored me to look outside, look at the bird in the tree, even promising me that she'd get me an ice cream at the top. Disgusted at his only child's cowardice, my father said nothing. I knew I was a disappointment to him. His family had worked its way up from countryside farmers who used cow dung for heat to city merchants in dirt-floor houses. I'd been brought up with plentiful food and schooling. Yet I couldn't stay attentive in class, was forever doodling in my notebook, on my desk, and on the chalkboard, to the amusement of my classmates.

Finally, as the cable car neared the end of its laborious journey, I opened my eyes and moved my view from the top of my fat knees, clad in blue shorts, to the great green beyond. Outside the cable car window, the unending pattern of trees on the mountain opposite me repeated itself on my retinas so that I saw them every time I blinked. I remained stunned even as I sat on a bench at our destination, outside a flimsy stand for tourists, eating an ice cream cone with great hungry licks, which I threw back up during the cable car's descent. My father blamed my mother for indulging me; she blamed the ice cream for being too cold. Later, many years after I'd immigrated to America, the land of milk and honey, I learned I was lactose intolerant.

This mountain that I had seen during my terrifying ascent, however, had been imprinted on my mind. Objectively it was an unremarkable peak, but through my brush, it took on massive proportions. I painted it from various angles, in the winter, at sunset, in the fog. I was like Monet, painting the same Japanese bridge over and over, except at least he (and now I, by painting replicas) had made money off of his repetitiveness. For the past few years, I had painted nothing but variations on this mountain, and to what end?

I thought Caroline Lowry was late to our appointment, but she'd actually been pressing the doorbell for the apartment above me and got a man who only spoke Spanish and was annoyed at being woken from sleeping off a graveyard shift. She stepped gingerly into my living room, where the traces of Jin still remained even three months after her departure.

"Tea?" I asked.

Caroline nodded. "With lemon, please." I had the feeling she often made this request of her assistant.

I went into the kitchen in a bit of a panic. Of course I should have anticipated that to Americans, tea couldn't just be tea, but stuff adulterated with milk, sugar, citrus. I set up a tray, then at the last minute looked in the refrigerator, which I had not paid much attention to since Jin had left. Miraculously, I spotted the glow of a plastic lemon on a back shelf. I remembered Jin making fun of it after she brought it home from the supermarket, wondering why there weren't plastic oranges or plastic apples with orange and apple juice inside.

I placed the plastic lemon like a little yellow football next to Caroline's teacup, like a half-formed apology. She ignored it and took a sip of the tea.

"This has an interesting flavor, what is it?" she asked.

"Gunpowder tea, from Fujian Province. That is in the southeast of China and where I am from." I played the tour guide.

"Oh." She gave a hint of a smile. "I should have known better than to ask for lemon juice with Chinese tea."

I shrugged and indicated the ridiculous lemon. "I tried."

Now that the formalities of tea were over, I led Caroline into my studio and turned on the lights that I had angled to show off my work. I couldn't tell by her impassive face what she thought as she walked from one end of the tiny space to the other. I tried to see the paintings through her eyes: a mountain in the mist, a mountain in the sun, a mountain in the rain.

"This is all very nice," she finally said. "But this isn't exactly what I had in mind. Or rather, what my client has in mind."

So she *was* acting on someone else's behalf. "What do they want?" I asked.

From her handbag, Caroline removed an old catalog listing of shows at the Lowry Gallery in 1970. She opened it to a painting called *Elegy,* by an artist named Andrew Cantrell. The name was vaguely familiar to me, although more to do with the artist's reputation than his work. According to the description, the painting had been done in 1969 and measured five feet by three feet. The image was of a swirling gray background with a nimbus of white in the center; representative, I guess, of the era's tastes. As to how it was elegiac, I couldn't tell.

"This," Caroline said, "was one of Andrew Cantrell's most famous works, that he supposedly was offered two million dollars for—a good amount back then—but he refused to sell. It was only shown once, at the Lowry Gallery, and then he kept it in his East Hampton studio until five years later."

"Until the fire that killed him." I was beginning to remember more about the artist. Andrew Cantrell had achieved some fame in the late 1960s, but he was perhaps best known for his death in a fire in 1975 that was supposedly set by his old mistress. Even I had read about that.

Caroline raised her eyebrows. "Yes. This was the most well-known painting that was lost. My client wants to resurrect it, so to speak. He's hoping to get a replica made."

"A copy?"

"As close as you can make it. The client is prepared to pay a good price for it."

"How much?"

"Two thousand dollars." She must have read the shift in my face because she quickly amended, "I can probably get him up to three thousand. Will that be enough?"

Now it was my turn to guess what was going on behind her funky reader glasses. Some impatience was there; if I didn't agree, she could easily find a starving art student to take my place. Plus, this was the most lucrative job I'd had in ages. If only Jin could see me now.

"Okay," I said.

"How long do you think it would take you to do it?"

The canvas she was asking for was larger than I usually worked with, but I didn't let on. "I'll need a month. Do you have anything I can work off of?"

"Anything that wasn't in a museum or private collection

was lost in the fire. There's one piece in the Museum of Modern Art. I'm sorry, but all I can give you is the catalog." Caroline paused. "To make it look as authentic as possible, you'll have to make sure the right kind of materials are used. Materials from the appropriate time period. Do you know how to do that?"

I nodded, certain I could figure this out. "When will the payment be made?"

"I can give you half the money next week. It'll be in cash, of course."

"Of course," I echoed, and we shook hands on it.

After I cleared the tray with the tea, which Caroline had hardly touched, the first thought that something might not be quite right with this scenario entered my mind. Copying a painting was common. Selling a replica was, as well. However, if Caroline's intentions were to try to pass this off as a genuine Andrew Cantrell, then that could mean trouble if the painting was traced back to me. But why would she do that? Say that she didn't, in fact, have a prospective client lined up and was intending to sell it on the open market? I had never heard of there being a market for Andrew Cantrell's paintings, as much as I knew about these things.

And, if she were intending to sell the painting as authentic, how could she be so sure that I wouldn't go to the police? Perhaps she was banking on the possibility that I had issues with my citizenship, which I did. I had come over on a student visa that had never been renewed, and throughout my scattershot work history I'd never been forced to provide anything as official as a green card. Look at where and how I lived. There had been no opportunity before for anyone to come after me.

Yes, I'd keep silent about a forgery, if that was what Caroline intended. But I couldn't tell what was going on in her glossy, bobbed head. The gallery that bore her name had once shown the painting, so she obviously had ties to the painter. Whatever it was, I would stick to the story, that she wanted me to paint a replica for a private client. There was nothing wrong with that.

After Caroline left, I looked again at the page in the catalog she had left me. It contained a brief bio of the artist, but not anything about what might have inspired him to paint such an obscure work. I squinted at the page. If I looked hard enough, the gray swirls turned into a version of my own mountain, the one that I painted over and over. Perhaps Andrew Cantrell had something he was compulsive about, as well.

When my eyes started to cross, I closed the catalog. It was clear that in order to pull this project off, I needed expertise I didn't have.

I pulled out my phone. "Wang?" I said. "I need your help."

# Chapter 2

Although no one had asked her in years, Caroline Lowry told people that her first memory was at her mother's funeral, when she was five years old, at a cemetery on Long Island. It wasn't of her father, who had been a dark, shapeless mass standing off to the side, consumed by grief. Instead, she remembered her aunt Hazel Lowry, her mother's younger sister. Hazel, always fashionable, wore a brown fur pillbox hat above her black lambskin coat.

Caroline tugged on her aunt's glove. "Can I hold your hat?" she asked.

Hazel looked down at her distractedly. "Of course, darling." She removed her hat, exposing her smooth, chestnut head to the chilly autumn day, and handed it to Caroline.

Instead of putting it on her own head, or even stuffing her hands into it like a muff, Caroline cradled the hat against her cheek, as though it were an animal. In fact, she was pretending it was a cat, the cat that she had always wanted as a pet and her father had promised to get her after her mother recovered from her illness. Now that her mother would never get better, she supposed this was closest thing she would ever have to a pet.

Caroline's father told her that her mother had died of bone cancer. Caroline didn't know what that meant, and even when she was a little older, she assumed that some kind of disease had eaten out the insides of her mother's bones, the way you could lick the marrow out of the beef bones her father bought from the butcher's down the street. Later, when she was fifteen, she happened to mention this to Hazel when she was spending the weekend with her aunt in the city.

"Your father told you what?" Hazel turned around from the stove, where she had been fixing them cocoa before bed.

"Mom died of bone cancer?" Caroline repeated tentatively from her seat at the kitchen table.

Hazel slammed her hands down on the sides of the stove. "Your mother died of *breast* cancer. Honestly, Catholics!"

Later that night, from the living room sofa where she was sleeping, Caroline could hear Hazel talking to her father on the telephone in the kitchen. "John, I don't care that you're not supposed to talk about certain parts of a woman's body. This is a life-and-death matter. What if Caroline ends up with the same disease as her mother? What are you going to tell her then?"

Caroline knew that Hazel believed in women's progress, and controversial things like the Pill; embarrassingly, she had asked Caroline whether she was dating any boys and assured her that she could get her contraception if necessary. Caroline shook her head so that her long, dark brown hair covered the flush creeping up her face. She barely spoke to the boys in her class, and they to her.

If she'd looked like her aunt Hazel, she was sure that boys would do more than want to talk with her. Hazel was in her early thirties but she wore her skirts short, her hair long, and her heels high. When Caroline walked down the street with her, she could see how men's eyes followed Hazel: deliverymen, businessmen; black, white; young, old. Hazel was an equal-opportunity attractor.

One weekend a month, Caroline's father allowed her to take the train to the city to visit Hazel. She much preferred Hazel's cheerful, eclectic apartment in Chelsea, even though there was no hot water and the rooms were stacked one after the other, railroad-style. In the decade after her mother's death, her father had never remarried and had hired a housekeeper to do the cleaning and the cooking. Once a week he went out with a coworker from the insurance company, a gray-faced woman named Jeanine Smalls. Caroline shuddered to think what went on during their dates, or if Jeanine stayed over on the weekends when she was visiting her aunt.

Hazel took her to nice restaurants, art galleries, snuck her into nightclubs, calling Caroline her younger sister. She knew a number of artists and later represented them, making enough to open her own gallery in the first floor of the apartment building she had lived in since her twenties. By that time Caroline was in college, at an all-girls' school in Massachusetts, and she mostly only saw Hazel at holidays. Once she took her roommate, Rose, with her to an art opening, an experience Rose inevitably reminisced about years later whenever the two women met for lunch in the city.

"Do you remember what Hazel was wearing, Caro?" Rose would say over a glass of white wine. "Do you remember when she introduced us to Andrew Cantrell? I couldn't believe my eyes."

While the Lowry Gallery was relatively small, it could accommodate fifty people, tightly packed, within its walls. Giggling, Caroline and Rose secured themselves drinks and wove through the crowd of people who all looked more sophisticated than they could ever hope of growing up to be.

They pretended to be absorbed in looking at the centerpiece of the art opening, a painting that commanded the entire room and that people stood back from in a reverent semicircle. The canvas was all gray except for a white blur in the center, like an indelible thumbprint. It was called *Elegy* and the painter was Andrew Cantrell. Both Caroline and Rose knew who Andrew Cantrell was, since he had been in the papers recently for turning down two million dollars for this very painting. Caroline looked at it again to see if she could tell what made it so special, what made it worth so much money, but she had no idea. The longer she looked at it, the more it resembled an inkblot out of a Rorschach test, which she'd recently learned about in psychology class.

Next to her, Rose was shaking her head. "I don't get it. Doesn't it look like a child could have painted it?"

Privately Caroline agreed, but she wasn't going to admit that to her friend, and especially in this company. Imagining what her aunt might say about it, she observed, "Well, that's the beauty of it. It's deceptively simple. But when you look closer at the brushstrokes—"

She was saved from trying to expound further on something she knew nothing about by Rose clutching her arm. "Is that *her*? Your aunt?"

Hazel was standing in a corner wearing what could only be described as a beaded caftan with a plunging neckline, paradoxically both modest and revealing. Her hair, which over the years had graduated to more red than brown, towered over her head. She looked like some kind of demented goddess.

"Caroline!" Hazel called. "Who is your darling friend?"

Rose looked like she was seriously contemplating whether to curtsy. The thing Caroline liked best about her roommate was that even though she came from an ordinary family unmarred by death or divorce, Rose often seemed more awkward and unsure of herself than Caroline was.

After Caroline made the introduction, Hazel placed her hand on the arm of the man behind her, turning him neatly to face them. "Girls, I'd like you to meet *my* darling friend, Andrew."

Beside her, Caroline could sense rather than see Rose's mouth falling open. What a Rose-ish response, she thought, which fortunately saved her from a similar reaction. Both of them had forgotten that they had been unimpressed by Andrew Cantrell's work, hadn't been able to understand the first thing about it, and were instead completely taken by being in the presence of the artist.

Later, when recalling the only time she'd met him, Caroline realized Andrew Cantrell was quite short, only coming up to her aunt's shoulder and barely taller than Caroline herself. What little hair remained on his head formed a fringe that partially obscured his ears, but his shoulders were broad and powerfully set. He shook hands with each girl with calloused fingers, looking intently into their faces as if resolving to remember the color of their eyes (Caroline, brown; Rose, blue).

"I will remember this night for the rest of my life," Rose declared afterward. She and Caroline remained at the edges of the room for the rest of the night, tipsy from their drinks and closeness to fame, but somehow Caroline was aware of where Hazel was all night. For one thing, it was hard to miss her red beehive bobbing above everyone else's heads. And always by her side—or rather, shoulder—was the gleaming orb of Andrew Cantrell's head. The two of them rarely touched or spoke to each other all night, but at one point Caroline realized, with astonishing clarity, that her aunt and the artist were lovers. She tried to picture a recent photo spread in *Life* magazine of Andrew Cantrell's summer home out on East Hampton, his studio overlooking the sea. His wife stood next to him with the afternoon tea she'd prepared on a tray, an apron tied around her trim waist.

Caroline never mentioned these thoughts to Rose, or her father, or anyone. After graduating from college, she moved to San Francisco for a job with a women's rights organization, as far away as she could get from her father's somber house. Two or three years later, she caught the headline in a newspaper that the artist Andrew Cantrell had died in a fire at his East Hampton home. The article suggested that it had been set by his former mistress, the gallery owner Hazel Lowry, but that paper was no better than a tabloid anyway. Still, Caroline was tempted to call her aunt to ask her if that was true, but decided against it. She'd talk to Hazel the next time she went back East to visit her father.

That visit didn't take place for another decade, when her father died of a stroke in the middle of winter. Caroline had become a social worker and was married to another social worker, Bob Kleinman, chosen primarily because his warm, unassuming demeanor was so different from her father's. Bob came with her to her father's funeral on Long Island, where he'd be laid to rest next to her mother.

Although she hadn't seen her aunt for many years, Caroline immediately spotted Hazel, her hair more brilliantly red than ever, in a leopard-print coat and hat. They kissed each other on the cheek, and then Hazel removed her hat and held it out to Caroline.

"Do you want to hold it?" she asked.

Caroline didn't know whether to laugh or cry. She introduced Bob to Hazel, and then saw a sallow-faced woman approaching her.

"You probably don't remember me," the woman said by way of greeting.

Caroline took in a breath. "Jeanine Smalls."

"Yes." Jeanine gave a small smile. "I was very close to your father. I even wanted us to get married, but he said he didn't think it was fair to you."

"Fair to me?" Caroline echoed.

"He thought you didn't like me."

Caroline hadn't known that her father had had such consideration for her feelings. Out of guilt, she invited Jeanine to come out to dinner afterward, but Jeanine declined, so Caroline, Bob, and Hazel set out on their own. They ended up in a diner off the highway, which wasn't very festive, but it had the kind of hearty, unembellished food that her father would have liked.

"How's business at the art gallery?" Caroline asked Hazel.

Hazel sighed. "Sales are down. But there are starting to be some foreign investors, from the Middle East and such, that's giving me hope."

Caroline noticed that her aunt's bright lipstick was bleeding into the fine lines around her mouth as she talked. For the first time in her life, she thought Hazel looked old. And why shouldn't she? Hazel must be around fifty by now.

When Bob left the table to settle the bill, Caroline said to Hazel, "I know it happened years ago, but I've always meant to tell you how sorry I was to hear your artist friend died."

"Who?"

Caroline flushed like a teenager. "The one who lived out on East Hampton. You introduced me and my friend Rose to him one night at a party in your gallery."

"Oh, Andrew Cantrell." Hazel tapped the ash off her cigarette and let out a stream of smoke from between her pursed lips. "That was an unfortunate death."

"The papers said..." Caroline paused.

Her aunt fixed her with a stern gaze. "I know what they said. Andrew and I weren't in a relationship anymore by that time. His wife had a better reason to set that fire than I did. Is that what you wanted to know?"

"I was just wondering... It was such a big news story at the time."

Hazel rolled her eyes. "Scandalous, I know. Well, that was a decade ago and people had a lot less to gossip about then. Speaking of friends, how's your old pal Rose?"

It was Caroline's turn to be confused by the abrupt change in subject. "She's fine. She lives in Connecticut now, married to a lawyer. She has two children, both boys."

"Sounds like a delightful life. Not something you want with Bob?"

"Children?" Caroline wondered where she and Bob would find the time, with their overload of cases, seeing every day what happened when parents were unable to provide for their own children. "You never had children," she pointed out, suddenly feeling bold.

Hazel took a long drag off her cigarette. "Not that I didn't have the opportunity. I just chose not to."

At that point, Bob came back to the table, and they left the diner, Hazel to take the train into the city, and he and Caroline to the house in which she'd grown up, where she spent the next week disposing of her childhood.

Not long after they got back to San Francisco, Bob announced he wanted a divorce, and Caroline calmly gave it to him. The transaction was relatively simple; they had no children or shared property, and had always kept separate bank accounts. There wasn't even a typical reason, such as an affair or a deadly disease or a midlife crisis, behind their disunion. Their lives had just gone off course, like a zipper that no longer went up to the top. The only saving grace, Caroline thought, was that her father hadn't been alive to see his daughter divorced, something his staunchly Catholic heart wouldn't have endured.

Bob ceded her the apartment, but at times Caroline wished she had started over in a new place, perhaps a new city. She'd welcome a new job, but she didn't know what else she was fit to do other than try and solve the familial problems of people she didn't know. After reconnecting with Hazel at her father's funeral, she and her aunt started talking weekly on the phone. Hazel was sympathetic about the divorce and would say things like, "I never got the sense that Bob was *there* there, you know what I mean?"

Since this was based on the one time she and Bob had met, Caroline didn't know what Hazel was talking about, and sometimes she suspected Hazel didn't, either. Often when she called her aunt, Hazel sounded sleepy, even when she insisted she wanted to talk, and she'd drift off into a tangent. Still, she was someone who would listen, and who understood what it was like to be single, unlike Caroline's friend Rose, who evinced the same amount of dismay when Caroline told her that she was getting divorced as when Caroline had told her that her father had died.

Then one night, after Caroline had complained yet again about how she wished she could start over, Hazel said, "Why don't you move to New York?" She sounded unusually alert and serious.

"What would I do? Where would I live?"

"You could stay with me. As for a job, you could help me at the gallery."

"I don't know anything about art."

"You don't need to know anything about art. Just what other people think they know about art."

Caroline thought Hazel was getting a little loopy again. But the idea of moving to New York City, where she'd been so close to growing up as a child without actually experiencing it, filled her with a sense of hope she hadn't felt for a long time. Within the month, she put in her notice at work, gave up her and Bob's old apartment, and moved across the country.

Caroline arrived at Hazel's apartment in Chelsea in the middle of the day. Hazel had left instructions to pick up the keys from a neighbor, as she would be out. When Caroline let herself in, her nose was instantly accosted with the smell of smoke—not cigarette smoke, but the skunky pinch of marijuana. That must explain Hazel's sounding so sleepy over the phone, the aimless trajectory of her conversations. Caroline pictured her aunt reclining on the sofa in one of her embroidered caftans, joint held between thumb and forefinger, a different kind of glamour.

In the noon darkness, the apartment looked older and more decrepit than Caroline remembered from her previous visits. The Moroccan glass chandelier that she'd thought so cheerfully bohemian, the Indian batik wall hangings that seemed so cosmopolitan—so *international*—struck her as tawdry now. No wonder she'd loved her aunt's apartment as a teenager. For the first time, she noticed that Hazel had no art at all on her walls.

By the time Hazel got home later that afternoon, Caroline had put away her few things in the spare room and was sitting at her old refuge, the kitchen table, drinking tea and flipping through a magazine.

"Welcome back, darling," Hazel said in the doorway.

Caroline nearly dropped her mug. In the year since she'd last seen her, Hazel's appearance had altered dramatically. All of the scarves and other layers of fabric draped around her body couldn't disguise how thin she'd gotten. Her face was long and gaunt, the grooves of her clavicle deep. The only aspects that were the same were the red of her hair and the corresponding crimson slash of her mouth.

She helped Hazel sit down and offered her some tea.

"Thank you," Hazel said. "I should be acting the hostess here. But this is your home now."

There was no point in trying to hide anything. "Aunt Hazel," Caroline said. "What's wrong?"

"I'm afraid that I've gotten you here under false pretenses. You probably thought I was being so generous, offering you a place to stay and a job. But the truth is, I need someone here to help me. For the first time in my life, I can't be alone."

"You're sick." When Hazel did not bother to contradict this statement, Caroline asked, "What is it?"

"Cancer. Not breast cancer, like your mother," Hazel added quickly. "Lung cancer. We're a lucky family."

"How long have you known?"

"Before your father passed away. I didn't want to tell you then, with you having to deal with the funeral and selling the house."

"And then Bob and I got divorced."

"It was easier just to talk to you on the phone as if nothing was wrong."

"I could tell something was going on with you. With the way you talked."

"Ah." Hazel pantomimed smoking a joint.

"Is that wise?"

"It's the only thing that keeps my mind calm. And am I really going to do more harm to my lungs?"

Unexpectedly, Caroline laughed, which she tried to hide behind a cough, but Hazel just nodded in understanding.

Caroline took a deep breath and then took her aunt's hand, fragile and clawlike, in her own. "You *are* being generous. Thank you for letting me help you."

Gratitude was the overwhelming emotion Caroline felt in the final few months of Hazel's life, accompanying her to doctor's appointments, cleaning up after her, cooking and keeping house; gratitude that she could be there when she had been too young for her mother and too distant and unaware for her father. On days when Hazel was feeling well, they'd take walks in the neighborhood, usually ending up by the Hudson River. On days when she wasn't, they'd stay inside and smoke pot, until Caroline felt like her existence was being drawn out as thin as thread.

When Hazel died, five months after Caroline had come to

live with her, Caroline inherited the rent-controlled apartment, the gallery, and, although she only came to realize it years later, despite the friends and lovers that rotated throughout the years, the solitariness of her aunt's life.

This morning, when Caroline looked around her kitchen, she thought how not much had changed about the kitchen since Hazel's day. She had kept the avocado-green appliances, the Formica table, the curtains, now yellowed with age. The rest of the apartment, however, Caroline had gradually converted to her own style. Gone were the Middle- and Far Eastern influences, replaced with modern furniture. A few paintings hung on the walls, by artists she'd been unable to sell in the gallery but considered too promising to let go. None of them ever turned out to be worth much, but she felt she owed these artists something.

She couldn't do much else to mitigate the age of the apartment, which hadn't been renovated since Hazel had moved there in the 1950s, since she didn't own the place. If she'd been smart, even as late as ten years ago, she should have borrowed to purchase the apartment and the gallery below. But rent control had lulled her into complacency, and now she was in danger of losing both places.

A few weeks ago, her landlord had sent everyone in the building a letter stating his intention to turn co-op, meaning they'd have to purchase into the building at its current value or leave. This wasn't the landlord whom Aunt Hazel had dealt with, who'd given her an unprecedented deal for renting both the apartment and gallery space sixty years ago, but that landlord's grandson, who lived out on Long Island. Caroline had commiserated with her other neighbors—an elderly couple who was fit for the retirement home anyway, a young couple who needed more room for their growing family, and two female roommates in their twenties who should be living in Brooklyn instead—but she doubted that any of them were in quite her situation. Simply put, Caroline had no other place to go if she wanted to stay in business. She was willing to find another place to live, but if she lost the gallery, she'd lose the only thing she'd inherited from her family.

The gallery didn't make enough money to warrant moving it to another location; and, if Caroline was being honest with herself, to preserve its current one. When Caroline had inherited it, it was in a steady decline. Resuscitation had come from an unlikely source. After Hazel's death, Caroline discovered her aunt had a storage space in the basement of the building that contained paintings by artists whose work had become quite sought after. At first Caroline had wondered whether Hazel had some kind of sentimental attachment to them and if so, why she hadn't displayed them in her own home. Then she realized they were collateral, to be used judiciously when needed. So she moved the paintings to a climate-controlled storage locker and sold them one by one during lean times at the gallery, usually when she was on the brink of shutting it down, and somehow they always pulled her through.

Now, though, there were no more paintings, and even if there were, she'd need something spectacular to save the gallery. What she currently had on exhibition wouldn't do. Sandro Hess, a middle-aged painter of German and Argentine descent, used vibrant colors but his work paled in comparison to what other galleries in the area were showing: multitextual, multimedia installations by artists barely into their twenties. Also, for some reason, Sandro had gotten fixated on the motif of Mickey Mouse. Caroline didn't know if this was indicative of the artist regressing in age or nostalgia for a childhood he'd never had. When she asked her assistant, Molly, who was in her early twenties, what she thought, Molly merely shrugged and said,

"It's all subjective, right?" As if she were talking to a professor and afraid she had been asked a trick question.

Caroline had been concerned Molly would turn out to be the kind of assistant she saw at other galleries, girls who thought that their proximity to art meant they needed to dress up like abstract paintings themselves, who hung on to artists and buyers with the hope that some of their fame or wealth would rub off on them. But Molly came to work every day wearing interchangeable tops and skirts of mismatched shades of black, scuffed black ballet flats, and her mousy brown hair pulled back in a ponytail. Without complaint, she did whatever task was given her, whether it was cleaning up years of spreadsheets and files on the computer or running minor errands for her boss.

This morning, when Caroline made the ridiculously short commute down the front stairs of her apartment building and into the gallery, Molly was sitting at the front desk looking at her laptop screen. The vase of flowers next to her were half dead, which went against Caroline's belief that there be fresh flowers on the front desk every day.

She was just about to comment on it when Molly said, "Sorry I didn't have a chance to pick up fresh flowers this morning. The train was late today."

Caroline wondered why young people always seemed to place the blame on anything other than themselves, and preferably on inanimate objects. She handed Molly a twenty-dollar bill. "You can get the flowers now, please. Plus a tea for me." She assessed the dark circles under the girl's eyes and added, "And a coffee for you. You look like you could use it."

As Molly stepped out from behind the desk, Caroline prompted, "Were there any calls waiting for me this morning?"

"Just Sandro Hess."

"Did he say what he wanted?"

"The usual, whether you had any potential buyers lined up."

Caroline rolled her eyes. The opening of Sandro's show had been almost a month ago, at the beginning of summer, and while he'd gotten more media coverage than she'd expected, nothing had come out of it. It wasn't the first time she'd thought it was a mistake to take Sandro on as a client. Really, as more than a client. But he had been so charming when they'd met, with his dark eyes and unplaceable accent. Sandro's money woes were well known to anyone who spent more than five minutes in conversation with him—the support to an ex-wife and child—and while it could garner some sympathy, it usually just made him look vulnerable and weak.

"If he calls again, just say I'm out at a meeting," Caroline told Molly.

The girl nodded and said, "And I'm not sure when you'll be back, but you'll call him if you have anything positive to report."

"Exactly."

How different Molly was from her vivacious mother, Caroline's college roommate, Rose Calhoun. She was Rose Schaeffer now, of course, had been for more than thirty years. When Caroline moved back to the East Coast, she and Rose had started meeting up for lunches in the city every few months or so. They managed to keep it up for years, as Caroline went from one financial struggle at the gallery to another, and Rose went from new mother to PTA volunteer to empty nester.

At one recent lunch, Rose mentioned her daughter, Molly, who was the youngest of her three children. For some reason Molly had quit school two months before she was set to graduate, and was moving to the city that summer to live with her college boyfriend.

"She was studying art history," Rose said. "Guess she was influenced by all the postcards from the Metropolitan Museum of Art you sent her over the years."

"May I remind you that I never studied art history?"

Rose laughed. "True. Well, it's not like an art history degree will get you a job."

Caroline knew what Rose was going to ask next, but she tried to stave it off by pretending to be interested in other aspects of the girl's life. "And you think it's a good idea that she's moving in with her boyfriend?"

"Sam's nice enough. They've been dating since the beginning of senior year. He works in a municipal garden."

Caroline pictured one of the city's green-clad sanitation workers, moving through the park with their plastic bags and trash pickers. Surely Rose meant something else.

"As for moving to the city, even though it'll be the two of them sharing a place, Caleb and I are probably going to have to help cover her part of the rent. I know, but it's hard for her father and I to deny her anything, especially after what she's been through at school. She had this roommate..."

Mentally, Caroline checked her schedule and wondered whether she could cut this lunch short by saying she had a meeting with a client.

"...so, I was wondering if maybe Molly could come work at your gallery? As your assistant? She did have some experience working as an admin at school."

Caroline was reluctant to admit to her old friend that she hadn't been able to afford an assistant in years. As if aware of what she was thinking, Rose added, "You wouldn't have to pay her much."

"She's probably overqualified, but I'll give it a chance," Caroline finally said.

"Great." Rose's smile lit her face in the way that Caroline remembered. "Thanks so much, Caro. I know she'll do well. She already looks up to you."

Since Molly had studied art history, Caroline thought of pawning her off on her friend Peter, who had been Hazel's assistant at the Lowry Gallery back in the day. Peter was now an art historian who was currently copyediting the arts section of a free newspaper and living off of his wealthier partner. But when she'd suggested it to him, Peter had said, "What would she help me with, catching all the times someone writes a letter to the editor and spells *Pollock* as *Pollack*? It's the *fish*, not a misspelling of the ethnicity."

Now whenever they met for dinner, Peter would inquire after Molly.

"How's your little protégé?" he asked at their most recent encounter.

"She's not my protégé."

"You must be teaching her something."

"I guess she's about to get a master lesson in the business of running an art gallery." Caroline told Peter about her landlord's ultimatum concerning the building. "The situation is just as bad as when Hazel left me the gallery the first time, if not worse."

"And there's nothing left in her private gallery in the basement?"

"Not one thing."

Peter had been instrumental in identifying the valuable paintings in the basement and instructing Caroline on what to do with them. Now he regarded her thoughtfully. "Too bad she never had an Andrew Cantrell."

"You'd think she would, given their relationship. But maybe she felt it was too painful after all they'd been through together."

"All the more reason to have one. Tell me, is Cantrell's wife still alive?"

"Naomi Cantrell? She must be in her eighties by now. She supposedly doesn't have anything by him, either—all his work was in his studio in East Hampton when it went up in flames."

"Now, that's hard to believe."

"No one bothered to dispute it. They didn't have any children or relatives who laid claim to his estate. Cantrell didn't have money of his own anyway, it all came from his wife."

Peter looked around the dimly lit restaurant with an exaggerated air of secrecy. "I'm not disputing that fact about Naomi Cantrell. But I think Hazel had an Andrew Cantrell painting."

"She didn't..." Caroline trailed off when she was beginning to grasp what he was saying.

"Have you ever heard of Zhang Daqian?"

"Who?"

"One of the most influential Chinese artists of the twentieth century, in his country and outside of it. Of course, outside of it he was better known as a forger. He produced paintings attributed to the great Chinese painting masters from centuries ago that were sold to places like the Boston Museum of Fine Arts and the Metropolitan Museum of Art."

"How did he do it?"

"He was a skilled artist, but he also made sure all of the technical details lined up—the age of the paper, the kind of ink, the appearance of the seal, that kind of thing. That's what makes forgeries of classical art so much more difficult than, say, post–World War II art, because the painting has to use materials plausible from that age and the artwork itself has to seem hundreds, or in Daqian's case, thousands of years old."

"Meaning?"

"That you, my dear, need to find yourself a Zhang Daqian."

"And if I find him?"

"Give him something worth copying."

When Caroline didn't respond, Peter pressed the palms of his hands together and looked skyward, as if in a benediction. "WWAHD." When Caroline looked confused, he added, "What Would Aunt Hazel Do."

Hazel would have told that landlord exactly what she thought of him, how he was a disgrace to his father's name and the names of all of his ancestors before him, but in the end she would have done whatever it took to preserve the gallery. So that's what Caroline decided she would do, too.

Provenance, or the origin of the painting, was a big issue, but there were stories all the time about paintings mysteriously showing up. A canvas belonging to a Nazi sympathizer that turned out to have been looted from a Jewish family. A work that had formerly been attributed to an apprentice now discovered to have been executed by his master. Andrew Cantrell had no institute or estate that could authenticate or verify his work. All Caroline had to go on was Hazel's relationship with Cantrell, and the fact that she had inherited everything that had belonged to her aunt.

Through Peter she learned more about the mistakes that contemporary forgers made: using the wrong kind of canvas, the wrong kind of paint, chemicals that hadn't been invented at the time the painting had supposedly been made. Peter suggested that rather than pretending to have discovered a completely unknown work by Cantrell, that she choose something that had existed and was said to have been lost in the fire.

Down in the basement of the building Hazel had a stack of catalogs from the year the Lowry Gallery had shown Andrew Cantrell's painting *Elegy*. Opening to the faded image on the page, Caroline recalled seeing it not only the time Hazel had introduced her and Rose to Cantrell, but in another context. She had been in San Francisco, in front of a newsstand, looking at the paper whose sensational headline declared the death of an American artist. No matter that Cantrell hadn't sold anything since the two-million-dollar offer for *Elegy*, and his style of painting had since gone out of favor. In his picture on the front page, he didn't look that different from the man she'd seen at the gallery opening, except perhaps with more hair; maybe the newspaper had run a photo from an earlier, more prosperous time. Accompanying it was an image of *Elegy*, describing it as one of the paintings lost in the fire. Even in newspaper ink, the painting seemed to leap from the page. This, Caroline decided, would be the work she would resurrect.

She didn't doubt that she could find someone with the technical skill to pull it off. She had worked with enough artists over the years to recognize that technical prowess was very easy to come by; what was difficult was to find the right blend of vision and confidence. What she needed was to find someone who knew enough about the artist but not so much as to be intimidated. And someone who would be willing to do the job for very little money. Perhaps a disgruntled artist who had watched his cohort leave him behind in terms of money and prestige? A cocky young art student who wanted to thumb her nose at the establishment? Caroline decided that Peter was right, she needed to find her Zhang Daqian, in more ways than one. She didn't need a renowned master, but a foreigner who knew enough English to understand the deal but not enough to feel comfortable going to the authorities. Someone who lived on the outskirts of life as well as fame.

Where would she find an artist like that? She couldn't ask anyone she knew, at the risk of ruining her reputation. If she put an ad online, she could be traced. She had spent weeks pondering this when she happened to stop in front of the Metropolitan Museum of Art, arrested by a Monet reproduction being sold at a stall. This Chinese man, Liu, was the perfect candidate. He certainly knew how to play a part—witness the traditional clothes he wore and the tea he served when she visited his meager living conditions in Queens. He must have thought she was one of those women of a certain age whose homes were filled with souvenirs of another culture, as proof they were worldly.

According to the canvases he showed her in the studio, Liu appeared to be stuck artistically as well as financially. He'd have to paint dozens of his Impressionist replicas to make the three thousand dollars she was offering him. Fortunately, he didn't seem to catch on that the client for the painting was fictitious, and neither did he blink an eye about being paid in cash. She figured that was how he must usually operate. And it could be that this job would break him out of his rut, of drawing the same image—was it a mountain or something else phallic?— over and over. Caroline convinced herself she was doing him a favor.

That had been a few weeks ago. She'd delivered half of the payment to Liu but hadn't heard from him since. He'd said he'd need a month to finish the painting. Caroline supposed she was being paranoid, but she didn't trust e-mailing or even tele-phoning him to find out how he was doing. And she wasn't about to go all the way out to his studio unless she had to.

Molly had returned to the gallery by now, bearing a bouquet of chrysanthemums with pathetic-size blooms. Caroline should have told her to go the Korean grocer two avenues over instead of two blocks up, where the chrysanthemums looked like mop heads. Leaving Molly to arrange the flowers, she went into her office and had taken the first sip of her tea when the ex-tension on her phone rang.

"It's Peter on line one," Molly's tinny voice rang out when she pressed the button.

"That's fine, Molly, I'll take it."

"You know how we were talking about that Andrew Cantrell painting?" Peter said. "I think I have someone who's interested in buying it. He's a Taiwanese businessman, last name Yu. Damian met him at a company event. Turns out he's looking for Western art as an investment piece. Someone like Cantrell would be right up his alley, not a huge name but could possibly be big in a few years."

Damian was Peter's partner, who worked for a foreign in-vestment bank. Caroline didn't like him much, finding him too sleek in his well-cut suits, but somehow he and Peter had been together for nearly a decade. Caroline frowned, thinking about how much Peter must have told Damian over the years about her family history. There was no way Peter could have kept the latest twist in the story to himself. Already too many people knew about this scheme for her comfort.

As if he could tell what she was thinking, Peter said, "I only told Damian that you had an Andrew Cantrell painting that you were trying to find a private buyer for."

Caroline doubted that Damian would be so incurious as not to want to know more, but she merely said, "What makes you think this Taiwanese businessman can afford to buy art?"

"He's the head of some kind of manufacturing company. Computer parts, I think Damian said. What are you planning to sell the painting for?"

"How much do you think I should sell it for?" Caroline had estimated a few hundred thousand dollars, but she wanted Peter's opinion.

"Two million," was Peter's immediate reply.

"You've got to be joking."

"Not at all. That's how much Andrew Cantrell was offered for it back in the day, right? It's a bargain, considering inflation. Anything less, and the buyer won't think you're serious. Or even that the painting's real."

"Won't he want verification?"

"If he needs a professional opinion, I'm happy to step in."

"You're just an art historian. What if he finds an actual art authenticator?"

"Trust me, he won't. These things happen all the time in art sales. People who won't blink an eye at paying a few hundred thousand dollars for a painting balk at spending a few hundred dollars for X-ray imaging or paint analysis. They're the ones who want to believe the most that a painting is real, and the desire to believe is a powerful thing."

Caroline leaned her head against her hands. "Okay, Peter. I

trust you." After all, she'd trusted him before when it came to selling art, with positive results. Also, she was beginning to think she needed an ally, that she wasn't strong enough to pull this plan off herself.

"Good," Peter replied, "because Damian passed your number on to this man Yu so he can stop by your gallery before he leaves the country. That should be in the next couple of days."

A momentary sense of panic rose in Caroline, which she quickly quelled. Even though *Elegy* didn't exist in reality yet, it existed on paper. She'd show Yu the catalog and tell him she was getting the painting restored, its condition not being the best after spending years in storage. This wouldn't be so different from what she did every day, trying not only to sell a piece of art to someone, but her thoughts about its aesthetic merit and value, which were usually not the same thing. Sometimes she wondered if she and the client were even looking at the same painting.

"This has to work," she spoke her thoughts out loud. "Otherwise I'll lose the gallery." Catching herself, she shook her head. Together, she and Peter would have made the worst spies in the world.

"Of course it'll work," Peter assured her.

After she hung up the phone, Caroline went to the front desk, where Molly had her head studiously bent over her laptop.

"Molly, I should let you know that an important client will be coming around in the next day or so. Someone by the name of—" She paused, not knowing the man's first name. "His last name is Yu. He's from Taiwan, so keep an ear out. If he calls, please put him straight through to me."

Molly nodded, catching on to the importance of the event.

Everything seemed to be coming together nicely: the painting, the artist, and the buyer. It was all thanks to Peter, Caroline thought. Maybe she should take him out to dinner and invite Damian along. It might be a good idea to find out just how much

Damian knew and impress upon him the need to stay silent. Because if anyone was going to take the fall, it was her. As far as Liu knew, he had been hired to paint a replica. Peter had done nothing more than plant the seed for the idea, and Damian had simply made the client connection.

As long as no else found out about the forgery, she'd be safe.

# Chapter 3

"Is there anything else you need me to do?" I asked my boss at the end of the day.

Caroline looked at me over the rims of her glasses, which I thought were fancy but ugly. "No thanks, Molly. You can go home now."

On the subway ride back home, I watched the faces of the people getting grimmer and grimmer the farther the train went into Queens. I wondered what it would be like to have the kinds of jobs I imagined they had, the men in their wrinkled suits and the women in support hose. Some kind of sales rep or government administrator. If a seat opened up, I pretended not to see it. I was probably the least deserving person among them to sit down. Not that I didn't sit all day at work anyway.

Compared to them, I felt like a fake. Although in a different way from Lauren and Sabrina, girls I'd known in college, whom I occasionally met up with for drinks. Lauren worked in a public relations firm, while Sabrina was an assistant to an ad executive. I'd listen to them, stirring the ice at the bottom of a drink that was way too sweet and pricey, as they talked about sample sales, one-hundred-dollar blowouts, and terrible dates with junior investment bankers. They shared an apartment on the Upper East Side and complained about how difficult it was to walk to the subway in new heels purchased at the aforementioned sample sales. I didn't feel like I was younger than them or older than them, just that I lived in an entirely different city.

What could I say that would interest them? That, aside from my boss and the deli worker from whom I bought lunch, I hardly had any face-to-face interactions all day? That I spent my mornings purchasing flowers and tea for my boss, and my afternoons fielding calls from disgruntled artists or my boss's gay art historian friend? That after work I went home to the apartment I shared with my college boyfriend, Sam? And that our relationship was as convivial and dull as anyone's who had moved in together too young?

I got off the train and followed everyone else down the stairs and into the street. Over the past few months the signs had stopped being a jangle of unfamiliar words and colors and turned into what was just my daily routine. On the corner was the bar Sam and I went to sometimes on Friday nights. Opposite it was the Dominican bakery where we got milky sweet coffee and cheese rolls on Sunday. Down the street was the salon—excessively called Number One Modern Beauty Parlor—that I had gone to once, when I'd first arrived in the city in the heat of late summer and been totally disgusted by the state of my toes. I'd worn my nicest pair of sandals but after walking around all day, my toes turned completely black.

After rounding the corner, I walked down a series of side streets before reaching our apartment. Sam and I had always planned to move to the city after we graduated, only I had screwed up the plan by dropping out of school before the end of our senior year. We'd kept up our long-distance relationship, with him at school while I lived at home and figured out what to do with my life. When I told my parents I was moving to the city to be with him in the summer, I think they were worried this meant I wasn't going back to school to finish my degree. *What's the point?* I wanted to tell them, but knew they wouldn't understand.

Predictably, my mother was also worried whether the neighborhood was safe. It went without saying that she only knew the city from lunches with her friend and my boss, Caroline Lowry. While I was growing up, she was always talking about her fascinating friend Caroline, who lived in the city and wore bright scarves and oversize jewelry. When Caroline came up to Connecticut for a visit, which was not very often, she struck me as less mystical than my mother had described, but that was a good thing. I was still a little afraid of her, because whenever my mother talked about her at the dinner table, my father would make disagreeable noises, like she was something that caused him indigestion.

Also, Caroline would occasionally send me postcards from the Metropolitan Museum of Art, which my mother would treat as if they were as precious as the paintings themselves. And they were never postcards of paintings suitable for children, like one of Edgar Degas's dancers or a garden scene by Renoir, but ones that hinted of more adult desires, like John Singer Sargent's *Portrait of Madame X* or Henri Rousseau's *The Repast of the Lion*. When I finally went to the Met as a teenager, I would walk by a certain painting and feel a certain tingle of recognition, as if someone had whispered into my ear or touched my shoulder. Then I thought, *Oh, Caroline sent me a postcard of that one.*

My mother was the one who arranged for me to work for Caroline. I don't think she had any faith I could find a job on my own, and maybe she was right. I mean, I didn't have a degree. Sam worked for an urban farm in Brooklyn, conducting class field trips for kids who evidently had no idea where their food came from. "Can you believe some of them didn't know that carrots grow in the ground?" he'd marvel. He came home at night bearing seasonal vegetables and stories about some ridiculously cute thing a child had said. I thought of it as his "quote of the day." His major had been early childhood education, and privately I wondered if he would end up dumping me for a blond Midwestern girl who worked for Teach for America. Maybe I even hoped he would.

Today, when I got home, he was already there starting dinner. From the smell of it, we were still stuck in summer squash season. Sam tried every way to get rid of it, in bread and fritters and soup, making me think of the zucchini in my mother's garden. For a moment, I wondered whether it was too late to sneak out the door and get takeout. But Sam had already heard me come in and kissed me, his beard scratchy against my face.

"You know what this kid said today?" was the first thing he said.

"What?" I asked patiently.

"He said *vegans* are eaten by carnivores. I think he meant to say *herbivores*."

I had to laugh at that one. What a different world Sam occupied during the day, filled with living, growing things, both vegetable and human.

"Anything interesting happen to you today?" he asked.

"Nothing much. Except I overheard this conversation between my boss and her art historian friend this morning." I hadn't meant to listen in on the phone, except that they had mentioned Andrew Cantrell. I'd recognized his name from one of my art history classes.

"What'd they say?"

"Something about an Asian collector coming by to visit the gallery." I thought of the two Asian men who'd stopped in the gallery about a month ago. Neither of them had looked like they were involved in business, though. One was a graying bohemian and the other could have been a takeout delivery person.

"And that's unusual?"

"I don't know," I said. "There was just something weird about it. How secretive she was being. I guess it's none of my business." I didn't add that Caroline had basically admitted to needing to sell this painting in order the save the gallery. I could tell Sam was already checking out of the conversation by the way he was turning his head toward our miniscule kitchen.

"Sorry, babe," he said. "Got something in the oven."

After dinner, which was baked summer squash, I did the dishes while Sam watched a Web series on his laptop. We didn't own a television, and wouldn't have paid for cable even if we did, but a large part of our utilities went to high-speed Internet. Occasionally a burst of laughter came from the living room, and while once that might have made me smile or ask what was so funny, now I just blocked it out as I did the noise coming in through the open windows. Our building was close enough to our neighbors that I could hear the clatter of someone else doing their dishes, a door slamming downstairs, a person whistling as they walked down the street. Farther away was the low, ever-present hum of traffic from the expressway, occasionally interrupted by a motorcycle or police siren.

Sam was one of those people who went to bed early so he could get in a run before work the next morning. As soon as I heard the bedroom door close, I went to the small second bedroom. It was around the size of a walk-in closet with a window, and it contained an easel, some half-finished canvases, half-finished tubes of pigment, a can of primer, crumpled and stained newspapers. This was my studio, and Sam's big selling point for the apartment.

"This room gets really good morning light," he'd said. "I'd never come in here, it'd be all your own."

I was too self-conscious to paint around Sam, even when I knew he was awake. I had barely made any art in college. As an art history major, with all the theory and philosophy and examination of the past, there was just no room for it. Then, when I'd moved back home, I'd gone upstairs to the attic and found inspiration for my latest project in a box of old photos. It would be a triptych of portraits depicting the women on my mother's side of the family. So far I'd been able to identify three generations back: my mother, my grandmother, and my great-grandmother, although there were few photos of the last one. The best was a black-and-white photograph of a woman from what I guessed was the 1920s. She stood confidently against a wall, one hand placed against the stone, her chin tilted up so that her face was turned away from the camera.

When I got the job at the Lowry Gallery, I pictured a finished project that I could take to Caroline. My boss would say it was the most promising work she'd seen by a young painter in years and offer me a show on the spot. Or, she'd recommend me to an agent or the owner of a larger gallery, and, just like that, I'd have my first solo show.

Once I started working at the gallery, though, I knew that would never happen. In my first month on the job, I'd walked around to other galleries in Chelsea. After getting over the sleekness of their interiors and the receptionists who worked there, I was thoroughly confused by the art they represented. Nothing spoke to me, not even a murmur. Everything, from neon-light installations to videos that required 3-D glasses, left me cold.

So I went to the museums, the Whitney, the Frick Collection, the Guggenheim, the Museum of Modern Art, and, as a last resort, the Metropolitan Museum of Art, where I wandered its dusky halls as if looking for old friends. Secretly, I liked the French Impressionists. Even though I also realized that made me about as unique in my tastes as my mother, who carried an umbrella imprinted with Monet's water lilies.

Now I fixed myself a cup of coffee in anticipation for a long night ahead and took it into my studio. I pulled back the old sheet draped over the canvas on the easel and really looked it. The outline of my great-grandmother's face gazed back at me, at this point revealing as little as a mask.

A few hours later, I got into bed and nestled against Sam's warm back. He stirred slightly but didn't wake up. I wrapped one arm as far as it would go around his chest and held on as if it were the only thing anchoring me to this earth.

My mother called me the first day of my job at the Lowry Gallery, wanting to know how it went, how was my commute, how Caroline was as a boss.

"She's fine, Mom," I said.

"She's not working you too hard already, is she?"

I thought about what I'd done that day: edit a press release for the Sandro Hess exhibition and compile a spreadsheet of the guests invited to the opening. Basic admin stuff, but maybe it would change as Caroline started to trust me more. I imagined her consulting me as to how to frame paintings and where to hang them, us going around to other galleries, her telling me gossip about artists and dealers. Although Caroline was my mother's age, she seemed and looked younger, with the potential for more fun. As the weeks passed, though, the work stayed the same. It really was like spending time with my mother, except unlike my mother, Caroline didn't ask me a million questions about the safety of my neighborhood.

The one thing I had looked forward to was Sandro Hess's opening. I'd met him once before then, after his paintings had been delivered and he came to talk with Caroline about how they should be hung. I had also spoken to him on the phone, his peculiar transcontinental accent immediately clueing me in since he never identified himself by name. From Caroline I knew he had been born in Argentina to a German father and an Argentine mother, who had divorced early in his childhood, and he had spent many years shuttling between those two countries.

He had been married and had a young son; he and his wife had also gotten divorced and he was constantly needing funds to pay for child support. He had been considered promising twenty years ago when he'd come to America and won some grants. Now, in his early fifties, he was trying to reinvent himself. Caroline had met him at the gallery opening of a friend of his, another South American artist, who made death masks of celebrities everyone wished were actually dead.

When Sandro walked into the gallery, he immediately came to my desk and said, "Ah, you must be Caroline's assistant. I can tell from your lovely voice."

This was despite the fact I hadn't spoken to him in person yet. I knew what Sandro looked like from preparing press release material and the Internet, but from what I could tell, those pictures were at least ten years out of date. His temples were now streaked with gray, contrasting with a fully dark, roughly trimmed goatee.

"What do they call you?" he asked, as opposed to "*What is your name?*" That must come from growing up in another country.

"Molly," I said.

"Oh, like the drug." He winked at me, as if to intimate that he knew what all the young people were into these days. Since no one had ever said that to me in college, even as a lame pickup line, I didn't buy his act.

"Caroline is out to lunch and should be back shortly," I told him.

"No matter," he said. "Maybe you can help me decide what paintings should go where?"

I came out from behind the desk and together we looked at the paintings that the framer had delivered, now leaning against the walls. I didn't have much opinion of Sandro's work and actually thought his repeated Mickey Mouse motif was juvenile.

After a few minutes of silence, Sandro asked, "What do you

think should go here?" He gestured at the wall that faced the front of the gallery. Any painting hung there would be visible from the window and draw the attention of someone stepping through the door.

"That one." I pointed toward a painting featuring a kaleidoscope of colors with Mickey's head in the center.

A grin spread across Sandro's face. "You have a very good eye, young lady."

I shrugged. "It's the most sellable one." I didn't mean to make it sound like I didn't think the others would sell, but Sandro didn't seem to take offense.

We'd moved that canvas against the front wall and had stepped back to take a look at it when Caroline swept in through the door. "Sandro! I hope you're pleased with the framer's job. You've really outdone yourself with this show." Then she looked at the painting we had just positioned. "Why is that one here?"

"Molly"—Sandro tilted his head toward me—"thinks this one should go in the front window. Because it's the most 'sellable' of the lot." I wasn't sure whether he was making fun of me or not.

"And why do you think that?" Caroline asked.

I tried to think of any art history terms I had learned in class, but those wouldn't work in this situation; they weren't looking for an analysis. "The colors," I said, trying to sound more assured than I really was. "People associate Mickey Mouse and rainbows with happy, positive things, right? A parent might want this for a kid's bedroom, or the head of a start-up for their boardroom." Surprisingly, both Caroline and Sandro nodded as if what I said made sense.

"Let's price this at ten thousand dollars," Caroline said. Sandro made a protesting noise, but she cut him off. "Affordable enough for both Upper East Side parents and Brooklynite entrepreneurs in their twenties."

She and Sandro went on to talk about the pricing of the

other paintings. Sensing that I was no longer needed, I went back to my desk. On a whim, I looked up Sandro's first solo show, at a downtown art gallery in 1990. There was one write-up, accompanied by a photo of the show. From the paintings I could see, Sandro's style was very different back then. According to the article, the main focus of the show was a series of landscapes from his native Argentina. One in particular depicted a landscape with snow-covered mountains. I looked from the computer screen to Sandro's present-day paintings, and then back again. It was as if I was looking at the work of two different artists. How did you evolve into being such a different kind of painter?

The day of the opening, I decided to wear my only black dress and a pair of heels instead of my usual flats. I spent the entire day in this outfit for no one's benefit but my own, and then after closing hours, set up a makeshift bar in the back with wine and beer.

"That looks good, Molly," Caroline said. She had gone upstairs and changed into a black pantsuit with a silvery scarf the size of a shawl draped over one shoulder. The scarf reminded me of one of my mother's that was made out of recycled plastic bottles.

I glanced up as two people entered the gallery. I expected one to be Sandro but, as if reading my mind, Caroline said, "Sandro will be at least an hour late. He likes to make an entrance." Then she moved past me to greet her guests. "This is Peter." She indicated the older, shorter man. "And his partner, Damian."

Peter, I knew from answering the phone, was Caroline's art historian friend. His appearance seemed to match his voice: a slight, pale man in his forties with a receding hairline and rumpled clothes that suggested he sat down all day in the presence of other people as opposed to the privacy of an office. His partner seemed to be at least a decade younger, with an expression on his face that suggested he was already bored.

"Nice to meet you in person," I murmured. "Do you want something to drink?"

Peter asked for a beer; Damian, red wine. I handed them their glasses as Peter was expounding on Sandro's work: "Mickey Mouse, how precious! Derivative of early Roy Lichtenstein, of course, without the comic intent…"

Other people came in, and I skittered about on my heels like a crab trying to serve them. It seemed like they were in three categories: older people around Caroline's age who looked like they might be her friends; middle-aged ones who were involved in the media; and a younger, less well-dressed set who might have wandered in off the street looking for a free drink. Someone draped a familiar arm across my shoulder and I turned, expecting it to be Sam, whom I'd invited.

"Molly, my dear," Sandro said. "Can you get me the strongest drink in the room?" The way the shininess of his suit was reflected in his face made me think he'd already had a strong drink.

"Sure." I ducked under his arm and went into Caroline's office, where I knew she kept a bottle of whiskey. I didn't think she'd mind.

"That's perfect," Sandro said when I handed him the drink. Then Caroline spotted him and whisked him off to meet somebody more important.

Finally, I noticed Sam's face, or rather the glint of his glasses, above the crowd. "You made it," I said, unable to hide how glad I was to see someone I knew. To my relief, he must have stopped home before coming to the gallery, for he'd changed from his usual uniform of dirt-streaked T-shirt and jeans into a button-down and khakis.

"You look nice," he whispered in my ear.

I got each of us a beer, and we stood at the side of the room, observing the crowd.

"This is a decent turnout," I remarked. Because of the gallery's size, the fifty or so people packed inside made it seem like it was overflowing. In some places it was hard to see the paintings because of them.

"It's not what I expected, after you talked about how empty it is during the day," Sam replied.

"Once the clock strikes twelve, the magic of this place is over."

Sam cocked his head. "Someone's looking for you."

Caroline materialized at my elbow. After I introduced her to Sam, she said, "Can you please go find Sandro? He seems to have disappeared."

I handed my beer to Sam. "Hold this, will you? I'll be right back."

Sandro wasn't in Caroline's office, where I suspected he might be looking for more of the whiskey, nor in the restroom. I went outside and looked up and down the street, then crossed it. Opposite me, the gallery window was filled with the bobbing heads of people talking and drinking, backlit like a scene out of a film.

Going into the gallery again, I exited out the back door, which I thought of as Caroline's secret passageway, to the building's stairs. On the third floor, the door of Caroline's apartment was ajar. I knocked on it softly and stepped through.

"Hello?"

No one answered, so I flipped on the light. I had never been in Caroline's apartment before, but it looked just as I thought, with sparse, modern furniture and a few pictures adorning the walls. The paintings looked like they were originals, and I wondered what had happened to the artists. Then I noticed a framed photograph on an end table. I sat down on the sofa and picked it up, turning it to the light so that the figure became illuminated. It was a color photo of a woman with bright red hair, wearing a short beaded dress that appeared to be from the

1960s. Behind her I could make out the outlines of the front of the gallery.

"That's her aunt," a voice behind me said, so close that I almost dropped the photograph.

"Who?"

Sandro sat down beside me. "Her aunt, Hazel Lowry. She was the one who started the gallery." He had removed his suit jacket and was holding a glass of some kind of liquor in his hand, probably refilled from Caroline's kitchen.

"What are you doing here?" I asked. "How did you get in..."

I didn't want to know any more. Caroline wasn't the kind of person who accidentally left her door open, so that could only mean that Sandro had his own keys, which she must have given him.

"Oh, don't look like that," Sandro said, tossing back the rest of his drink.

"Like what?"

"Like you're disgusted at the thought. How do you think I got this show? Who else would want to display the work of an artist whose best days were twenty years ago, when he first started?"

I held up my hands. "I didn't say anything."

Sandro seemed to not have heard and continued with his monologue. "This show is the only way I can make some money. And I need it, to pay Claudia." I guessed that was his wife. "She's the one I care about. But"—he gestured so widely I was afraid the glass would go flying against the wall—"this is what I have to do. This is how the world goes 'round. And you'd better learn that's what you have to do, too."

"Let me take that." I reached out for the glass. Our fingers met, and then suddenly the glass went tumbling on the floor. He was so close to me that I could smell the whiskey, and perhaps something else, on his breath, as he pushed me onto the sofa, which would have been uncomfortable even without being pawed by a middle-aged, washed-up artist.

"Sandro!" I shouted in his ear, and he recoiled. I stood up, trembling with indignation and possibly fear. I straightened myself on my heels. Looking down on him, I said, "What could you possibly offer me?"

He lowered his head into his hands. "Nothing," I barely heard him say. "You're so young, you have everything before you. You have no idea what it's like."

No, I had no idea what it was like, but I couldn't help but feel sorry for him. "Let's go back downstairs. Caroline's looking for you."

"I can't."

"Why not?"

He lifted mournful eyes to me. "I'm scared."

I wanted to laugh. "Of who? Those people? You have to go back. At least if not for yourself, for your work."

"Okay," he finally said. A reluctant grin crossed his face. "You make a lot of sense, Miss Molly."

I wasn't about to forgive him, but I wasn't angry anymore. It would be like being angry at a toad. "You go down first," I said, and watched as he shuffled out of the room.

When I was sure he had left, I picked up the glass on the floor and took it into the oddly old-fashioned kitchen, where I rinsed it and placed it facedown on a dish towel. Then I went back into the living room. Before I switched off the light, I glanced once more at the photograph of Hazel Lowry. I could see a slight resemblance in the eyes between her and Caroline, even though Hazel must have been twenty years younger than Caroline's current age in the picture.

The rest of the night went smoothly. I didn't interact with Sandro again, and the last I saw of him, he was being carted off to a nearby bar by some young admirers. After everyone had left, I made a feeble attempt to clean up the mess left behind, with Sam helping me, but Caroline told us to go home. I tried not to think of what I'd learned about her and Sandro, of them together.

"God, just wear flats next time," Sam said as, clutching his arm, I hobbled up what seemed like an endless flight of stairs from the subway into the warm June night.

Once I got to our corner, I couldn't stand it anymore, took off my heels, and threw them into the trash can. Sam looked at me in disbelief, and then we started laughing. I think we were both a little drunk. Then he picked me up and carried me the rest of the way down the block, so my feet wouldn't get dirty.

A few days after Caroline had warned me about the very special client, he appeared.

I knew it was him immediately. He was the first Asian person to visit since the bohemian and the deliveryman about a month ago. I noticed him pausing in front of the gallery, looking at what must have been an address written on a piece of paper, peering through the window, and then looking at the paper again. Just as I was about to go outside and ask whether he needed assistance, he came in.

It was hard for me to tell whether he was twenty, thirty, or forty years old. He was casually dressed, not like a tourist, but in a linen shirt and tan pants, expensive-looking loafers, a light jacket draped over his arm. The planes of his face were pale and smooth, topped by a shock of thick dark hair. A silver watch with a complex face gleamed on his wrist just below the cuff of his shirt.

"Can I help you?" I asked.

He approached me, and I saw the thin silver of a wedding band on his ring finger. So maybe he wasn't twenty. "This is the Lowry Gallery?" His English was clear and precise.

"Yes," I replied.

"And you are...Caroline Lowry?" The faintest hint of confusion on his face.

I laughed. "No, I'm her assistant, Molly Schaeffer." I had no idea why I had given my full name.

"Molly Schaeffer," he said, "can you tell me where I can find Caroline Lowry?"

His use of the first and last names made me feel like I was in a language textbook exercise. I couldn't keep from speaking loudly and slowly. "Caroline has stepped out for a moment, but she will be back soon. I'm sure she will be pleased to see you. Would you like to sit down?"

"I prefer to walk around and look at the art," he said.

"Would you like something to drink? Water? Coffee?" Reminded by his Asian-ness, I blurted out, "Tea?"

I hadn't meant to sound so pushy, but he nodded. I went into the back room, looked through the various boxes and tins that had migrated downstairs from Caroline's apartment, and decided on Earl Grey. In the gallery, the client had paused thoughtfully in front of what was my least favorite of Sandro's work, a variation on Manet's *Olympia* except the nude's head had been replaced with that of—who else—Mickey Mouse.

I handed the man the cup of tea and he nodded again in thanks.

"What do you think?" I asked, tilting my head toward Olympia-Mickey.

"It is—how do you say—humorous?"

"Yes," I said, laughing a little too forcefully. "It's very funny."

He took a sip of his tea and I noticed a barely perceptible frown cross his face. Had I picked the wrong flavor? Maybe I should have asked him if he took lemon, like Caroline. Flustered, I excused myself and went into the back room to tidy up. When I returned to the gallery space, I noticed the cup had been placed on the front desk, apparently not having been touched again.

Thankfully, Caroline came in through the door a few minutes later. I said to her in a low voice, "The client's here. The one you told me to expect."

On cue, the client stepped out from behind one of the walls

dividing the gallery and, putting a wide smile on her face, Caroline stepped forward to greet him. "You must be...Mr. Yu."

"Harold Yu." He removed a slim, silver card case from an inner pocket in his jacket and presented her a card with both hands.

Then, to my surprise and secret delight, Mr. Yu turned to me and gave me a card, as well, which I took with one hand.

"Please come with me," Caroline said to him. "We can speak privately in my office. I'm so glad that you're interested in this acquisition."

I couldn't hear any more as they went down the hallway.

From the conversation I'd overheard on the phone between Caroline and Peter the other day, I knew Mr. Yu was here to purchase a painting by Andrew Cantrell, which I'd never heard Caroline speak of, nor seen mentioned in any of the files, records, or papers I'd been assigned to organize since I'd been hired at the Lowry Gallery. Caroline would probably keep a painting as valuable as a Cantrell in a vault. I recalled seeing records from a warehouse on Long Island that detailed paintings from well-known contemporaries of Cantrell. Those, I guess, had been sold or moved elsewhere long ago.

Then I pictured the interior of Caroline's apartment. I wondered if the Cantrell was one of the paintings on her walls. Nothing I had seen looked like a Cantrell to me, as much as I knew what they looked like from an art history class. Idly, I typed Andrew Cantrell's name into my laptop's search engine and looked at the images. Some of his most famous paintings came into view, including *Meditation,* which was at the Museum of Modern Art. That had been the painting in my class textbook, a black canvas with a single, horizontal, dark-blue band in the middle that seemed to shimmer off the surface.

There were a few pictures of Andrew Cantrell, as well. He was not a very good-looking man. I found a black-and-white photo of him with an aproned woman who I guessed was his wife. Then another photo of him, in color, accompanied by a different woman with shimmering red hair. I had seen that woman's face before, in the framed photograph on Caroline Lowry's end table.

Feverishly, I clicked on that image, which led me to an article about a show at the Lowry Gallery run by Hazel Lowry, a "good friend" of Andrew Cantrell. I scanned the article, but didn't find much else that was of interest, just a list of names of famous artists and celebrities who had attended the event. Then, at the end, a single line: "Notably absent was the artist's wife, Naomi Cantrell, but Hazel Lowry eagerly stepped in to fill that role."

So Hazel Lowry had been Andrew Cantrell's mistress? I searched both their names together and found a number of tabloid articles about their being seen together at dinner, at the theater, walking down Fifth Avenue. Then I spotted an article about Cantrell's death in a suspicious fire that destroyed most of his work, suggesting that Hazel Lowry had been involved. "Scorned Mistress Sets Artist Studio Ablaze!" was the headline.

Caroline and Mr. Yu came out from her office, and I quickly closed the page.

"I look forward to showing you the painting in person," Caroline was saying to Mr. Yu. They shook hands, and I watched as Mr. Yu exited the gallery. In the same, deliberate fashion as when he'd arrived, he looked up the street, down the street, and began walking toward the corner.

Caroline had a distant but pleased look on her face.

"So he was interested in a Sandro Hess?" I asked innocently.

Her face shifted. "He's interested in another painting. It isn't anything you need to know about."

So, for whatever reason, Caroline wasn't going to tell me that Mr. Yu was interested in an Andrew Cantrell. And why should she? It was none of my business.

That night, when Sam was comfortably ensconced on the

sofa for his nightly binge-watching, I went into my studio and called my mother. Her overjoyed response to find I was on the other end of the line, as always, sent a pang of guilt through me.

"Did you know that Caroline's aunt, Hazel Lowry, was the artist Andrew Cantrell's mistress?"

"Why, yes. I remember when we were in college, we went into the city for a show exhibiting one of his paintings."

"Which one?"

"Oh, I don't know. This ridiculously dark painting that neither Caroline nor I could make any sense of. But Hazel was there. She was just sublime."

"What do you mean, 'sublime'?"

"She was wearing this incredible dress. And her hairdo! So red and massive. You have to remember, this was the sixties."

The way my mother sounded, I could easily imagine her around my age, awestruck by a famous artist and a beautiful woman, even if she didn't understand why. I was having a harder time picturing Caroline, even though I had once seen an old college photo of my mother's, her fair head next to Caroline's dark one. Caroline must have started dyeing her hair red, just as Hazel must have done, because there was no way Hazel's hair color was found in nature.

"Did you know Hazel was Cantrell's mistress?"

My mother hesitated. "I don't think so. I remember when he died, though, and the awful tabloids that came out afterward about her."

"What happened to her?"

"She died of cancer, poor thing. Less than two years after Caroline's father died. She was very important to Caroline, her only family, really. Caroline's mother died when she was young, and her father didn't sound like the warmest man. And then she got married and divorced out in San Francisco. She had pretty much no one but Hazel when she came back to New York. And she's lived like a nun ever since."

*Not quite like a nun,* I thought.

After I had assured my mother that I was being careful walking home from the subway, I hung up. I looked at the unfinished canvas before me, the portrait of my great-grandmother. In the blank space where her face should have been, I imagined the fine features, the radiant smile, from the photograph I had seen in Caroline's apartment. For the first portrait in my triptych, I needed a strong-willed, self-assured woman like Hazel Lowry.

# Chapter 4

On the flight home to Taipei from New York City, Harold Yu thought about the painting by the American artist he was going to buy, which he'd only seen in a catalog presented to him by the woman gallery owner.

"We're currently restoring it," she told him as they sat in her office, which was shabbier than he'd expected. The gallery was small and displayed some kind of child's artwork. The picture of the painting she'd presented him was quite different, though, a moody, gray-and-white piece.

Harold didn't pretend he knew anything about art, or that he wanted to buy this particular painting because it spoke to something within him. He didn't even know anything about the painter, Andrew Cantrell, whom the dealer said "would have been considered the next Jackson Pollock if he had lived." But one of his works hung in the Museum of Modern Art, and that was good enough for Harold.

"Where did you get this painting?" he asked the gallery owner.

She didn't miss a beat. "My aunt knew the painter himself

and received it from him as a present. She kept it a secret and I only found out recently that she had it, while looking through the things I inherited from her after she died."

"You don't want to put it up for auction?"

She sighed. "Mr. Yu, I'll be honest. I would hold on to this painting if I could afford to. The next best thing is to sell it to an individual buyer rather than an investment group, and that's not likely to happen if I take it to an auction house. I want it to have a real home."

Harold wasn't sure what she imagined his home environment to be like. "I will need independent verification," he told her.

"Of course. I can direct you to an expert if you want."

Harold knew most people would consider his decision foolhardy. Perhaps he should have looked for something via a reliable auction house like Sotheby's or Christie's, but that would have raised the price. He was willing to pay the two million dollars the gallery owner had asked for, with the hope that the value would increase over time. Besides, he liked taking a risk, for perhaps the first time in his life.

At Taoyuan International Airport, he flagged a taxi and was soon on his way home, north of Taipei. Last year his wife had convinced him to buy a town house out in Shilin District at the edge of Yangmingshan National Park. She convinced him the air would be better for their son, and Harold had to admit that being surrounded by greenery, with the promise of more greenery in the park just beyond, was refreshing. Like his wife, he'd grown up in the middle of Taipei, in an apartment block where the streets were overrun with stray dogs and cats howled late into the night. This apartment was newly constructed and would have not looked out of place in Singapore or Hong Kong, even Manhattan.

At first, he'd been a little discomfited by the change. Traditionally, the suburban area of Shilin District had been populated by politicians and diplomats, since they were the ones who had money. Then, all sorts of people who made their fortunes off of real estate, transportation, and the manufacturing business, as Harold's father had done, became well off enough to live there, too. The area was somewhat isolated, but Harold's wife could still employ a Filipino housekeeper, and she was able to take trips into the city to go shopping with her friends at the latest Western stores in the Xinyi Planning District.

Then, he started to appreciate how, on the commute to and from the office, sitting in the back of his chauffeured car, he could allow his mind to wander. When he passed the National Palace Museum, the ornate, palatial complex filled with artifacts brought over from the mainland in 1949, he began to draw together his thoughts, either toward work or home. Usually, on the way home, he'd wonder what expensive purchase his wife had made when she was out shopping.

On his trip back from New York, when he stepped through the door, he was greeted by his four-year-old son, Adrian, who had been allowed to stay up past his bedtime.

"I have a present for you," he said, after disentangling himself from the child's clinging arms.

"Where?" Adrian grabbed at the pockets of his jacket.

"Not there, silly. In my bag. I'll get it for you in a moment."

But his son was already crouching at his suitcase and tugging at the zipper so that Harold's careful packing spilled out onto the varnished floor.

"Did you get me something, too?" This from his wife, whose English name was Victoria; she went by the nickname Vicki. She stood backlit in the hallway so he couldn't quite tell whether there was a welcoming look on her face or not.

"Of course."

A squeal from Adrian as he discovered inside the shopping bag from FAO Schwarz a twelve-inch-long replica of the Staten Island Ferry. Harold hadn't known exactly where Staten Island was, but he remembered how much Adrian loved taking the ferry from Keelung Harbor, just outside of Taipei, to Xiamen

Island off of mainland China. Vicki had wondered why they couldn't take their vacation on an island in the Pacific, like her friends, and the entire time they were in Xiamen she'd been critical of the Chinese tourists, so crude and unfashionable. The worst thing anyone could say to Vicki was that she was Chinese instead of Taiwanese, despite—or because of—the fact that her grandfather had come to Taiwan from the mainland in 1949 as part of the nationalist government. In college, as she liked to remind people, she'd been the first runner-up to Miss Taipei.

Meanwhile, Harold thought it was important that his son have some exposure to the mainland, where much of his business had shifted over the past ten years. Someday, when Adrian was old enough to take over the company, as Harold had when his father died, it would be useful not to consider himself so different from the people across the Taiwan Straits. When they'd arrived in Xiamen, Harold couldn't see much difference between it and a Taiwanese city, except for the signage.

"The way they speak is terrible," Vicki would say. "My ears are bleeding. And the simplified characters on the signs everywhere hurt my eyes." Obviously she thought that mainland people were inferior, possibly more stupid, because instead of using traditionally written Chinese characters, as the people of Hong Kong and Taiwan did, mainlanders used characters with fewer strokes.

Adrian, however, seemed perfectly happy and excited by everything, the ferry, the beach, the guesthouse they stayed in, even if it did, as Vicki pointed out, lack the amenities of a five-star hotel.

Now Adrian rushed off to his room to play with the ferry, while Harold knelt and rummaged through his suitcase for Vicki's present.

"This is for you," he said, holding out a dark brown shopping bag.

As Vicki stepped into the light, he thought, as he almost always did when first seeing her after some time away, how lovely she was. Although in her midthirties, her face was as dewy as it had been when she'd competed for Miss Taipei. Of course, a lot of that was due to the various skin-whitening, wrinkle-reducing creams she applied every night.

"How thoughtful," she said, when she opened the bag to discover a Louis Vuitton purse with a pattern by a Japanese artist. She seemed pleased enough, even though he suspected she didn't know who the artist was and might have preferred a monogram that her friends could understand. And he hadn't thought very much about it all, other than passing by the flagship store on the way to FAO Schwarz.

"Glad you like it," he said. He glanced toward the kitchen. "Is there anything to eat? The meal on the plane was awful."

"I think the housekeeper left something."

Their housekeeper, Maribel, had been hired expressly because she could cook simple, traditional Taiwanese dishes. Every morning she took the bus from the city, laden with fresh produce, fish, and meats from the market, arriving just after the sun rose. Harold had no idea what she did when she wasn't at their house, on her day off, or whether she even had a family of her own.

After Harold had eaten some leftover three-cup chicken and made a few preparations for work the next day, he got ready to turn in for the night. In the meantime, Vicki had put Adrian to bed—Harold could hear Adrian's wails as his mother took his new toy away from him. Harold expected Vicki to be asleep, too, when he went into their bedroom, but she stirred when he lay down beside her.

"I got something for myself while I was in New York," he told her.

Drowsily, she asked, "What?"

"A painting."

"That's nice." She turned over so that her back faced him.

Beyond them, the night pressed in through the floor-to-ceiling windows. Harold wasn't quite used to the noises this environment presented: crickets instead of fighting cats, the sighing of the wind through the trees instead of rumbling mopeds. Sometimes he missed where he'd grown up, the aging apartment block where all the kids knew one another and played in the streets among the trash and stray animals. Here, Adrian's nanny took him to scheduled playdates with the children of families he didn't know, although the mothers were often friends of Vicki's. None of these women thought this was unusual, having been raised by nannies themselves. Harold was an only child, and although his family could have afforded a nanny by the time he was born, his mother had preferred to take care of him herself. At times, when watching his son, he wondered whether he should have let Vicki decide how their child should be raised.

But altogether, this kind of life, he told himself, was better for Adrian and for Vicki, and thus better for him, too.

At around the same time Vicki's grandfather had come to Taiwan with Chiang Kai-shek's government, Harold's grandfather had smuggled himself over the Taiwan Straits, although as a merchant fisherman. He lived in Keelung Harbor, raising his children on the docks. Harold's father was the youngest son and thus promised nothing. But when he was six years old, he was spotted and taken in by a wealthy but childless couple who put him through school. It was not a formal adoption, and Harold's father kept the last name of Yu, but it was very unusual for someone to take in a non-relative.

Improving on the previous generation, Harold had gone to Tai Da, or Taiwan National University, the best school in Taiwan. After college and finishing his compulsory military service, he went to work for his father's business, an electronics exporter that benefited greatly from moving production in the mid-2000s to China. Around that time, his old classmate Charlie Lin introduced him to his friend, who happened to be Vicki.

In the beginning, Harold had been intimidated by Vicki and her accomplishments, as well as those of her family. They still had ties to the government, and Vicki herself had studied abroad at Oxford; traveled throughout Europe; and seen the finest art in the Louvre and the Prado. Not to mention, she was the most beautiful girl who had ever agreed to go out with him. He was afraid that she would look down on him because the source of his family's wealth was so different from her own, but she seemed to take him on as her special project. She introduced him to the right people, told him what clothes to wear, where to get the proper haircut, which foreign car to drive. The president of Taiwan had been invited to their wedding.

On schedule, two years after they were married, they had Adrian. Harold thought finally Vicki would be satisfied, but she often talked wistfully about having another child.

"You're an only child," she said. "Weren't you lonely?"

Harold thought of his mother's attention, the neighborhood children whom he had played with, and shook his head. "I believe in the one-child policy," he tried to joke, before realizing it was the worst possible response he could have given.

"Like a mainlander!" Vicki spat. "Now that you have a son who can carry your name and inherit your precious business, that's all you care about."

Harold let her think that. He couldn't tell her that he didn't think having another child would make her happy. She was increasingly restless, seemingly bored with the regimen of shopping, entertaining, and keeping the process of aging at bay. She was so educated and had seen so much of the world, Harold often thought she should start her own business. But someone from Vicki's background did not work, or even take care of her own children. Her mother, the wife of a judge, had led a similar kind of existence.

In revenge for his one-child-policy stance, Vicki drew away from him. They still slept in the same bed, but nothing other than sleep had gone on in that bed for months. She got up after he'd left for work, allowing the nanny to feed and dress Adrian, and went to bed before he returned. He was away frequently enough on business trips to the mainland and abroad that they could go for weeks without spending a waking hour together. When Harold told her he was planning to return to New York in a month's time, he thought she looked relieved. He let her assume it was for business, whereas that was when he had been told the Andrew Cantrell painting would be restored and ready for purchase. He imagined unveiling the painting to Vicki and how surprised—maybe even impressed—she would be at how much he'd paid for it.

Before going to New York again, Harold had another trip planned, a legitimate one, visiting a factory on the mainland. There he would meet up with Charlie Lin, who over the years had evolved from classmate to colleague. Charlie's wife, Serena, was one of Vicki's best friends, and they had a daughter around Adrian's age. It was a well-known fact, both among their friends and their wives, that Charlie had a mistress in Shanghai whom he saw whenever he spent time on the mainland, which was as much as six months a year. A "little third," this mistress was called, referring to the third leg in a love triangle. Back when they still had conversations with each other, Harold and Vicki used to laugh at how short, square-faced Charlie had a "little third."

A week after he returned from New York, Harold took the two-hour-long flight from Taipei to Shanghai, and Charlie met him with a private car that delivered them to the Qingpu Industrial Zone on the city's outskirts, where many of the manufacturers were located. Often, migrant workers from the surrounding provinces stopped here to find jobs instead of venturing into the city itself, and there was an endless supply of them. A whole makeshift city appeared to have cropped up around the factory grounds, with flimsy stalls selling plastic slippers, batteries, and likely knockoffs of the products being manufactured inside.

Harold and Charlie were greeted outside the factory by a representative, a young woman who went by Miss Hao. She wore a cheap-looking skirt and suit set, but her eyes were bright and her cheeks flushed a little when Charlie remarked on how capable she looked.

After a preliminary meeting with some of the factory higher-ups, Miss Hao took them onto the work floor, where hundreds of young people, clad in white dusters and caps, blue masks shielding their noses and mouths, assembled electronics. Most of them were young women; Miss Hao, Harold thought, was probably the luckiest one out of all of them. He half-listened as she talked about workers' conditions, their twelve-hour days with paid overtime, their ninety-minute rest periods, and instead swept his eyes over the scene before him, each person a pixel on a screen. Then his eyes settled on one worker who had nodded off, her cap askew.

"Is there anything else you'd like to know?" Miss Hao asked.

Charlie said, "After the 'unfortunate incident' last year, have there been any further disturbances?" The unfortunate incident was that a female worker at the factory had died from taking rat poison, supposedly after discovering she'd been dumped by her boyfriend.

Miss Hao looked flustered. "None at all. We have a hotline set up if workers feel like they need to talk to someone. If they get too stressed, there are a lot of places here for them to relax. We have our own movie theater, basketball court, hair salon, Internet café where they can play computer games..."

"What about their dormitories?" Harold asked.

"Excuse me?"

Harold ignored the questioning, slightly annoyed look Charlie shot him. "We'd like to see their dormitories, too."

"I will have to speak to my bosses," Miss Hao hedged.

"We'd like to see them now."

Uncertainly, Miss Hao looked toward Charlie, who looked heavenward as if for patience and then nodded. So she took them outside past what appeared to be the basketball court, a scrubby, poorly paved piece of land with a single hoop set up, and to another building. This appeared to be a women's dorm, judging by the nature of the toiletries in the rooms; the plush animals on the metal bunk beds, eight to a room; and the floral-patterned clothes drying on the balconies. Very few people were inside during the day, only those who appeared to be sick. The youth of the women and their possessions made Harold think of a boarding school, only these girls would never gradu-ate to a better job.

He nodded at Miss Hao, satisfied, and with visible relief she led them out onto the campus.

"Well, that was depressing," Charlie said when they were back in their car and speeding toward Shanghai. "I think we need to do something tonight to cheer ourselves up. I'll call Jenny and have her find a restaurant. Maybe she can bring a friend for you."

"You know what my answer is to that." Every time they were in Shanghai, Charlie made Harold the same offer.

Charlie laughed and clapped him on the knee. "My incor-ruptible friend, Harold Yu! Someday we'll find out what he truly wants."

Harold had met Jenny, Charlie's mistress, before, and she had also insinuated that she could find Harold a "little third." She lived in an upscale neighborhood called Shanghai Villas and had a personal driver, all paid for by Charlie. Unlike most women in her profession, Jenny was older, well into her thir-ties, and had no desire for anything more from Charlie, such as children or a divorce from his wife. Charlie had confided in Harold that Jenny had grown up in a rural part of Jiangsu Province. She'd had a disastrous early marriage that resulted in a child, who lived with her parents. Five years ago she had come to Shanghai to start over and found work in a nightclub, which was where she had met Charlie. This was around the time Charlie's daughter had been born.

Jenny was not an unattractive woman, Harold thought, when she met them at a Mongolian hot pot restaurant along with two of Charlie's friends. She was, however, overdressed, in a silver sequined dress that showed off her legs. With her hair cut in a shiny bob that grazed her elegant jawline, she looked as polished as any one of Vicki's friends. Although Vicki would have seen right through her to her Jiangsu village origins.

Charlie introduced Harold to his friends, Jay and Yan, and then the food began to flow: thinly sliced beef, abalone, cubes of congealed duck blood, fish balls, lotus root, chrysanthemum leaves, all cooked in a steaming metal pot and washed down with cheap beer.

Harold didn't pay much attention to the conversation, until Jay mentioned something about purchasing a piece of what he thought was Ming dynasty porcelain at an auction.

"Turns out it was made by a factory in Jingdezhen," Jay said. "Three years ago! They have these places that turn out so-called ancient artifacts, just like they were shoes or phones. The workers actually look at auction catalogs and copy them. There's no honor in what they do."

"That's the problem with the Chinese art market," Yan remarked, and Harold remembered that he worked for some kind of anti-corruption board. "No oversight. Not like what we have in place for our factories."

"What made you decide to invest in porcelain?" Harold asked Jay.

"Easy. Have you looked at the Chinese stock market lately?

Completely unreliable. And Chinese property value has slowed down. People are so dissatisfied that they're starting to buy outside the country, in London and New York. In China, art is the only thing that lasts."

"Would you ever think of investing in a piece of American art? They've got to have more oversight."

Jay waved that away. "I don't know the difference between a Picasso and Matisse"—he pronounced the names as "*Bi jia suo*" and "*Ma di si*"—"and if I try to resell here, a Chinese investor won't know, either. Best stick to the artists whose names are known."

"Like who?"

"Qi Baishi. Xu Beihong. Zhang Daqian. You sell one of Qi Baishi's shrimp paintings, and you're set for life."

Charlie gazed at Harold over the rim of his beer glass. "I didn't know you were interested in art, Chinese or American."

"I'm not," Harold said. "Just looking for something dependable to invest in, like the rest of you."

Charlie gave a shout of laughter and drained his glass. "This is the most dependable investment I have," he declared, sliding his arm around Jenny's waist, and she smiled in a way that hid her teeth.

After dinner, Jenny suggested they go to a karaoke bar. She knew just the place, where the *xiaojie* were particularly pretty and obliging. But the one she took them to appeared to be crawling with foreigners, which made Harold doubt her taste. She and the four men settled themselves into a small, dim room illuminated by the blue screen of a flat-screen TV, where they flipped through laminated notebooks, smoked Zhonghua cigarettes, snacked on boiled peanuts, and drank watered-down whiskey.

At one point, a knock came at the door and three young women entered. They were dressed not unlike Jenny, who acted like their big sister and introduced them. Each girl was assigned to one of the men; Harold's was a waifish-looking one with big eyes, who for some reason reminded him of Miss Hao. The way she kept looking at Jenny for guidance made him think she hadn't been doing this job for very long.

Harold glanced at the watch on his wrist, a Patek Philippe that had been a gift from Vicki for his last birthday.

"You shouldn't have," he'd said when she'd presented him with it. "I can go to the night market and get a knockoff that works just as well."

Vicki's face had crumpled, and it had taken her a few days to forgive him, even after he'd repeatedly apologized.

The time was past midnight, too late to call Vicki, although he doubted she would care. In front of the room, Yan was swaying before the screen, slurring the words to a Taiwanese pop song. Everyone else watched him with seemingly rapt attention, although Jay's hand had slid down the cleavage of his girl's dress, and the girl who'd been assigned to Yan was sitting on Charlie's lap. Jenny, who sat next to Charlie, didn't seem to mind.

Harold felt a slight pressure on his thigh and looked down to see the hand of his girl lying upon it, as timid as a slug. Not wanting to offend her, he shifted so that her hand fell into the crack between them. In a moment, her hand had crept back. He grabbed her wrist and she looked up at him, confused and frightened.

He stood up. "We're going outside for a bit," he announced to the others. Charlie raised his whiskey glass to Harold with a knowing grin.

With his hand against her back, Harold hustled the girl down the hallway. "Did I do something wrong?" she asked him, and he shook his head.

At the entrance to the bar, she balked. "I'm not allowed to leave the bar."

He glanced at her impatiently. "You're being paid for your time, aren't you?"

"I guess." She indicated her short dress. "I can't go out like this."

"Can you change?" Some of the other patrons, including the foreigners, were staring at them now, and he was afraid he would get her in trouble.

She nodded.

"Meet me outside in five minutes."

When the girl arrived, she was wearing jeans and a fitted shirt, her long black hair pulled back into a ponytail. She'd scrubbed most of her makeup off, and in the streetlight she looked to be in her early twenties.

"Where are we going?" she asked.

"Where do you usually go?"

"I don't really go with customers—"

He sighed. "I mean, where do you go when you're off work? With your friends?"

"The night market, I guess."

"Then let's go there."

Harold followed the girl down a warren of side streets, newly brushed black by the rain, until they emerged into a splash of lights and color, raucous vendors and diners and sizzling food. It reminded him of the Taiwanese night markets he used to go to as a child with his parents, then as a college student and a young man, where almost everything one could ever want to eat was on display, as well as things one didn't want to eat, such as snakes. They walked by stalls displaying skewers strung with pieces of seasoned lamb and chicken hearts, plates of fresh clams on ice, piles of boiled and salted crayfish with their living counterparts scrambling in buckets behind them. Smoke from braziers hovered between the stalls and the night sky.

"What do you want to eat?" the girl asked Harold.

He thought back to his childhood, of walking down a night market street littered with refuse, each hand held by a parent. They stopped in front of a stall, and he watched as the vendor poured a circle of batter on a hot griddle, cracked an egg into it, and added a handful of oysters. His mother handed him the warm, eggy packet and he toddled down the street nibbling on the savory oyster omelet.

"Do you have *o-a-chian?*" he asked the girl.

"What? Oh, you mean *muli jian*. We have that here, too."

Harold purchased one for each of them, and they sat at a low plastic table with the other diners.

"What's your name again?" he asked her.

She thought for a moment as if trying to remember. "Tina."

"Your real name."

"Xiu Xing. Everyone calls me Xiao Xiu." *Little Xiu.*

"I'm Harold."

She laughed. "Where did you get such a funny English name?"

"My father chose it for me." His father couldn't even pronounce it properly. "Are you in school?" he asked her.

She laughed again. "What, you think I'm some college student working as a KTV girl on the side? That's a businessman's fantasy. This is my only job."

Little Xiu went on to tell Harold that she was from a small village in the neighboring Shandong Province. She'd dropped out of school at sixteen to work in a factory that made wedding dresses, but after six years got tired of the low wages and long hours.

"I was miserable," she said. "I couldn't stay awake on the floor so I took pills, and that made me anxious and jittery. I couldn't concentrate and made mistakes in my stitching and was penalized for shoddy work."

Harold thought of the factory he had visited earlier that day. "Didn't you have time off? Places you could relax in?"

"You mean like the Internet cafés?" she scoffed. "People go there to play on computers that are poor versions of the ones they just spent all day putting together. I wouldn't be caught dead there."

On a trip to Shanghai, Little Xiu found out through a friend that she could make more money in a KTV bar while only working nights. As Harold had suspected, she'd only started this job a month ago. Her parents, whom she visited every Spring Festival, thought she still worked at the factory.

Little Xiu asked Harold where he was from, and when he said Taiwan, she said, "I knew it! You don't seem like you're from the mainland. But not one of those *huaqiao*, either, from overseas. You're from Taiwan and you don't have a girlfriend on the mainland?"

Although he wasn't sure how true it was anymore, Harold replied stiffly, "I'm very happily married to my wife. She was first runner-up to Miss—" He stopped himself from echoing Vicki; this girl wouldn't care.

"All of them are happily married," Little Xiu said. "Otherwise they wouldn't want to share their happiness with another woman."

"And how do you think their wives feel?"

Little Xiu shrugged. "I heard a story somewhere, that a wife found out about her husband's mistress and threatened her. The mistress ended up poisoning herself. The husband was so upset that he divorced the wife, who lost her social status. You know who ended up with the best life?"

"The husband," Harold guessed.

"Yes, but at least the mistress had fun while she could. She lived a full life."

"Is that what you want out of life?" Harold asked. "To become someone's mistress?"

Little Xiu considered for a moment. "What I want out of life is a Gucci handbag."

Harold had to laugh. "Well, that's easy enough to get."

"Not a real one. Not for me."

For a moment Harold wondered whether he should go to the Gucci store that he was sure must be located on Huaihai

Lu, Shanghai's premier shopping street, and get Little Xiu her coveted handbag, just as he had gotten Vicki her Louis Vuitton handbag in New York. It would possibly take a little more effort, as he was due to fly out early the next day. Maybe Vicki would find the receipt for it, realize she'd never received a present from him after his trip to Shanghai, that she didn't even have a Gucci handbag lined up in her closet, and think he had a mistress. Would she care then, or would she continue to let their marriage slip away?

He realized Little Xiu was talking to him. "It's getting late," she said. "I need to get back to the bar before my boss notices I'm missing and some new customers come in. This is just the beginning of the night for me."

Harold checked his watch; it was two thirty in the morning. Then, on impulse, he unclasped the watch and held it out to Little Xiu. "This isn't a Gucci bag"—it was actually much more expensive—"but you can have it."

"No way!" Her already large eyes widened as she took the watch from him, turning it over in her hands. "It is silver?"

"Stainless steel. It's expensive, made in Switzerland. You can sell it if you want."

She grinned, put it on, and held out her arm to admire the watch on her thin wrist. "I want to wear it. It's probably the closest I'll ever get to Switzerland."

As they walked back, Harold felt Little Xiu's hand creep into his. Her fingers were small and soft, reminding him of a child who didn't want to let go. The watch on her wrist felt cool where it came into contact with his skin. Already, it seemed to be a part of her in the way it had never been part of him.

At the entrance to the bar, she whispered, "Thank you," and went inside.

Harold returned to the karaoke room he thought he'd left Charlie, Jenny, and the others in, but saw he'd made a mistake as soon as he opened the door. A bunch of college-age boys were inside with bar girls, several of whom seemed to have lost their tops. Harold muttered an apology and got out of there as quickly as he could, after settling the bill; as usual, Charlie had expected him to pay.

It took a few days after he got home from the Shanghai trip for Vicki to notice that he wasn't wearing the watch.

"Did you lose it?" she asked.

Harold tried to sound contrite. "I forgot to tell you. Maybe I left it at the hotel in Shanghai."

"Have you called the hotel?"

"What's the use? Someone probably took it and it's on the black market as we speak."

"Well, that's a pity." She paused. "You never really liked wearing that watch, did you?"

"I liked it because you gave it to me."

"But you didn't *like* it."

"I wore it, didn't I?" He turned his eyes back to the financial section of the newspaper he was reading. As Charlie's friend Jay had said, Chinese stocks really were terrible.

For a moment Vicki subsided, paced around the living room, rearranged the cushions on the sofa, then returned them to the exact same place. "Did you have a good trip?" she asked.

"It was fine."

"Other than losing your watch."

Harold looked at her over the edge of the newspaper and held her gaze. "Yes, other than that."

"I suppose you spent a lot of time with Charlie Lin."

"Yes, I was there to tour a factory with Charlie. You know that."

"While you were gone, I had lunch with Serena." Vicki began to pick at her nails, a bad habit Harold had noticed when they'd first met. "She says you must have a 'little third' in Shanghai, just like him."

Harold laughed and put down his newspaper. "Do you really think I'm like Charlie? First of all, I'm almost never in Shanghai for more than a night. How would I find a mistress, let alone spend time with one?"

"All right, not Shanghai, then. Maybe New York. You seem eager to go back there. Serena says everyone does it."

"Serena is a bitter woman who wants to see everyone around her as unhappy as she is. Just stop talking to her."

"Don't tell me who I can talk to."

Vicki was more than just agitated, Harold realized. She might even be delusional. At another point in their marriage he might have gone to her and held her, but her entire body, in a silky gray sheath that clung to her slim form, seemed to be vibrating with tension.

"Vicki, there's no one but you and Adrian." He stood up. "You're welcome to sit here and think the worst about me. In the meantime, I'm going to take Adrian out for the afternoon."

"Where?"

"I was thinking Keelung Harbor."

Vicki nodded abstractedly, without seeing him.

Adrian seemed happy to be going on a trip with just his father and insisted on bringing his Staten Island Ferry replica. On the bus, he surfed the orange vessel alongside the cars speeding by the window. As they disembarked at the bus station and walked toward the water, Harold wondered what his grandfather would think of Keelung City now, with its skyscrapers and modern port, appearing like a miniature Hong Kong.

He and Adrian strolled along the harbor, admiring the boats.

"Which is bigger, Daddy?" Adrian asked, holding up his toy and pointing to a white fishing boat in the distance. "The real ferry or that boat?"

Harold had never seen the Staten Island Ferry, but he assured Adrian the Taiwanese boat was bigger. "Do you remember when we took the ferry to Xiamen, Adrian?"

He was pleased when his son nodded. The trip had required them to book a berth overnight, and Adrian had liked running from one end of the room to look out the porthole, balancing himself against the almost imperceptible swaying of the ship.

"This is how your great-grandfather Yu came from the mainland to Taiwan," Harold had told Adrian.

"On this ferry?" the little boy had asked.

"Well, not on this exact ferry. But probably something like it."

In fact, from the stories his father had told him, Harold's grandfather had come over with around fifty other people on a fishing boat that would normally accommodate ten. When their supplies ran out, they ate raw fish caught from the boat. Their goal had been Kaoshiung at the southern tip of the Taiwan island, but storms had blown them days off course and they'd arrived in Keelung in the north instead. They were lucky to have even gotten there; if they'd missed the island altogether, they would have drifted out into the East China Sea and either died from thirst or pirates. But this wasn't a story fit for a three-year-old.

When they got to Xiamen, although Vicki complained about the guesthouse conditions and mainlanders in general, she eventually calmed down and they spent three days on Gulangyu Island, walking along its beaches and down its winding lanes. The lack of cars made it feel like they had stepped back in time, and Harold allowed himself to think about his grandfather's family. Although his family hadn't come from Xiamen, they must have migrated from somewhere along the coast of Fujian Province, or perhaps Guangdong Province just to the south. What would his grandfather have thought of the relations between Taiwan and the mainland now? For decades, people said there were three things that would never pass directly between the two: planes, boats, and letters. The fact that all of these were happening now was unthinkable.

Harold also had wondered what his grandfather would have thought of Harold's own life, his company, his expensive apartment, his beautiful wife, his smart son. All at once, he felt like bursting with pride at his accomplishments. Walking down the beach, with Vicki at his side and Adrian running ahead, he felt like the luckiest man alive.

That trip to Xiamen had taken place over a year ago. Maybe it was the last time he and Vicki had been happy.

Behind him, Adrian had set his toy ferry on the ground and was busy chasing a white paper bag down the wharf, the wind keeping it just out of reach. Harold turned away from him and looked into the waters of Keelung Harbor. In his mind he saw the Andrew Cantrell painting and its grayness swirling around an uncertain center.

# Chapter 5

When I was in my last year in school in Xiamen, I won a contest in my art class to see who could most accurately copy the work of the great Chinese master painter Qi Baishi. In the early 1900s he was considered to be one of the best painters of nature in the country. While he did paint landscapes, his specialty was flora and fauna, especially shrimp.

Why shrimp? And why were people so obsessed with his depictions of them? I attribute it to the Chinese fascination with food, especially seafood, and more so, fresh seafood. Qi Baishi's shrimp are definitely fresh. Antennae waving, arms and legs scrabbling, they look as if they are about to crawl off the paper and into your mouth.

"The point of the contest is *lin mo*," my teacher, Master Zhuo, explained. "The art of imitating the masters. The winner will get one hundred *renminbi*." Back then, especially for students, that was an unheard-of amount of money.

Immediately, my classmates and I set about devising strategies for winning the contest. It was no question that we'd all paint shrimp, but there can be twenty different versions of shrimp, just as there can be twenty different versions of the same story. Which is the most believable?

My classmate Rong Jiawen and I decided to work together. I considered him my biggest rival, although considering our backgrounds, he had a far greater advantage in life. His family was from Shanghai, one of those merchants who had miraculously survived not only the Japanese Invasion, the civil war, and the worst of communism, but had actually come out better for it. Not to mention his father was friends with the principal, but I had to admit he had talent. As for me, it was a miracle that my parents were able to pay my tuition. I suspected my father, who hadn't gone beyond primary school, might have been proud of me for the first time in my life.

"I have an idea," Rong told me after class. "Let's study real shrimp."

"What's the point of that?" I asked. "We're supposed to copy Qi Baishi, not actual shrimp." I had anticipated holing up in my room with my textbooks and copying Qi Baishi's shrimp paintings a thousand times, or until I got a cramp in my hand.

"Just come with me."

I expected Rong to lead me to the market, or maybe to the harbor to see what the fishermen had caught, but instead he took us to a small restaurant tucked away down a side street. SPECIALTY, LIVE SHRIMP! the handwritten signboard proclaimed.

Of course Rong was taking us somewhere to eat. He loved his food and wine, and could afford lavish meals at restaurants while the rest of us made do with steamed vegetable buns that tasted like paste from the school cafeteria.

After we sat down at a table, Rong ordered beer and lifted his bottle to mine in a toast. "To whoever wins the contest!"

"To whoever wins," I echoed, and took a long swig. I hadn't eaten live shrimp before, and while the prospect did not disgust me, I did wonder about getting food poisoning. Better bathe the stomach in as much alcohol as possible beforehand.

As the waitress plunked down a bowl of shrimp, it was apparent that the shrimp themselves were also on their way to getting drunk. They were marinated in strong liquor and soy sauce, spiked with scallions, garlic, and chili. Some of them barely twitched as we poked at them, while others contorted themselves enthusiastically, as if dancing to get our attention. One particularly feisty one did a backflip onto the table, leaving behind dark spatters of sauce.

Rong laughed and grasped it in his chopsticks. "You ready?" he asked me.

I picked a large shrimp from the bowl, positioned it in front of my lips, and nodded. On the count of three, we both popped the shrimps into our mouths. I had gotten a real live one. It squirmed against my teeth and punched the top of my mouth. Amid its frantic wriggling I managed to bite off the head and worry off the shell with my tongue, both of which I spat out on the floor. Only then was I able to concentrate on the flavor of the meaty body. The explosion of salt and spicy heat was delicious.

"Wait," Rong said around his mouthful.

"What?" I stopped midchew.

"Feel the movement of the body in your mouth. The essence of the shrimp itself, its life as it drains away. Then draw it."

I thought he was joking until he withdrew from his schoolbag some paper and charcoal. "We're drawing here?" I asked.

Rong swallowed and shrugged. "What better way to practice?"

It was truly one of the most enjoyable live-drawing experiences I've ever had. Rong and I got progressively more drunk on beer and more full on shrimp as we ate and drew, drew and ate. The table became scattered with pieces of sauce-stained paper upon which insectlike creatures swarmed, devolving from detailed depictions to blurred scrawls. Beer bottles piled up under our feet and shrimp shells littered the ground. The waitress scowled at the mess we were making, but she didn't say anything as long as we continued to order. I was relieved at the end when Rong offered to pay for our meal, before we staggered out into the humid, subtropical night.

That turned out to be the only time we practiced together. Otherwise I did what I had planned, studying any picture of Qi Baishi's shrimp that I could get my hands on. The painting I decided to imitate was one that showed two shrimp, front claws angled slightly toward each other, as if getting ready for combat. I figured one shrimp wouldn't be enough to show off my skill, while more than two would look sloppy.

The day of the contest arrived. That morning, we students filed into the classroom under the watchful eye of Master Zhuo, armed with rice paper, brushes, and ink. We had an hour to complete our paintings. I concentrated on following what I had learned about Qi Baishi's technique, that he had automatically painted each shrimp with a set number of strokes and in the same pattern, the way one might write a Chinese ideogram. He hadn't been painting from live shrimp at all; he'd committed the very shrimpiness of the image to his memory.

About forty-five minutes later, Master Zhuo was unexpectedly called out of the classroom. He set a student to oversee the contest, but as soon as the door closed behind him, I glimpsed Rong remove something from his schoolbag.

"What are you doing?" I whispered.

He just shook his head and indicated the student watching at the front of the classroom. Before my unbelieving eyes, I saw him stealthily replace his painting—which was of a single shrimp, and quite well done, from what I could tell—with a completed painting of three shrimp. They were all facing to the left, the same direction as mine, claws outstretched, antennae gracefully streaming behind them. Had Rong painted this outside of class and, anticipating that nerves would get the better of him during the contest, brought this as a backup?

Master Zhuo returned and I snapped my eyes back to my painting. All at once, in comparison to Rong's three shrimp—let alone Qi Baishi's—mine looked puny and lifeless. I dipped my brush into the ink and poised it above the paper, thinking I should try to draw another shrimp. But Master Zhuo called time and I only had the chance to sign the painting with Qi Baishi's signature, which I'd also practiced.

After lunch, we students milled about outside the classroom waiting to hear the verdict. Master Zhuo had promised to let us know the results of the contest by the end of the day, and already some students were talking about what they were going to do with their prize money—go to a restaurant, hire a prostitute, find a gambling den. Most of them were boasting, I suspect, and the money would go straight to their parents.

Finally, Master Zhuo called us all in. As we sat at our desks, he said, "Rong Jiawen, please come to the front."

I took this to mean Rong had won, and I felt the weight of disappointment start to lower itself upon me. But looking at him standing before the class, I saw that his face was more flushed from nervousness than pride.

Master Zhuo held up Rong's painting of the three shrimp, and everyone nodded and murmured in admiration, until he demanded, "Where did you get this?"

"I painted it," Rong stammered in the silence that followed.

"You did not. This was painted years ago. I can tell from the condition of the ink, the age of the paper." Master Zhuo rubbed the corner of the page. "It has oxidized over time. Let me ask you again, where did you get this?"

Rong hung his head and said so softly the rest of us could barely hear him, "I got it from home. It belongs to my family."

Master Zhuo all but threw the painting at him. "Rong Jiawen, you have disqualified yourself from the contest. If this were an exam, I would suspend you for cheating, but I've decided to be merciful. You will have to live with your shame."

As Rong slunk back to his seat, Master Zhuo continued addressing the class. "All of your paintings were very good. But the one I was most impressed by, the one that achieves the very soul of Qi Baishi's shrimp paintings, is the one by Liu Qingwu." And he held up my measly two shrimp.

While of course I was happy to have won, I was still confused by Rong's attempt to cheat. I understood that it wasn't about money, since his family could easily afford to give him the one hundred *renminbi,* but that for some reason he hadn't trusted his own work enough.

After class I followed him. "Congratulations," he muttered, trying to get by me, but I blocked his way.

"Why did you do that?" I asked. "And where did you really get that painting?"

"It belongs to my family," he said. "I didn't lie about that. We've had it for years, before the Japanese Invasion. My grandfather says it's a real Qi Baishi, although no one knows for sure. I thought maybe if Master Zhuo thought it was good enough to win the contest, that would mean it was real. And"—he lowered his eyes—"I did want to win that contest."

"Can I look at it again?"

Reluctantly, Rong handed me the painting. I tried to look at it with new eyes, but despite all that I had read about the artist's technique and the many times I had copied his pictures, I couldn't tell whether it was a real Qi Baishi, either. I rubbed the corner of the paper the way Master Zhuo had. Looking at it closer, I could tell that the paper appeared worn, the coloring different from the fresh white paper we usually used. The ink, too, did not look like it had recently dried, but was faded from age.

Rong observed my actions. "I didn't consider the materials," he admitted. "I didn't think Master Zho would look that carefully at the ink or paper, just at the images."

I handed the painting back to him. "Well," I said, "I think I liked the painting you did of the single shrimp better."

He gave me a half grin. "So, what are you going to do with your prize money?"

I thought about what my father's reaction would be when I told him I had won the contest. He'd be even more excited to know that I had gotten some money, which he undoubtedly would take away from me and use for next semester's tuition. But maybe he didn't have to know the contest had involved winning money.

"I think I'll go out to dinner," I said to Rong. "Want to come?"

By the time I decided to go to America, two years after leaving school, I had lost touch with Rong Jiawen. I figured he had abandoned the idea of being an artist and gone to work for his family. It was what any sensible person would do, given the opportunity.

When I met Wang Muping in New York, something about him reminded me of my old classmate Rong. They had the same easy way of living, the ability to act as if the world owed them something instead of the opposite. Without Wang, I wouldn't have been able to pull off the Andrew Cantrell replica. That's what I told him it was, a replica, a reproduction, a simulation; but I could tell from the way he looked at me, that first time we met up after I asked him for help, he was also suspicious of Caroline Lowry.

"Did she pay you?" was his first question.

"Yes, half up front," I said. I didn't tell him how much, knowing that he made much more off of one of his pornographic *shanshui* paintings than I would imitating a famous artist.

"Good, because you'll need that money. What's the date of the painting?"

I checked the Lowry Gallery catalog and told him 1969.

Our first stop was not an art supply store, as would have been my instinct, but to an antiques dealer upstate. We took the train up the Hudson and stopped in one of the small, sleepy river towns that reminded me of the towns you might see traveling along the Yangtze River in China, the ones that had been evacuated and flooded after the installation of the Three Gorges Dam. The main street was lined with antique stores, all seeming to display the same Revolutionary War–era chests of drawers and chairs, fireplace andirons, and decorative mantelpieces, so I was confused when Wang headed straight to one particular store.

We stepped into the clutter of furniture, and as we moved farther into the store, we seemed to move backward in time. Cherrywood tallboys gave way to art deco cabinets to midcentury-modern lamps, until we reached a section entirely filled with canvases. Some of them were the worst that American kitsch could offer—velvet paintings, paint-by-numbers, saccharine portraits of wide-eyed children and fluffy pets.

I jumped when an elderly man appeared at my elbow, but he seemed to know my friend well. Wang introduced him to me and we shook hands, but I instantly forgot his name, which was probably for the best given the secretive nature of the project.

Wang asked, "Do you have a canvas from the late sixties, oil, size five feet by three feet?"

"Ah," the elderly man said. "I have just the thing."

The canvas he extracted from the jumble was a color field painting, its bold, confident strokes not entirely unprofessional to my eye. "We'll take it for a hundred dollars," Wang informed the proprietor.

"Two hundred. You never know, this might be an undiscovered Rothko."

"Ha!" I exclaimed, a little too forcefully.

The elderly man winked at me. "You never know."

After getting the price down to a hundred and fifty dollars, we said good-bye and made our way to the train station, carrying the wrapped canvas between us.

"How do you know about this place?" I asked Wang as we huffed down the street.

"I like to collect porcelain," he said.

"Oh, like porcelain from Jingdezhen?"

"Actually," Wang said, without a trace of embarrassment, "I like Delftware. The store owner calls me whenever a plate shows up at an estate sale."

"Do you eat off of it?"

"I just like looking at it. The blue and white pattern makes me happy."

I shook my head. Even though I'd known him for thirty years, my friend was still full of surprises.

Wang instructed me to contact him once I'd stripped the canvas. I was used to doing this, for I often stripped and painted over many of my own, as a way to obliterate my failures. Only this time I didn't have my wife to complain how I smelled of acetone and turpentine when I went into the house.

"You smell like a house painter," Jin would say when I sat down at the kitchen table, even though I'd scrubbed my skin raw in the shower. "Maybe you should become a house painter. There's more of a future in that."

I would ignore her grumblings, and didn't point out that whenever I went to pick her up from the hair salon, the odors that emanated from that place—from women getting their hair dyed, straightened, permed, or whatever was necessary to achieve the opposite of their natural state of hair—could make a strong man faint.

As promised, when I was done with stripping the canvas, I called Wang and he stopped by my studio.

"This canvas doesn't look aged enough," he said. "Do you have any tea?"

I wondered if he had suddenly gotten thirsty. "Of course I have tea. What kind do you want, Chinese or American?"

"Black tea," he said and sized up the canvas. "About five tea bags."

Intrigued, I did as I was told and he pressed the wet tea bags one by one against the canvas until he had achieved a dull beige shade. Once, I asked him, "Where did you learn how to do this?"

He grinned. "Ancient Chinese secret."

Afterward, we went inside the apartment while I made us some tea for real.

"Not so bad being a bachelor again, is it?" Wang observed, looking around the kitchen at the dirty dishes piled in the sink and the grimy countertop. "Why'd Jin leave?"

He'd never so much as mentioned her name before. When I invited him to our wedding, which had taken place at city hall with a lunch in Chinatown afterward, he had sent his regrets. I suspected that he preferred to stay away from anything that hinted at commitment.

"The usual," I said. "She wanted more from me than I could give."

"I see," he replied knowingly. "It's always about money, isn't it? Get a better job, find a better place to live, give me a better life."

There was more to it than that, but I let Wang think what he would. Most of the women he became involved with, if he ever let a relationship get very far, probably thought that way.

He leaned forward and clapped me on the shoulder. "Believe me, you're better off without her. We artists, we need our freedom."

Many years ago I might have thought this, too.

The next step in the process I took alone. I visited the Museum of Modern Art to look at its Andrew Cantrell painting, the only one in a public collection. Although some overlap was to be expected, the breed of tourists here was somewhat different from those I observed from my stall in front of the Metropolitan Museum of Art: fewer families, more couples; fewer sneakers and backpacks, more fashionable footwear and designer bags. I

thought by going in the middle of the day and in the middle of
the week, I might avoid the crowds, but it seemed to be a holiday in another part of the world and the place was deluged with
European tourists, apparently looking for more recent master-
pieces than their centuries-old museums could provide.

The MoMA's Andrew Cantrell was located on the second
floor, in what I considered to be the most ignominious place
possible, opposite the escalators and only a few feet from an information desk on one side and the bathrooms on the other.
Most visitors probably walked by it without giving it a second
thought. I tried not to get in the way of the people looking to
either find a more famous painting or to relieve themselves.
Finally, I stood with my back against the escalator divider and
attempted to ignore the heads that passed in front of me, block-
ing my view.

*Meditation*, painted in 1967, was smaller than *Elegy*, about
three feet by two feet. But the single dark blue band across the
black background was mesmerizing, shimmering with the
strength of a neon sign in the dark night. I tried to imagine
what Cantrell had been thinking when he'd produced this
painting, at what point he was in his life. From what I'd read,
at the time he'd been married for five years to Naomi Jordan,
the daughter of a New York City corporate lawyer. Two years
later, when he'd painted *Elegy*, the marriage was said to have
gone sour over charges of infidelity. They'd moved out to East
Hampton, to the summer house that her family owned, to escape the rumors—and, supposedly, to get away from Hazel
Lowry.

I visualized the movement from *Meditation* to *Elegy*, from
the strength of black and dark blue to the chaotic gray and
white, and wondered how much of Cantrell's personal life had
affected that progression. Of course, there may have been no
connection at all, just the graspings of a desperate man looking
at the paintings almost forty years later.

I removed a sketchbook and pencil from my backpack, and

began to trace the brushstrokes of the painting in front of me. I especially made sure to copy the signature exactly, as it was one of the more identifiable features. Because of the black background of *Meditation,* the signature was in a lighter color and clearer on this painting than the image of *Elegy* in the Lowry Gallery catalog or any other I'd been able to find. Sketching the painting was not easy to do, with all the people passing back and forth between us. I wanted to stop them, to make them take notice, to ask them what they saw. Finally, after a half hour or so, I gave up and went home.

Over the next few weeks, *Elegy* entered my dreams. I awoke drowning in its gray waters, sucked into the white eye of the storm in its middle. Somehow I became confused and instead of the ocean I was in the mountains, descending too fast in a cable car, rushing toward the ground as my stomach lurched with indigestion and perhaps guilt.

While my nights were spent battling waves, during the days I sought to find the right mix of paints. I couldn't use anything with chemicals developed past 1969. Wang and I had taken such care to "age" the canvas that I couldn't spoil everything now by covering it with something completely anachronistic.

After I was done with the first coat, Wang paid another visit to my studio. I watched anxiously as he evaluated what I'd done, but all he said was, "Do you have a hair dryer?"

Jin must have left one behind—it was ridiculous, as a hairdresser, for her not to have owned one—but after a thorough search, it looked like she had taken it with her. I couldn't keep Wang waiting much longer.

"I'll be back in a moment," I said, and ran out the door and down the few blocks to the salon where Jin had worked. I always thought Number One Modern Beauty Parlor was a ridiculous name, especially since the faded glamour shots on the walls featured feathered haircuts from the eighties. I recalled the many times I'd come by to see Jin at work, during my lunch hour, when I needed to take a break from my work in the afternoon, or in the evening just to walk her home. Her station was next to the front window, and when she caught sight of me, her face would brighten.

The first time I'd gone looking for her was the day after we'd met at the continuing education class. When she recognized me in the salon, she looked more wary than pleased, but relaxed when I said, "I'd like to get a haircut." She must have known it was an excuse to see her, as my hair, which I cut myself with a pair of clippers whenever I remembered to, was already quite short. But she played along with me, asked me to sit in a chair, and abstractedly plopped a women's fashion magazine in my lap. I pretended to flip through it, watching out of the corner of my eye as she continued to color a white lady's hair a shade that looked like buttered popcorn.

When Jin was ready, she beckoned for me to come to her, but I announced, "My hair needs to be washed." This was even more preposterous, as there was barely half an inch to wash, but she led me to the back of the room, where I sank into a recliner-like contraption with my head at an impossible angle. Perhaps in retaliation, she ran the water too hot, then too cold, but I endured it. She briskly kneaded my shoulders, allowing me to fantasize for a moment what our physical relations might be like, until she jabbed too hard with her fingernails and I gave a little yelp of pain.

Finally, I let her lead me to her chair, where she draped a plastic sheet around me as impersonally as if I were a corpse, and produced her shears.

"Just a little off the top, please," I said, although I sensed she was going to do what she wanted with me.

"Why did you come here?" she asked in between snips.

"You came to where I work, now I've come to yours. Besides, you said you could get rid of my gray."

She paused and tilted her head. "Is that what you want?

Maybe a little streaking would help you. I'm thinking red." She couldn't help but smile at my horrified expression.

After a few minutes of silence, punctuated only by the snipping shears, I said, "I liked what you drew in class."

"I was trying to follow what you said. About looking into the person's soul. It's not so different from what I do here."

"Here?" I asked skeptically of the room filled with hairdressers and their clients.

"I'm also trying to look into people's souls, into what their true appearance is. Then I cut their hair according to what I see."

"I had no idea cutting hair was such an artistic activity."

"It takes as much skill as painting a picture," she retorted. "And I probably make more money at it, too."

This, I did not bother to deny. I was only aware of her nearness, of her presence just over my shoulder with a dangerous weapon in her hand, especially when she cut close to my ears. I watched her in the mirror, and although she mostly kept her eyes on her work, occasionally her gaze would meet mine. Then, just as quickly, she'd avert her eyes, but I'd catch a trace of color on her cheeks.

When Jin had finished cutting my hair and whisked away the plastic sheet, I turned my head to one side, then the other, pretending to admire her handiwork. In reality, I couldn't tell much of a difference, but that didn't matter. What mattered was that in the space of an hour, I had fallen in love with this woman.

I gave her a large tip, which she seemed to ignore as she stuffed it into the pocket of her apron, and then I blurted out, "Will you have dinner with me after you finish work?"

"We're open until nine," she pointed out.

"I'll come back then."

I did, half-expecting her to already be gone, but she was still there, sweeping up the hair from the floor so it appeared there was a dark, furry animal clinging to the end of her broom. I took her to a local Sichuan restaurant that I knew to be cheap but good, and that was all we needed to begin our courtship.

Now, as I approached the Number One Modern Beauty Parlor, I pictured seeing Jin in the front window. But there was another hairdresser at her station, a young Chinese man with bleached blond hair whom I'd never seen before. I took a deep breath to steel myself against the noxious fumes, and the inevitable questioning looks from those of Jin's coworkers who knew me, and stepped inside. Her former boss, Old Guo, approached me.

"She isn't here," he immediately said.

"I know," I said. "I have a favor to ask of you."

Old Guo and I did not have the best of relationships. Jin had told me he was a fair boss; unlike many others, he allowed his workers to keep their tips. He didn't try anything shady with the female hairdressers, and he allowed them one day off a week. But when Jin announced that she was leaving the salon, he accused me of taking away his most reliable worker. I tried to tell him that Jin's decision was as unexpected to me as it was to him, as well as troublesome, because that meant we had lost the steadier of our two incomes. But Jin had her reasons, which at the time I didn't know.

"What do you want?" Old Guo asked me, seemingly not antagonistic anymore.

"I need to borrow a hair dryer."

"What for?"

"I'm...painting my house and need to dry some...varnish."

I must have looked as desperate as I felt, for Old Guo relented. He motioned toward the fake-blond male hairdresser to bring over a hair dryer. "Be sure to return it!" he called after me as I ran out the door.

"Professional grade," I told Wang when I got home, triumphantly waving the hair dryer in his face.

He ignored me, plugged in the dryer, tested it, and then turned it full-blast toward the painting.

"What are you doing?" I cried, thinking the heat was going to ruin my work.

"Don't be stupid," he yelled over the industrial-strength hum. "You need to dry out this layer before adding the next one. The heat will make the paint crack just enough so that it looks aged. But don't do it too much, otherwise it'll look like it's from the nineteenth century."

When he was done, I had to admit that his methods seemed to work. The canvas now had a sheen of age and, in my mind, authenticity. I'd never doubt Wang and his peculiar tactics again.

A month to the day I had told Caroline Lowry I would take the job, I was done. I invited Wang over one last time to look at the painting and celebrate with a bottle of *baijiu,* the strongest Chinese alcohol. This liquor was usually poured into tiny, handleless cups, but I only had teacups, so we used those.

The painting was propped against the wall of the garage under the light of a bare bulb, which I'd turned on even though it was early afternoon. I'd covered all the windows with black plastic trash bags in case my neighbors or passersby got too nosy. Nervously, I awaited my friend's reaction.

Wang raised his cup to me. "Congratulations," he said. "You've created a masterpiece."

"Do you think?" I tried to look at the painting as if I'd never seen it before—or rather, only from a catalog, as Caroline Lowry's client must have. The brushstrokes were assertive, indicating fluid and clear movement. Even more important, the painting looked forty years old. Without Wang's help, I wouldn't have paid as much attention to those details as I should have, instead dreaming about what might have motivated Andrew Cantrell to create the painting in the first place. I wouldn't have concentrated on what was known, like the year the painting was made, and found materials that could convincingly be dated from then.

"This is all due to you," I told Wang. "I should really split the money with you."

"You must be drunk already," Wang responded, and then grinned to lighten his words. "No, this is all your doing. You're the artist here."

"You're right," I said, deliriously. "I am the painter of this picture."

If only for a moment. I still needed to add the signature. I had wanted to wait until Wang was with me to christen the painting. Ever since I'd seen it on *Meditation*, I'd practiced Andrew Cantrell's signature until I had gotten it down quite well. I especially wanted to make sure that I spelled his name correctly, although perhaps it didn't matter as much as one would think. I had heard about a Jackson Pollock forgery in which the artist's last name had been signed as *Pollack*, a common misspelling, and no one, from the dealer to the buyer who had paid millions of dollars for the painting, had noticed until later.

"For the final touch," I said, and dramatically poised my brush over the lower right corner of the painting. Wang cheered me on.

Then, in a moment, it was done. I was no longer the painting's creator; that person was Andrew Cantrell. I was relieved, yet also a little regretful, as if something had been taken away from me. If I couldn't claim ownership of something I'd painted, what kind of artist was I?

The ultimate test was whether Caroline Lowry would approve of this painting. After all, she'd seen it in person, although it had been many years ago.

"It made a great impression on me," she'd said. "I can remember it like it was yesterday, hanging on the wall of my aunt's gallery. I'd never seen anything so striking, so brooding."

I wasn't sure if she meant what she was saying, or whether she was trying to impress upon me the importance of the task.

This time when she visited my studio, she came with a man whom she introduced as her art historian friend. Though he was small and unassuming, I immediately felt like I was being given some kind of test. I regretted not having asked Wang to join me as backup, but then thought Caroline would not like so many people witnessing this act of verification.

I made no preamble with costumes or tea and took Caroline and her friend straight into the garage, where they appeared a little disturbed by the trash bags covering the windows. I have to admit, they made the place resemble the scene of a crime about to happen. Then their full attention was drawn to the painting. Caroline acted as if she had seen a dead person come to life.

"This is exactly as I remembered it," she said, more to her companion than to me.

I breathed an inner sigh of relief that she approved. But then her companion started asking me questions, such as where I'd purchased my materials. He seemed particularly interested in the people I'd dealt with, which made me glad that perhaps Wang wasn't with me after all. I assured him that the antiques dealer that I'd gotten the canvas from was someone I'd dealt with many times before, that I'd paid cash. I decided to leave out the tea-staining and the hair dryer, as even those methods seemed a bit dubious to me.

Amid this interrogation, I shot a look at Caroline as if to ask her whether all the attention to detail was necessary.

"It's just that the client is very particular," she said.

"Can you tell me who he is?" Ever since I'd finished the painting, I'd felt some responsibility toward it. I'd spent a month of my life working on it. I wanted to know where it was going, whether it would be hung in someone's workplace or bedroom, or tucked away in storage, never to see the light of day.

Caroline and her companion exchanged glances. "It's a foreign businessman," she finally said. "Actually, he's from China, too."

The knowledge that the painting was going to a compatriot helped a little bit, I supposed. "Where in China?" I asked.

"Taiwan."

I shook my head. "Then he probably would rather be called Taiwanese than Chinese. If he's in business, it's likely his family came over after the communist takeover in 1949."

Caroline nodded, but her companion appeared impatient at this impromptu history lesson. "Chinese, Taiwanese, whatever," he said under his breath.

"Is the painting to your satisfaction?" I addressed the both of them.

"Yes," Caroline said and handed me an envelope of cash. "Very nice doing business with you, Mr. Liu." She paused. "You really are a talented artist."

*Talented as an imitator,* I thought, but I thanked her.

She and her companion packed up the painting and took it out with them to a van parked at the curb. Her companion got behind the driver's seat, and they left.

Afterward, I sat in my apartment, counting the money in the envelope. Caroline had given me a two-hundred-dollar bonus. I wondered what she would have done if she'd been displeased with my work. We hadn't signed a contract or a confidentiality agreement. But the truth was, there was no one I could tell about this event in my life. Wang knew, but the only other person I would have told would have been my wife.

The day Jin left me, I had come home from one of my teaching jobs at the Chinese Baptist Church senior center to find she'd left a note saying she'd gone to stay with friends, for me not to worry about her, and most of all, not to look for her. I expected her to turn up, but after a few days with no further word from her, I went to the salon and asked if she was staying with anyone there. Other than her former coworkers, I didn't know who her friends were. I also called Jin's sister in Sunset Park, who told me she didn't know where Jin was, either. I suspected the sister was lying, but had no way to prove it.

I wonder if my slowness in finding out where Jin had really gone was influenced by my reaction to her abandonment. I was angry at her, for leaving me for no conceivable reason. Unlike some stories she'd told me about her former coworkers' husbands, I did not beat her when drunk, waste my money by gambling, or sit at home watching television while she worked overtime.

I should have known something was wrong when she left her job at the salon. At first I thought something must have happened there, a fight with a coworker, or perhaps her boss, Old Guo, had tried something with her. But from the times I had met him, he didn't seem the type, and Jin was not the kind of person who would tolerate abuse from someone else by walking away. I asked her what she planned to do, thinking about whether I could pick up more classes at the senior center, but Jin admitted she didn't know, mumbled something about getting her old clients to come to our apartment to get their hair cut.

I should have connected her decision with what had happened a month or so before that, when she'd fainted on the job. At first she'd thought she was pregnant and had been ecstatic. Maybe I'd blocked that memory because my reaction had been the exact opposite. The last thing I wanted, at my age and given my livelihood, was to bring up a child. I told her this, and we'd argued about it, and she called me a selfish bastard who was only interested in my art, and that we shouldn't have gotten married in the first place if I wasn't willing to make sacrifices for her happiness. This resulted in much time spent apart, even if we were physically in the same space, even after she took a pregnancy test and it turned out negative. A wedge had been driven between us, and she could not forgive me for the things I'd said.

Then I thought she had found someone else, someone who could give her everything she'd ever wanted, financially and otherwise. Perhaps she'd gone back to an old lover from her hometown in China, or she'd met a man who'd also gone into the salon asking for a haircut when what he really wanted was to get to know her better. If that was the case, if another man had bested me, I could accept it. To be left hanging from a precipice was infinitely worse.

I combined the money I'd just received for the painting with what remained from the first half of the installment. Most of it was still there, as I'd just paid a few hundred dollars for the materials. It was the most money I'd ever received for painting a single work. But it still wasn't enough for me to give up teaching classes or selling replicas from a stall. Ten thousand dollars wouldn't have been enough.

But I was beginning to realize that millions of dollars weren't going to be enough for me to become the artist I wanted to be. And no amount of money would bring Jin back.

# Chapter 6

Caroline leaned the copy of *Elegy* against the wall in her living room, just out of the light coming in through the windows but enough to illuminate its textured surface. In the many years since she'd seen it in person, it had taken on mythic proportions—the painting lost in the fire that had claimed its artist's life. Now resurrected, its power was more palpable than ever. She was already beginning to think of it not as a copy, but as even more real than the painting she had seen hung in the Lowry Gallery as a college student, when she had met Andrew Cantrell and realized that her aunt Hazel was his mistress.

At the time, she'd thought their relationship so thrilling, so dramatic. Of course, Andrew Cantrell wasn't much to look at—and neither was his work, she'd thought at the time—but the fact that Hazel had chosen him and his painting to exhibit made him rise inestimably in Caroline's eyes. Suddenly, the boys she and her roommate, Rose, knew, like those from the coed college in town, seemed so young and flimsy. Take Caleb Schaeffer, for example, who took Rose on dates to the local diner or the movies or, on one memorable occasion, hiking. No wonder Rose thought Caroline's trips to the city and Hazel's life were so glamorous.

There was also something glamorous about being attached to a painter, and a married one at that. Had Cantrell ever asked Hazel to pose for him? Had he considered her his muse? How early had his wife known about their affair? From the *Life* magazine article, Caroline knew that Andrew and Naomi Cantrell had moved out to a farmhouse in East Hampton that year; the tabloids suggested the main reason was to get Cantrell away from Hazel, although it obviously hadn't stopped him from coming into the city to see her.

When Caroline started to have her own flings with artists, they were always short-lived and never as exciting as she had been led to believe. It had taken her a few years to get over the divorce from Bob, who had essentially been her first and only real relationship, and then taking care of Hazel before her death and figuring out how to run the gallery afterward required much of her time. But then she met an abstract painter who was in town for the weekend to attend an art fair, and she surprised herself by her physical response. She hadn't realized how much she had missed the touch of another person.

For about a decade starting from her late thirties, there had been one or two encounters a year, with men who were married and who were not, younger than her or not, some of them who went on to become artists she exhibited in her gallery or not. None of them lasted, not that she expected them to, but sometimes she wondered if she was lacking some personality trait. One that Hazel had. While Caroline didn't envy a relationship quite like Hazel and Cantrell's, given how tragically it had turned out, she wanted to radiate togetherness in the way they had, so strongly that it was apparent to everyone who looked at them.

Sandro Hess had started out just like the others. It had been years since Caroline had taken a lover, and she was beginning to resign herself to the trappings of old ladyhood—going to events and eating in restaurants alone, depending on her landlord to fix things in her apartment. Although she hadn't had any work done on her face, she knew she looked at least ten years younger than her age. However, she didn't count on a man who was actually ten years younger than her to be interested, as Sandro was.

When she met him, at the gallery opening of a South American friend of his, she was immediately struck by his accent and his old-fashioned, if a little sexist, behavior. The kissing of the hand instead of the cheek, the shirt that was open a little too much at the neck, the pomaded hair and equally groomed goatee. She found it all oddly attractive, especially that he paid her so much attention even though there were plenty of young, long-limbed women in attendance that night.

"Do you like what he has done here?" Sandro asked, indicating the celebrity death masks that made up the exhibition.

"It's a unique idea," Caroline admitted. "Rather...interactive." While some of the masks were displayed in a traditional way, erected upon pedestals, others were suspended from the ceiling, where people accidentally walked into them. She considered that a safety hazard.

"But what do you think of the masks themselves?"

Caroline caught herself. Of course he wanted to know what she thought of the art rather than how it was being presented to an audience. She guessed he must be associated with the artist in some way, as a friend or a fan, so she replied cautiously, "It's quite a commentary on pop culture."

"Glad to hear it," Sandro said, and introduced himself. When Caroline said she owned an art gallery in Chelsea, he seemed to be taken aback. "But surely you are an artist yourself."

"Not in the least bit, I'm afraid."

"You know, I would love to show you what I'm working on at the moment."

Caroline expected this; almost every time she went to an event and revealed her occupation, someone would ask her to visit their studio. Usually she'd take their card rather than give hers out, saying she'd get in touch if she was interested, and throw the card away when she got home. But this time, something about the pleading in this man's dark eyes made her offer her card to him instead.

Within the week she had visited Sandro's studio. He had received a grant to work in a government-subsidized building in the West Thirties. The space had tall windows that let in the sunlight and possibly dazzled her into thinking his Mickey Mouse–rainbow pastiches were more clever than they were. In any case, by the end of the visit, she had agreed to give him a show that summer. She had made that deal before they slept together, she liked to remind herself, so there was no conflict of interest. No conflict of interest at all.

Even before the opening, Caroline was starting to tire of Sandro. Almost every conversation now, in and out of bed, was about his need for money to support his ex-wife, Claudia, and their seven-year-old son, Sebastian. Claudia and Sebastian lived in their former apartment in the East Village, and Sebastian had some kind of learning disability that required therapy. Claudia sounded high-maintenance, although Caroline wasn't sure whether Sandro was portraying her accurately. Alternately, she pictured his former wife as a dark-haired Argentine beauty dealing with a difficult child or a stern Germanic woman obsessed with controlling her ex's life. Sometimes Sandro would speak dismissively of her; other times he referred to her with such longing that Caroline wished long-departed Bob had felt that way about her.

Once, she asked Sandro where he and Claudia had met.

"In high school. We were what you call 'high school sweethearts'?"

"This must have been in Argentina, right? Or Germany?"

"Ah." Sandro looked a little embarrassed. "It is true that my mother is from Argentina and my father is from Germany. However, I grew up in the Bronx."

"But the accent, the…" Caroline gestured feebly at Sandro's entire person.

"You have to admit," Sandro said, "it makes a much better story." He spoke without any accent at all, not even a Bronx one. All at once, Sandro didn't sound or look like he was from anywhere.

Neither of them mentioned his origins after this exchange, and Caroline continued to introduce Sandro as her "German-Argentine" client, but something about him was beginning to unnerve her. She wondered whether it had been prudent to give him the keys to her apartment, which she had never done with anyone else, but he had talked about how uncomfortable his studio was, which was where he had slept since Claudia had kicked him out of their apartment.

Finally, in the week before his opening, she told him she wanted her keys back.

"Is this it between us?" Sandro had asked.

"I'm sorry, but I don't know how long you thought this would last," Caroline had replied. "Besides, your show opens next week. Haven't you gotten what you wanted?"

Sandro put his hand over his heart. "It hurts me that you think our relationship was simply about that."

"Oh, stop it," Caroline snapped. "Stop talking like *that*." She wasn't sure whether she meant his words or his put-on accent. She gathered herself. "Again, I apologize for having to do it this way. But let's just make this clean. Give me the keys, you'll have a great opening next week, all of the paintings will sell, and you can give the money to your ex-wife."

"That's all I want."

"And if you do as I say, you'll get what you want." Caroline held out her hand, and Sandro reluctantly dropped her keys into it.

During the opening, Caroline worried that Sandro might make a scene, especially if he drank a lot, but he seemed to be in good spirits and more attentive toward her assistant, Molly, than Caroline herself. She congratulated herself on having averted a crisis.

Since then, although Sandro called nearly every day asking whether she had any leads on a sale, she diverted him to Molly. Of course she would talk to him if anyone contacted her, but although the opening had been well attended, no one was actually interested in buying one of his paintings. Maybe she shouldn't have given him a show, but he had thoroughly charmed her—a charm that was beginning to wear thin.

As the summer progressed, Sandro faded into the background as Caroline concentrated instead on the copy of *Elegy*. Now it stood finished, in her living room. At first she thought she should keep it somewhere safer, a storage locker or even temporarily in the building's basement, but then decided there was no danger of anyone seeing it, as she hardly invited anyone to her apartment. Now that she was able to look at the finished painting every day, it began to take on an indefinable presence. She didn't believe in ghosts, but she couldn't help thinking that Hazel was there with her, guiding her next step.

Although Hazel had been dead for twenty years by the time Chelsea became the epicenter of the art world in New York City, Caroline couldn't help wondering if her aunt had had some kind of premonition when she'd started her gallery there in the 1960s. At that time, her neighborhood was bordered by warehouses and packing plants, serviced by an elevated rail line that gradually became dismantled throughout that decade. In the mid-1980s, when Caroline moved in with her, most galleries were concentrated in Soho, although artists were being squeezed out of their loft spaces by rising rents.

"Someday they'll all come here," Hazel had said. Caroline looked behind her at the skyline of dilapidated buildings, their broken windows and stained bricks, and wondered if her aunt was hallucinating.

She and Hazel were sitting in a pocket park facing the Hudson River in the West Twenties, watching the ships come into port. On Hazel's good days, they would venture out of the apartment and walk down the two long avenues to the water. They never saw anyone else in the park, nor signs of life in the form of litter or rats or even pigeons; this was too far west for most living creatures. However, this also made it easier for Hazel to smoke as many joints in public as she wanted, and sometimes Caroline would join her, sinking into a pleasant, muzzy haze along with the sun below the waterline.

It was then that Caroline felt uninhibited enough to ask Hazel questions about her relationship with Andrew Cantrell, such as when they met.

"It must have been around 1965," Hazel recounted dreamily. "Andrew was in his thirties, so not that young, although he still had most of his hair. I remember he'd just gotten married to Naomi. Naomi Jordan, she was. Their nuptials were announced in all the papers. Of course, most people who cared to read wedding announcements were scandalized that the daughter of one of New York's oldest families had chosen to marry a starving artist."

The image of the woman in an apron, meekly carrying a tray, materialized in Caroline's mind. "What was she like?"

"I only met her once, if you can even call it a meeting. Andrew and I were sitting in a restaurant when she came in, with her furs and jewelry, and she slapped me in the face."

So maybe not that meek. "What did you do?"

"Slapped her back, of course. There happened to be a tabloid photographer following us, and he got a picture of my slap, not hers. So I was the one who became known as the hussy, the home wrecker. Sometimes both in the same headline. How they loved alliteration! Naomi, however, was infinitely worse than a home wrecker. She wrecked Andrew's creativity. You have to admit, his two most famous paintings, *Meditation* and *Elegy,* were done when their marriage was over."

"He never wanted to leave her?"

"You mean leave her for me?" Hazel laughed. "Andrew knew he could only afford to paint because of her. She provided everything for him—food, shelter, business contacts. Although she gave him terrible advice. When Andrew got the two-million-dollar offer for *Elegy,* she wanted him to take it. I told him to turn it down, and he became better known than ever."

"And you never asked him to leave her?"

"Our relationship wasn't like that."

In the mellowing silence that followed, Caroline thought about her marriage to Bob, how perhaps they'd been too compatible. They'd traveled on parallel tracks in career and life, agreeing on nearly everything from not having children to where they'd live, with no obstacles. Caroline had felt she could have followed that path until she and her husband were graying retirees, but obviously Bob had wanted something else. They'd kept in touch since the divorce had been finalized, and soon Caroline had learned that he had a new girlfriend, whom he ended up marrying within the year. Caroline had been invited to the wedding, but by that time Hazel had been so sick that she couldn't be left. When Hazel passed away, Bob had sent his condolences, and then over the next few years had intermittently let Caroline know the more pertinent details about his life, including the birth of his two daughters. Then the trail turned cold and dark, and Caroline never heard from him again.

But back when she was still raw and smarting over the divorce, she wondered whether the kind of relationship Hazel had had with Andrew Cantrell, even if it didn't come with marriage or any sort of security, was preferable to what she'd had with her own husband.

"I don't want to be too personal..." she started hesitantly.

Hazel indicated the joint in her hand. "You'd better do it now while I'm an open book."

"Why did you stay with Andrew? There must have been other men, other artists, who you could be with."

"Who didn't have a rabidly jealous wife? I thought about it," Hazel admitted. "More times than you know. Especially after Naomi and Andrew moved out to the family's summer home in East Hampton. I know that makes the place sound impressive, but it was really just a farmhouse with a barn that Andrew used as his studio. He was never able to paint anything worthwhile there. And it definitely didn't keep him from coming into the city and continuing to have shows. Naomi couldn't stop him from doing that."

"Did you ever go out to their house in East Hampton?" Caroline asked, before remembering the newspaper article suggesting Hazel had set the fire that killed Cantrell. She could tell, as Hazel stubbed out her joint, that her aunt was thinking the same thing.

"You want to know whether it's true? That I tried to kill Andrew because he had decided to end our relationship?"

"I didn't mean to—"

"Yes, I was in his home that night. Naomi was away at a charity function, so we thought it would be safe. Yes, by that time we weren't together anymore. And yes, grief does terrible things to people. But I had come to discuss art, not our personal problems. I was as shocked as anyone to find out the next day, when I was back in the city, about the fire." Hazel looked directly at Caroline, her vision unclouded. "Naomi found out I had been there and blamed me. I can see why. She'd just lost the love of her life. But she wasn't the only one. I'd lost part of myself, too. And the whole world lost a great artist and some of the finest work he'd ever done."

"What was the funeral like?"

"I don't know, I didn't go. Naomi wouldn't let me. But I didn't care. Part of me had already said good-bye anyway."

Hazel leaned back into the bench and closed her eyes against the sunlight, as if she had become exhausted by too many questions. Instantly, Caroline regretted her own nosiness. Who cared whether Hazel had played a part in Andrew Cantrell's death? It had happened close to ten years ago, and anyone who cared about it, like Naomi Cantrell, must have made her peace with it. Or Hazel, who would soon be gone herself. Once that occurred, there wouldn't be anyone left who cared about the details of Andrew Cantrell's death anymore.

Hazel's memorial was held in the gallery, as she had requested. There was no current show, and the white walls made a stark contrast with the somberly dressed crowd. A woman who had been Hazel's first assistant said a few words about how much of a mentor Hazel had been for her. An art dealer spoke of her knack for finding up-and-coming young artists. One of those artists—or at least someone who had fit that description at one time—detailed how supportive she had been of him over the years.

Then it was Caroline's turn. She had scribbled some notes on a piece of paper, but now that she had it unfolded in front of her, the writing seemed like it had come from someone else's hand. Finally she crumpled it up.

"My mother died when I was five years old," she started. "It was a Catholic funeral, with a wake the night before and a priest. It probably wasn't what my mother wanted, but my father insisted on it. What you see before you, however, is exactly what Hazel would have wanted. She was my mother's younger sister, and since my mother died, she was not only my aunt, but my friend. Although there were years when we lost touch, I always knew she would be there when I needed her. And I would be there when she needed me."

At that moment, Caroline looked up to see a woman who had just entered the gallery and was hovering at its edge. She appeared to be in her fifties and didn't look connected to the art world in any way or, in a colorful patterned dress beneath a tan trench coat, dressed appropriately for a funeral. Her hair was a bright blond, and gold jewelry winked at her neck and wrists. Other people had noticed Caroline's hesitation and were starting to look at the woman, too, but she seemed unaware of their gaze.

"So, thank you all for attending and fulfilling Hazel's last wishes," Caroline finished lamely.

Afterward, as she circulated through the crowd and accepted people's condolences, she looked for the woman who had arrived late. She noticed several people nodding their heads in acknowledgment at her, although no one bothered to engage her in conversation. When Caroline saw Hazel's old assistant, Peter, she went over to him.

"Do you know who that woman is?"

Peter seemed to know exactly whom she was talking about. "That's Naomi Cantrell. The nerve of her, right?"

"I'll say."

The adrenaline left over from her speech was enough to make Caroline march directly over to Naomi Cantrell. "You aren't welcome here," she said.

"Excuse me?"

Caroline was struck by how immediately Andrew Cantrell's widow signaled that she was a different kind of moneyed human being in the leisurely way she turned her head, the faint whiff of expensive fragrance that came with that movement. "You told Hazel that she wasn't welcome at your husband's funeral," she said.

Naomi held up a hand with exquisitely tapered nails. "Surely you don't want to talk about that here."

"Why not?"

"Not in front of these people. Is there somewhere private we can go?"

Ignoring the stares that followed them, Caroline led Naomi into the back office. "I'd offer you a seat but I don't want you wrinkling your clothes," she said, not caring if she sounded rude.

"I do apologize for the way I'm dressed," Naomi replied easily. "It was a last-minute decision to come here. Hazel wasn't much for protocol anyway."

Caroline unconsciously clenched her fists, feeling like a five-year-old again. "Don't talk about her like that."

"You don't think that after almost ten years of being my husband's mistress, she was completely unknown to me? I had a private investigator following them for years. I don't suppose she ever told you this."

"She told me that you were a hindrance to your husband's creativity."

The expression on Naomi's face hardened. "I wouldn't say such things about another person's relationship. You think everything your aunt Hazel told you was true? Such as she told you that I didn't want her at Andrew's funeral? I invited her, and she refused to come."

After a while, Caroline said, "Even so, you weren't invited to Hazel's funeral. I'd like you to leave."

"If that's what you want." At the door to the office, Naomi turned and asked, "Do you know what will happen to the gallery?"

Caroline shook her head.

Naomi gestured at what could be seen of the crowd through the slightly opened door. "It would be a shame to let all this go to waste."

She left Caroline in the dimness with the muffled sound of people just outside. Succumbing to waves of fatigue, Caroline put her head down on the desk. She didn't wake until Peter came in to find her and tell her everyone had left.

The next day, Caroline took Hazel's ashes to the pocket park they'd spent so many afternoons in and scattered them over the water. Likely illegal, but that also had been one of Hazel's last wishes. In Hazel's apartment, after keeping some choice outfits, Caroline gathered up decades of her aunt's clothes—all of her elegant animal-print coats and hats, her showy embroidered caftans—and donated them to charity. The same went for her aunt's wall hangings and knickknacks. Every night before she fell into an exhausted sleep, Caroline reminded herself that she should start looking for another place to live. As for the gallery, she hadn't received any directions on it at all.

But within the week Caroline received a telephone call from Hazel's lawyer about her aunt's will. Apparently Hazel had left everything she owned to Caroline, including the rent-controlled apartment and gallery, and the contents of a storage space in the building's basement. However, rent on the gallery space had been overdue for months, and while the landlord was sympathetic, she needed to pay up before the end of the month.

Caroline called Peter and asked him to come over and walk her through the gallery's books. Apparently the last sale had been the year before, and Hazel hadn't held a show since her diagnosis.

"Basically you're running on empty," Peter said.

"Is there anything that can be done?"

Peter shrugged. "Miracles happen."

That it would take a miracle seemed about right. While Caroline was grateful that her aunt had left her a place to live and a reason to work, Hazel must have known what financial straits the gallery had been left in. What had made her think Caroline knew how to handle the situation? Although Caroline didn't feel she was worthy of that trust, she knew she couldn't fail Hazel's final directive.

Caroline asked Peter to go with her down into the building's storage basement and help her move whatever was there upstairs. Most of it was outdated furniture and more clothes, but then Peter discovered some canvases in a corner, inadequately covered by old sheets. He and Caroline dragged them out into the light, and then Peter gasped.

"What is it?" Caroline asked. The painting Peter was looking at appeared unremarkable to her, a red circle on what had once been a white canvas but now was a dingy gray.

"It's a Mark Finnegan. Color field painter from the early 1960s." Peter quickly went through the other canvases, seven in all. "And works by his contemporaries." He turned to Caroline, his smile so wide that she could see it in the poor basement light. "You're sitting on a treasure trove of museum-worthy contemporary art."

"Why would Hazel keep them down here?"

Peter shook his head. "She should have known better. Dust, mold, rats—anything could have ruined them. They seem to be in pretty good shape, though."

"What would you suggest doing with them?"

"First, get them cleaned up and put into a climate-controlled storage unit. They'll be safer there, too. Good thing the landlord isn't an art connoisseur. Then choose one to sell."

"They're that valuable?"

"You sell one of these, and the gallery is back in business."

As Caroline did what Peter suggested, she still wondered, if the paintings were worth that much, why Hazel had never mentioned them, either to her in person or in her will. Perhaps she had meant to but the pain medication toward the end had affected her mind. Or maybe she'd wanted it to be a secret for Caroline to discover, in the same way she'd never told Caroline she was leaving the gallery to her in her will.

Caroline had an appraiser from one of the larger auction houses take a look at the Mark Finnegan, and it was accepted for sale. Together, she and Peter went to the auction. It was the first time she'd been in that kind of environment; she supposed she should get used to it. She thought the room would be filled with Naomi Cantrell types, but instead the attendees mostly seemed to be businesspeople, many on phones.

"Don't the actual bidders come to the auction?" she whispered to Peter.

"Most don't," he replied. "Many are overseas, Europe or Russia or increasingly Asia, and have someone here to do the job for them."

Caroline passed the time by flipping through the catalog. The starting bid on the Mark Finnegan was $100,000, which, now looking at the other offerings, she realized was toward the bottom of the listings. Her ears perked when the British-accented auctioneer announced, "Lot 20, *Untitled* by Mark Finnegan, painted in 1968, starting at one hundred thousand dollars. Do I have one hundred and fifty thousand?"

Several paddles were raised.

"Two hundred thousand. Two hundred and fifty thousand."

As the amounts went up in increments of fifty thousand dollars, the bids began to fall away, aside from one person on the far side of the room, and another person on the opposite side. Caroline felt like she was watching a tennis match between two equally proficient players.

Finally, the auctioneer called for one million dollars. Caroline clutched Peter's arm, and he responded with a pinch. "You're not dreaming," he said.

The gavel went down on 1.2 million dollars. In vain, Caroline tried to see who'd had the winning bid, but all she saw was a dark-suited man, probably someone acting on the orders of another person.

She continued to be curious about who had purchased the painting, but pushed it to the back of her mind as she planned the resurgence of the Lowry Gallery. Now she had more than enough money to secure the place, have a new show, and hire an assistant. She first offered the job to Peter, of course, but he told her he had moved on and was going back to grad school to study art history.

Now that she was officially the owner of the Lowry Gallery, Caroline decided to adopt her mother's maiden name—Hazel's last name. She had never liked her father's last name of Russo and Bob's last name, Kleinman, had never sounded right to her. By changing her name, she felt closer to Hazel than ever.

After a few days of reveling in the sight of *Elegy* in her own home, Caroline contacted Harold Yu to tell him the painting had been restored and was ready for purchase. He replied within the day that he had scheduled a trip to New York at the end of the following week, and would meet with her then. Meanwhile, could she line up an expert to verify the painting's authenticity?

Caroline planned carefully for that Friday. Peter, of course, would serve as the expert. She told Molly to take the day off, as she couldn't have the girl, with her sharp eyes and inquisitive nature, hanging around. Molly said she'd take the opportunity to go visit her parents for a long weekend, and even asked Caroline what she thought would be a good gift to take for her mother. Caroline had no idea what Rose's tastes were like now, but recommended a local store that sold handmade ceramics at ridiculous prices.

That morning she was nervous and skipped breakfast. Peter, who had come early for moral support as well as his later role, told her she had nothing to worry about.

"Where did this painting hang the last time you saw it?" he asked.

Caroline assessed the gallery, which hadn't changed in configuration since Hazel had owned it. She walked over to one of the walls. "Here," she said.

"Then let's put it where it belongs."

Together, she and Peter removed the Sandro Hess painting that hung there and replaced it with *Elegy*. Peter was right, it did look like it belonged there; although perhaps, she thought to herself, less so than in her own living room.

"Much more impressive," Peter observed, then put a hand on her arm. "Caro, you're shaking."

"I just haven't had anything to eat this morning. Aren't you concerned?"

"Why should I be? There's no way Mr. Yu has connected the two of us, and even if he did, why does it matter? I still have the credentials. I can still give a good talk."

"I'm sure you can."

Caroline had just allowed herself to relax slightly when Peter tilted his head. "There's our man."

She conjured a smile to her face and went to let Harold Yu in, taking care to lock the door after him and make sure the TEMPORARILY CLOSED sign she'd asked Molly to make the day before was affixed to the outside. She didn't want to take the chance of anyone walking in on them.

Harold Yu was as impeccably dressed as last time. He refused any refreshment, and went straight to the painting displayed on the wall. He looked at it for so long and without saying a word that Caroline wondered whether he had changed his mind.

Then he turned to Peter. "This is the expert?" he asked.

Peter rushed forward to introduce himself—too eagerly, Caroline thought—with his hand extended. Yu took it, and then mid-shake looked over Peter's head toward the front of the gallery, where someone was trying to rattle the door open.

"I'll get that," Caroline said hastily. "Probably the mailman." *Who can't read.*

Before she could move, though, Molly's voice tentatively rang out, "Is anyone there?"

Caroline went to intercept her untimely assistant while Peter attempted to regain Yu's attention. She tried to keep the irritation from her voice as she asked the girl, "Molly, what are you doing here? I gave you the day off. I thought you were going to visit your parents."

Molly emerged from behind the front desk, having dropped an overnight bag on her chair. "I was," she said, pushing back her hair from her face. "I just forgot this." She held up a bag from the ceramics store Caroline had mentioned. "I got my mom something from there, like you suggested. Do you want to see it?"

With one ear alert as to what was happening on the other side of the room, Caroline said, "Sure." Probably best to go along with the girl and hopefully she'd leave soon.

From the bag Molly withdrew a white porcelain vase in the shape of a squirrel. "You think she'll like it?"

"Of course. It's a great choice." Privately, it was one of the most ridiculous things Caroline had ever seen, more like a joke gift. But it had probably cost Molly half her week's wages, given what little she was paid.

Peter's voice could be heard from across the room and Molly said, "Oh, do you have a client?" Before Caroline could react, she left her desk and Caroline heard her say, "Hey, Peter, nice to see you again. And Mr. Yu, isn't it?" Caroline recalled that Yu had given Molly his card, as well.

When Caroline caught up with Molly, she and Peter gave each other resigned looks over the girl's head. Might as well proceed as planned; there was nothing about the situation that would lead Molly to think this wasn't a regular sale. Perhaps she would even learn something.

"Isn't that an Andrew Cantrell?" Molly said next. Now the look Peter shot Caroline was tinged with alarm.

"Yes," Caroline replied easily, thinking that the girl must have recognized it from the catalogs she'd asked her to clear out of the basement.

But Molly added, "I've seen it in one of my art history classes."

"You have?" Yu seemed to find this an interesting fact. "This painting is well-known enough to be in an American textbook?"

"It was quite well known during its time." Peter stepped in.

"But I thought it was destroyed in a fire?" Molly turned questioning eyes to Caroline, who cleared her throat.

"Well, yes, it was assumed lost for many years. But it turned out my aunt Hazel, who owned this gallery before me, kept it in storage. I only found out about it recently."

Molly subsided as Peter continued his spiel about why he thought the painting was authentic. He had brought color reproductions of Cantrell's other paintings, which he used to compare brushstrokes. He sounded, Caroline had to admit, like he knew what he was talking about. Yu seemed to believe him, too, occasionally nodding, which Caroline found herself unconsciously imitating. Molly stood to the side, her arms folded, without an expression on her face.

"Does this meet with your satisfaction, Mr. Yu?" Caroline finally asked.

"It does. But I will need the weekend to make my final decision. I am flying back to Taiwan on Monday and will let you know that morning."

"Certainly," was all Caroline could say. She had thought Yu seemed convinced, but now she had no idea what was going on behind this man's polite, unreadable exterior.

She was about to tell Peter this, after Yu had left the gallery, when she realized Molly was still there. "Don't you have a train to catch?" she snapped, and Molly jumped to collect her bags and left.

# Chapter 7

When I called my mother to tell her I was coming to visit for the weekend, I could sense the knee-jerk panic in her hesitation, before she said cheerfully, "Of course! Your father and I will be happy to have you." You'd think she'd be more excited at the idea of a visit from her only daughter, but her hesitation was a natural reflex from earlier that year, when I'd announced two months before graduation that I was coming home.

"It isn't for long, is it?" she had asked that time. "Did you get into a fight with Sam? You're not in any kind of trouble, are you?" I could already tell the possibilities that were racing through her head: pregnancy, depression, an eating disorder, an altercation with the law.

"Can we talk about it later?" I replied.

"Sure, sweetheart, of course. Your father will pick you up at the train station."

When I'd called her that time, I was crossing campus with a duffel bag of things I'd retrieved from my dorm room. It hadn't taken me long to pack up. I barely slept there anyway, preferring to take advantage of Sam's perpetually absent roommate.

While I hadn't fought with Sam, he also didn't approve of my decision to leave school. At the moment, though, I had no choice. I had been suspended for the rest of the month, and I'd decided I wasn't coming back.

As I walked across the main lawn, I noticed all the signs of spring—students in short sleeves, tender green grass, white and pink flowers on the trees, the occasional sound of someone allergic sneezing. It was a picture straight out of a catalog. If not for the actual college, then for one selling preppy clothes that let you pretend you went there.

My school, Amberlin College, was known for its New Hampshire location, lenient pass/fail policy, and focus on sustainability. The most popular classes involved farming skills and food preservation, in which students learned how to can vegetables from the college's hundred-acre farm, which were then served in the cafeteria over the winter months. For someone like Sam, it was a perfect blend of food-based academics and practicality. For me, not so much. Amberlin had a small art history department but no applied arts.

The nearest town to Amberlin was so small that I had to take a bus to Boston before catching a train to Hartford. By the time my father picked me up from the station, it was after dark. He nodded amiably to me as I threw my bag into the backseat and got into the front. The radio was tuned to the Red Sox game so we didn't speak at all for the twenty-minute drive home, but that wasn't unusual. My mother was the one who worried for the both of them.

"Are you hungry?" was the first thing she asked when I arrived. Then, without waiting for an answer, "I put aside some dinner for you."

Although my mother made elaborate meals while my brothers and I were growing up—exotic stir-fries, pungent curries—she stopped after I left for college. One weekend I came home to find my father eating a microwaveable meal in front of his computer. Meanwhile, my mother had parked herself in front of the television in the living room with a prepackaged salad.

That night, though, I ate whatever my mother put in front of me, also so that there wouldn't be any opportunity for her to ask questions. She watched me scarf my food, a worried look on her face. When I was done, I said, "I'm feeling kind of tired. I think I'll go to bed."

"Okay," my mother replied reluctantly. "Sleep well."

My brothers' rooms and my room all had been transformed into something else—Josh's into an office for my dad, Ricky's into a craft room for my mother, and mine into a guest room. I was the only one who regularly came home. Josh was married and had two kids, so they rented a vacation house whenever they came for the holidays. Ricky, who had a rotating cast of girlfriends, preferred to stay in a hotel. They were twelve and ten years older than me, so we weren't that close growing up. Too old to even tease me about being an accident when my parents thought they were done with having kids.

I did once overhear Josh on the phone telling my mother she indulged me too much. He must have been in his late twenties and just thinking about settling down with his now wife, and worried about inheriting our mother and father's parenting skills. I would have been sixteen and had just decided to quit an expensive backpacking program, after my parents had paid the nonrefundable deposit, because my best friend had decided to drop out of it. Vanessa and I were supposed to have spent the summer hiking the Appalachian Trail, bonding with eight other girls and learning how to be self-sufficient. The only person I wanted to bond with—or rather, re-bond with—was my best friend since sixth grade, whom I was quickly losing to an older boyfriend and his pothead crowd at school. I'd explained it this way to my mother, who said she understood how important friendships were at that age, and helped convince my father to pull me from the program. So maybe they were indulging me, because there was no doubt spending three weeks in the woods would have toughened me up, and Vanessa and I lost touch after we'd gone to college anyway.

They were less enthusiastic about my choice of major, although they were also committed to letting their children make their own mistakes. I didn't know how they would take my deciding to leave school, though, especially with graduation so close. At some point I would be ready to tell them, but that first night back home in the guest room, lying between crisp, fresh sheets, I just didn't want to think about it anymore.

I did wonder, however, where my old roommate Kimi was. Whether she was currently tucked in bed at her parents' the way I was. Wherever she had ended up, I hoped she was safe.

Kimi Kitano was the one who had introduced me to Sam, if you can call it an introduction. She was half Japanese and half white, wore dyed blond dreads covered with a blue bandana, and printed Indian skirts over her jeans. Although she insisted her hair color was natural, the shape of her eyes gave her away. She told me she'd grown up with three sisters—all home-schooled, of course—in a yurt her father had built in upstate New York.

Although Kimi and I had shared a number of classes, I knew her better by reputation. She called herself a performance artist, and the previous spring had entertained the student body with a project in which she'd knitted wool sweaters and put them on Amberlin's flock of sheep after they'd been sheared. Then she'd released the sheep, and they'd run across the main lawn, disrupted classes, and snarled traffic in town. I'd watched them out of the window of the library, where I'd gone to study. Something about those sheep, dressed in their new, rainbow-colored coats, was pure joy.

When I told Kimi that I wanted to be an artist, too, although in a more traditional sense, she said, "Never apologize for who you are, Molly. You're already an artist by existing."

"What do you mean?"

"Our interaction right here." We were sitting opposite each other on our beds, and she pointed to the space between us. "We're performing right now."

"About what?"

"Daily rituals. Female friendship. The art of conversation."

"But there's no audience."

Kimi gave me a mysterious smile. "What makes you think there isn't?"

At night, I was the audience for Kimi's performances in bed. A few times a week she'd bring back boys and I'd try to ignore the sounds that ensued, the giggles and bed frame creaks and muffled groans, by turning my back and burying my head under my comforter. Then I eventually realized there was just one boy. I was beginning to identify the sound of his weight when he shifted on top of her, the sighing sound he made when he came. I started keeping my head uncovered so I could hear better, my right hand sneaking underneath the waistband of my pajamas and between my legs. In the morning, I waited until Kimi's boyfriend had left before pretending to wake up. When I did so, Kimi would give me a sly look and say, "I hope you slept well."

All I could do was nod, but both of us knew I had heard everything. I suspected Kimi wanted me to hear, that she was making such theatrical sounds for my benefit. Maybe I was jealous, although I wasn't sure of whom. What made Kimi so attractive? Was it her mixed ethnicity? She could be pretty if she tried, but her hair looked unwashed, and it went without saying that she didn't shave her underarms or legs. Although she only used baking soda as deodorant, her odor was not unpleasant, if a bit nutty, like coconut oil. Underneath her layers of clothes, which she wore like a form of protection, her body was sinewy and taut. Having sex with her, I thought, must be like having sex with a piece of twine.

Then one night, Kimi and her boyfriend were so loud with their grunting and yelping that I couldn't tolerate it anymore. I turned over in my bed and kicked the wall. They were silent for a moment, and then a giggle from Kimi, and then they resumed what they were doing, completely ignoring me. I couldn't help it, but I started to cry. Out of frustration, anger, or envy, I didn't know, but I couldn't keep the tears from running down my face. I had enough shame for all three of us.

The next morning I woke up with a massive headache, my eyes sandy and swollen. I got dressed without looking at the bed opposite me and headed to class. When I was only a few yards away from the dorm, I heard someone running after me. Kimi? No, a boy with brown hair, a rumpled flannel shirt, his glasses askew. So this was Kimi's boyfriend. He was serious-looking and weedy, not the type I thought she would go for, or, for that matter, the type I would go for.

"Why were you crying last night?" he asked, almost shyly.

"Because I can't stand hearing you guys fuck anymore." I started walking away.

He ran to keep up, his untied shoelaces slapping against his skinny ankles. "I'm sorry. Can I at least walk you to class?"

That was Sam. As far as I knew, he never slept with Kimi again, and soon it was my neck he was sighing into. Kimi didn't seem to care when I told her about Sam and me, and to keep things from getting awkward, I would spend nights in Sam's room, where his roommate, who was less tolerant than I had been, got driven out.

By spring of my senior year, I was barely spending any time in my dorm room, just stopping by to pick up fresh clothes or a book I needed for class. Most of my stuff had migrated to

Sam's anyway. I often missed seeing Kimi, although I observed that her side of the room was gradually being covered by laundry, dirty dishes from the cafeteria, and library books. I figured she was in the middle of writing her senior thesis, like me. I had chosen the most written-about and uninspired topic ever—light and dark in the works of Caravaggio—but the upside of that was I had plenty of resources and had almost finished writing the damn thing.

The next time I saw Kimi in our room, I was surprised at how thin she was, the way her clothes hung off her body. Her hair was as matted as it could get before becoming a complete rug.

"I haven't seen you for a while," I said. "How're you doing?"

"You know, working hard on the thesis," she replied. "I can't decide on a topic. Should I write about Chinese landscape painting during the Tang dynasty? A feminist interpretation of Klimt's *Portrait of Adele Bloch-Bauer*? At least I'm not writing about some clichéd, religious hack like Caravaggio."

I swallowed. "Well, good luck."

"Wait!"

I turned at the desperation in her voice.

"You have access to the department, right?"

"Yes." My work-study job for the past two years had been as an administrative assistant in the art history department.

"I think some materials there could inspire me."

"You can come in whenever you want and I'll help you find what you need," I offered.

"What I need is your help to get in there after-hours."

I thought about it for a moment. I didn't know what exactly Kimi had in mind, but it sounded suspicious. On the other hand, she did look like she needed some kind of help, and she was my friend. Besides, I had always felt guilty for taking Sam away from her, no matter how involved or not they had been. I owed my roommate one.

"Okay," I said.

We arranged to meet later that night. When I told Sam that I was helping Kimi with her thesis, a strange look came over his face.

"I don't think it's a good idea to get involved with any of her projects," he said.

"Why not?"

"Well, for one thing, that girl is unstable."

"And you slept with her for, like, a month?"

His face twisted a little from embarrassment. "In that context, she was a good kind of unstable."

"So you're saying that I'm boring?"

"No! I just mean, be careful with her, Molly. I know she looks like this free-spirited, artsy person"—the opposite of me—"but she's actually kind of fragile. Be careful," he repeated.

When I met Kimi outside of the art history department, I had to laugh. She was completely dressed in black, including a headband with cat ears. "I get it, you're a cat burglar," I said. I wondered if this was a joke, one of her performance pieces.

As I fumbled with my key card to open the department door and turned on the light in the office, I told myself I wasn't doing anything wrong. I had every right to be there as an employee. What if I'd forgotten something at my desk? Or just wanted to make some copies? Was stealing office supplies even a crime?

While I was pondering these things, Kimi wandered through the office. She sat down in the chair of the other admin, Lorene, a local woman in her fifties who had worked at Amberlin for twenty years so her son could go to college for free, and tried on the pair of reading glasses that Lorene kept on her desk. Then she got up and went to the faculty's mailboxes, where she removed some letters and stuck them recklessly into the wrong slots. I was about to tell her to quit it when she went straight to a cabinet to the side of the room that housed every senior thesis that had passed through the art history department. She opened a drawer and rifled through the papers until she seemed to find one that suited her, and stuffed it into her backpack.

"What are you doing?" I whispered. "You can't remove that from this room." Students were allowed to look at those files but not to check anything out.

Kimi waved me away. "I found what I needed. Let's get out of here."

The next day, when Lorene searched her desk and said, "Now, where did I put my glasses?" I didn't say anything. So what if Kimi had taken a thesis? It was one out of hundreds of papers that would never be noticed missing, unless the person who had actually written it came looking for it. Besides, I didn't know what she planned to do with it. Maybe she was going to cut it up and throw word scraps from the roof of the department, or set it on fire on the main lawn. It was true that I had no idea what she intended to do.

Over the next month, I turned in my thesis on Caravaggio and started talking with Sam about moving to New York after graduation. He wanted to work with inner city kids; I wanted to start some kind of art project, although I didn't know what. It had been a long time since I'd painted or even sketched for my own enjoyment. Then Dr. Renfeld, the chair of the art history department, called me into her office.

Dr. Renfeld was originally from Beijing and was one of Amberlin's first foreign students in the 1980s. Before she arrived, the only topics art history students studied were related to European art, and nothing after World War II. It was as if postmodernism didn't exist. She persuaded the school to add classes in Asian and Middle Eastern art, and then, after she became chair, contemporary art. She'd also married the biology professor, who now headed his respective department, and the "Drs. Renfeld" were a common fixture at campus events. I liked her; she had taught several of my classes and was my thesis advisor.

I assumed she had called me into her office to talk about my thesis now. Then I saw Kimi slouched in one of the chairs in front of Dr. Renfeld's desk.

"Molly," Dr. Renfeld said. "Please sit down."

As I did so, I snuck a look at Kimi, whose face revealed nothing. She didn't even appear to recognize me. I glanced at the paper lying on the desk and saw that it wasn't mine, but Kimi's thesis, entitled "The Garden Within: Landscape Painting during the Tang Dynasty."

"When I was growing up in China," Dr. Renfeld began, "there was no such thing as plagiarism. It was referred to as honoring the work of the masters. So I suppose I should have felt flattered when I read this thesis and found my views from twenty years ago quoted almost word for word. Of course, I went by the name Ming Lei back then, my Chinese name."

Kimi didn't respond. She was looking out the office window, which had a view of the central lawn, where several students were tossing a Frisbee back and forth. I followed her gaze, wishing I were outside, too.

"I'm sorry to say, Ms. Kitano," Dr. Renfeld continued, pulling our attention back to her, "that you're not the only student who's ever been caught plagiarizing their senior thesis, in this department or at this school."

Kimi finally spoke, jerking her head toward me. "What does this have to with her?"

"I thought you must have had some kind of help. There aren't many people who have access to the art history department. Security gave me a log of everyone who swiped their key card after-hours in the past month." Dr. Renfeld rested her gaze on me. "Turned out there were very few people on that list."

"How are we going to be punished?" I blurted out. "Will we be allowed to graduate?"

"Ms. Schaeffer, you've been relieved of your job in the department. Ms. Kitano, it goes without saying that you've failed your thesis. As of now, both of you are suspended from school for the rest of the month. After that, we'll talk about what you'll need to do if you want to graduate."

"I don't care if I graduate," Kimi said, standing up. "In fact, I'm dropping out right now."

I found myself standing up, as well. "Me too."

"Girls—" Dr. Renfeld started.

But Kimi had already pushed back her chair and was heading out the door. "God, why are you following me?" she snapped as I ran to keep up with her long strides across the main lawn.

"You're angry at *me?*" I demanded. "*You're* the one who got me into trouble. You're the one who plagiarized your thesis."

She stopped so suddenly that I almost ran into her. "It was… a pastiche."

"*Bullshit*. This isn't one of your stupid performance pieces. For whatever reason you couldn't write your paper, so you copied someone else's. Not just someone else's—Dr. Renfeld's."

"How was I to know that she's practically the only Chinese student to have ever attended Amberlin?" Kimi muttered. "I didn't think I would get caught, okay? But dropping out… who's copying who now?"

"I have my own reasons," I said. "They have nothing to do with you."

"Really? Because the way I see it, including Sam, you want to be just like me."

"Leave Sam out of it!" I shouted.

Kimi screamed as if I'd pulled her hair, causing everyone on the lawn to stare at us, and headed toward our dorm. I guessed it wasn't a good idea to follow her there and went to find Sam, where I choked out to him what had happened.

He kindly did not say "*I told you so*" about Kimi. "What're you going to do?"

"I guess I'm suspended. I'll have to go live with my parents for the rest of the month."

"And then? You're coming back to graduate, right?"

I shook my head. "I don't want to graduate. I just want us to go to New York as soon as possible. Isn't that what you want?"

"What'll your parents say?"

"I'll tell them I'm taking a break. That I'm planning to come back at some point."

Sam studied me carefully. "You *are* going to come back to school, aren't you?"

"Sure. Eventually. But I want to be an artist. I don't need a degree for that. I just need experience."

I was far from sure when I said that. But I was sure my parents would eventually come around to my decision. What could they do about it? Refuse to let me come home? They weren't like that. They'd be angry at first, especially my father, but I'd find a way to soothe them, tell them I was planning to go back to school in the fall, but first I wanted to get a taste of the real world. I was their beloved only daughter.

The next day I received a formal letter telling me I had been suspended from school, as well as an e-mail from Dr. Renfeld in which she implored me to come into her office to talk about my next step. "By the way," she added at the end, "I was very impressed with your thesis on Caravaggio."

That still didn't change my mind. I convinced Sam to let me keep most of my things in his room, and went back to my dorm to get what little remained there of my stuff.

Part of me hoped I would run into Kimi; part of me dreaded it. When I entered the room, no one was there. Most of her things had already been put into boxes, and her bed was stripped. I heard a sound behind me and turned around, expecting to see Kimi, but instead in the doorway there stood a middle-aged couple. The man was Japanese, with Kimi's eyes and mouth, dressed in a navy polo shirt and khakis. The woman was a tall blonde in a salmon-colored silk shell; I couldn't see anything of Kimi in her at all, but I knew she must be Kimi's mother.

"Hi," I said. "I'm Molly, Kimi's roommate."

"You mean Kimberly," the woman said, extending her hand.

Kimi's real name was *Kimberly?* No wonder she had changed her name.

"I've heard a lot about you," Kimi's mother continued. The way she pursed her lips afterward suggested that what she'd heard lately wasn't good.

I wondered what else Kimi had made up about her background. "You shouldn't blame her for what she did," I said. "I mean, how could she know about plagiarism, being *home-schooled with her sisters?*"

Kimi's father gave me a strange look, confirming my suspicions. "Kimberly's an only child. And she went to private school in New York."

He excused himself to take the boxes to the post office, but her mother stayed while I tried not to self-consciously pack up my clothes and books. Finally, as I wrestled with trying to fold my sheets, she stood up and took over, holding one end and then motioning me to walk the other over to her. She grasped all four corners and folded the sheets into a neat square, then handed them back to me.

"Kimberly told us you tried to help her," her mother said. "She said if it wasn't for you, she'd have done something much worse than plagiarize a paper. Hopefully when we get back home, she'll be able to see her therapist more regularly." She paused. "Her father and I appreciate you looking out for her."

"Of course," I said. But I hadn't looked out for Kimi at all. I'd stolen her boyfriend, was hardly around for most of the year, then had been her accomplice in something that had gotten us both kicked out of school. By helping her plagiarize I'd thought I was helping her, but I'd ended up hurting us both.

When I had finished packing, I said, "Please tell Kimi—I mean, Kimberly—good-bye for me."

Her mother nodded, and I left her there, sitting on the plastic surface of her daughter's stripped bed. I wasn't surprised that Kimi had fictionalized her background; it was all part of the performance. If I could, I'd probably have done it, too. I just wasn't brave enough. I couldn't even tell my parents why I was going home.

It turned out that I didn't have to explain myself. The day after I arrived home, I woke up at noon to hear my father roaring downstairs. The last time I'd heard him so angry was when Ricky was in high school and had gotten arrested for intoxication.

When I entered the kitchen, my parents fell silent.

"Caleb, let her get some breakfast in her first," my mother pleaded.

My father ignored her and addressed me. "Molly, I called your school this morning to see why you left, and they said you helped another student plagiarize her thesis. Is this true?"

"It was my roommate," I clarified. "And I didn't know what she was going to do. She only told me she needed to get into the department office for research material, and since I had access, I let her." This was not entirely true; from the moment Kimi waltzed into the office, I knew she wasn't going to be content to just look around.

"This is serious," my father said. "You're going back there once your suspension is up and apologize to the chair of the department. And then you're going to get your degree, no matter if you have to retake classes and work twice as hard."

"Sam and I are moving to New York," I announced. "Right after he graduates."

A sound was caught in my mother's throat. I hadn't given my parents any hint about my plans after college, but they must have suspected I wanted to go away. I wasn't going to come back and live at home, like I was doing now, was I?

"What about you?" my father asked. "When are you going to graduate?"

"I need to take some time off from school," I said.

My father laughed. "Don't most kids do that their junior year and go abroad? I think it's too late for that now. And if you don't agree, maybe you should find somewhere else to stay until you do."

"Caleb," my mother said and put a placating hand on his arm. "She just got home. We can talk about her future later."

"We're talking about it now!"

"I'm sitting right here," I pointed out. I wasn't going to tell them what I had told Sam about wanting to be an artist. "I'll make a plan. Maybe I'll go back in the fall. But I just can't do it right now." I got to my feet.

"Where are you going?" my mother asked.

"Out for a walk."

Still in the T-shirt and sweatpants I'd slept in, I shuffled out the door and down the sidewalk. My parents' neighborhood was filled with old, veranda-enclosed houses, colorful flower beds, pristine front lawns. One of the neighbors was outside in her garden and waved when she saw me.

"Yes, I'm home for a visit!" I preempted her question and walked more quickly.

When I got to the corner, I pulled out my phone and called Sam. "What day do you want to move?" I asked. "I don't think I can stand it here much longer."

Eventually, my father calmed down and accepted my refusal to immediately return to school, although I led him to believe that I was going back in the fall. I also convinced my mother about my plan to move to the city with Sam. For the next couple of weeks I moped around the house, sleeping until noon, my conversations with Sam serving as the highlight of the day.

He talked about parties I was missing, the end-of-the-year festivities, but I didn't miss them at all. Already, Amberlin seemed like it was in another country, and I'd lived there in another life.

Then, one day, while rummaging through the attic, I discovered the box of old photos of my mother's female relatives. For the first time in years, I felt like I wanted to create something outside of myself.

This weekend, the atmosphere at home was much calmer. My father gave little hints here and there about my enrolling for the fall semester, but I told him how much I loved my job at the Lowry Gallery, which pleased my mother.

"I'm learning so much from Caroline," I said, and she practically glowed with delight.

When I presented her with the gift I'd brought her, she looked at it blankly. "Is that a hedgehog?"

"It's a squirrel. You can use it as a vase! It came from a ceramics store near the gallery. Caroline thought you would like it."

"Well, I do like it," my mother recovered. "Thank you, sweetheart. I think I'll put it on the mantelpiece in the living room." I suspected she'd rather use it a doorstop and close the door a little too heavily on it.

It wasn't just Caroline's judgment on gifts for my mother I was starting to question. More than once I was tempted to ask my mother whether she thought her old college friend was capable of selling a forged painting, but I knew what the answer would be. My mother never thought the worst of anyone, least of all someone she considered family, or close to it.

Still, I couldn't keep my suspicions out of my head, or the image of the version of *Elegy* I had seen at the Lowry Gallery. Maybe I could compare it to the only real Cantrell that was accessible: *Meditation* at the Museum of Modern Art. So I told my parents that I had to cut my visit short and took the train back to the city Sunday morning, then walked the ten blocks or so from Grand Central to the museum.

After paying the entrance fee—and privately grumbling that a former art history major like myself could hardly afford it—I located *Meditation,* in its odd placement next to an information desk, and stared at it. I had seen the painting before only in photos, and in real life there was unexpected texture and nuance to the black and blue shades. It was a harsher work than *Elegy,* which reminded me of a painting by Turner—the grayness reminiscent of a seascape, with the pale white light at the center. His seascapes had always been my favorite paintings by him, before I learned that many of them looked that way because they were unfinished.

"Molly!" someone called.

I turned to see a girl who had just emerged from the women's restroom a few feet away. It was Kimi Kitano. Wearing a sleeveless blue sundress, she looked so different that I wouldn't have recognized her if I'd passed her in the street. Her dark brown hair was in a pixie cut, bringing out an odd beauty to her facial features.

"What are you doing here?" I asked.

"Came to see the Ad Reinhardt retrospective. Never knew there could be so many different shades of black." Kimi cocked her head to see the painting I had been perusing. "Are you interested in Andrew Cantrell?"

I shook my head, not wanting to explain. So many questions hung between us in the awkward silence that followed. *What happened after you left school? What are you doing now? Are you okay?* But instead, I said, "I was just leaving."

"Me too," Kimi said. "Let's get lunch and we can catch up."

In the second-floor museum café, sandwiched between a Euro-hipster couple wearing the exact same jeans and two elderly ladies in elaborately patterned scarves, we briefly updated each other on our lives. I told Kimi about my job at the gallery and living with Sam in Queens, and she told me how she was staying at her parents' in Brooklyn Heights and how she'd started volunteering at a summer school program for disadvantaged children.

"Have you been working on your art?" I asked.

Kimi fluttered her hand. "I haven't thought about art since the day I left Amberlin. I felt like I was performing all the time—it was just too exhausting."

"So, was the stunt you pulled with your thesis a 'performance'?"

Kimi looked down at the table. "About that...I'm sorry I dragged you into it. I guess I didn't believe enough in myself that I could write that silly paper. And everything seemed to come so easily to you—Sam, your thesis, your job. You seemed so sure of yourself."

"*Me?* You're the one with that reputation on campus."

"Yeah, because I was afraid that if I wasn't doing something outrageous, no one would pay attention to me. My mom says it's because I'm an only child." Kimi rolled her eyes. "Anything rather than put the blame on herself, I guess."

"So are you thinking of going back?" I asked. "To Amberlin?"

"I meant what I said, I'm done with that place. I like the volunteer work I'm doing now. Maybe in the fall I'll look into getting my teaching certification."

The idea of Kimi teaching young children was a little unnerving to me.

"What about you?" she queried. "Are you working on anything?"

I told her that I had a project, although not what it was.

"You should use your connections at the gallery," she said. "Get your first show."

I thought of Sandro Hess and how he'd gotten his show at the Lowry Gallery. It wasn't as simple as someone liking your work; you had to be able to offer them something in return.

"I don't know if I should start where I work," I said. "Besides, I don't know how long the place is going to stay open."

"Why? What's going on there?"

Little by little, my doubts concerning *Elegy* and Caroline came tumbling out. It was as if I was compelled to share my thoughts about them to someone, and Kimi was the most likely person. Who else was there? Sam would probably say I was imagining things and should stay out of trouble. When I mentioned the possibility of a forgery, Kimi's eyes gleamed.

"So, you need to find proof that the painting is a fake," she clarified.

"Yes. But maybe it's none of my business."

"Don't you want to know the truth?"

I had to admit I did. "How would I start trying to prove it?"

Kimi leaned the palms of her hands against the edge of the table. "Okay, pretend that you're writing a thesis on this painting by Andrew Cantrell. What would you do?"

This felt like a trick question. "Um, research?"

"Exactly."

"I already looked up these articles about Andrew Cantrell on the Internet—"

"Lazy!" Kimi shouted and the Euro-hipster couple stared at us through their thick-rimmed glasses. "You need to go to the library."

*So* now *you want to do research*, I thought.

Kimi pulled out her phone. "The New York Public Library is open until six. Come on!"

So Kimi and I retraced my steps from that morning, back the ten blocks down Fifth Avenue to the main branch of the New York Public Library, past the stone lions that flanked its entrance, and to the Microforms Reading Room on the first floor. Kimi was right. Although some of the articles about Andrew Cantrell that turned up had been ones I had seen before in my cursory Internet search about him and Hazel Lowry, there were others from obscure publications I had never heard of.

"Listen to this," I said, stopping on an article in a magazine called *Artsbeat*. I began to read out loud. "'Andrew Cantrell's latest painting, *Elegy*, comes from a very tender place. In an exclusive interview with yours truly, the artist revealed the painting was inspired by his childhood and was dedicated to a special someone. And where can you find this dedication? No one looking at the painting will be able to tell, but the artist himself showed me the initials on the back in the lower right-hand corner. I can confirm that they do belong to a certain red-haired gallery owner...'"

"Ugh," Kimi said. "Who wrote this?"

I checked the byline. "Someone named Marigold Guthrie."

Kimi rolled her eyes. "Total artist groupie. Well, now we know something about *Elegy* that isn't visible in a photo. Can you check to see if there's a dedication on the painting in the gallery?"

I told her I would do it the next day at work, and after promising her I'd let her know what I found out, we parted just as the library was starting to close.

When I got home, I flopped down sweatily on the sofa beside Sam and said, "You won't believe who I ran into today. Kimi Kitano!" When his reaction was not as surprised as I expected, I stated the obvious. "You already know she's been living in the city."

"Yeah," he admitted. "We've kept in touch."

"And you never told me?" I felt like throwing a sofa cushion at him.

"I didn't think you wanted anything to do with her ever again."

And I hadn't, until this afternoon. "Next time, please tell me if you are still in touch with my old roommate, *who you used to sleep with*."

"Okay," he wisely said, knowing that I wasn't in the mood for excuses. After a beat, he asked cautiously, "How did she seem?"

"Good. Really good."

And she had. In fact, I would have considered it a toss-up as to who had recovered better from our suspension from school. Sure, I was living with my boyfriend rather than my parents, but my parents were still contributing to my rent, so I couldn't exactly consider myself independent. My job at the Lowry Gallery paid so little that I was essentially a volunteer there, the same as Kimi at her summer school program. At least she seemed to be taking inspiration from that experience for the future, whereas every interaction or event I'd been a part of at the gallery had plunged me further into confusion. Now I was left to wonder whether I wanted to be an artist, when fraud—of the personal as well as literal kind—seemed to be the expected path.

I got to the Lowry Gallery early Monday morning, but when I opened the door, the alarm system had already been disabled. Caroline must have come down before me. *Elegy* had been removed from the wall where it had hung on Friday and taken to Caroline's office, or upstairs to her apartment, or wherever she stored it. A ding came from my phone and I saw that Kimi had sent me a text: *????*

*Painting is gone,* I texted back.

*!!!!* she replied.

Caroline's line was lit on her phone; she was talking to someone in her office. When she came out, a smile on her face, she saw me and looked perplexed. "Molly, you're here early."

"There was nothing wrong with the train," I replied easily. "Did you get some good news just now?"

"Some very good news. Mr. Yu is stopping by to pick up the painting at noon before his flight home to Taiwan."

"Do you want me to pack it?" I asked, even though I had no idea how.

Caroline looked me up and down as if it were an absurd question. "I've hired a packing service."

Of course she wouldn't entrust the packing of a painting worth two million dollars to her assistant. But I didn't know how I would be able check the back of the painting otherwise.

When the two packers arrived, they followed Caroline to her office, where apparently the painting was being kept. She stayed behind to keep an eye on them while I manned the front desk.

I texted Kimi. *Help! Need a diversion.* I was being melodramatic, but I knew that would get her attention.

*Be there soon,* she replied.

Kimi arrived at eleven o'clock wearing another cute sundress and oversize sunglasses perched on her head. I informed her that Mr. Yu was picking up the painting in an hour but that I hadn't been able to check the back of it because Caroline was always around.

Kimi raised her voice. "I really need to speak to your boss."

"What?" I asked.

"I told you, I need to speak to the gallery owner."

I raised my voice to meet hers. "Sure, I'll go get her right away."

Kimi gave me an exaggerated thumbs-up.

Caroline was sitting in her office amidst a pile of enough acid-free paper, foam corners, cardboard, and Bubble Wrap to outfit a post office.

"There's a client out front who wants to talk to you," I said. "I'll keep an eye on things here."

Caroline nodded and finally left her office. The packers had already wrapped the bottom of the painting but, putting as much authority in my voice as I could, I told them to redo it. Pretending to check their work, I examined the lower right-hand corner of the canvas.

Nothing was there.

"Something else wrong?" one of the packers asked me, impatient.

"No," I answered in a daze. "You can continue with your work."

Forgetting I had told Caroline I was keeping an eye on things, I wandered back out into the gallery. Although I had been convinced in my head that the painting was more likely a fake than not, to be faced with the actual proof was something else. Now I had to decide what to do with this information before Mr. Yu arrived.

In the gallery, I heard Kimi saying, "...I really want to get something unique for my parents' anniversary, and they *love* Disneyland...."

Just then, Mr. Yu showed up early.

Over Caroline's head, Kimi raised her eyebrows as if to ask, *Is that him?* I nodded, and she sprang into action.

"Excellent," she said. "I need an outsider's opinion." She approached Mr. Yu with her most flirtatious smile. "Pardon me, you look like someone who knows a lot about art. I'm thinking of buying this painting." She gestured toward Sandro Hess's painting in the gallery's front window. "Do you think it's worth ten thousand dollars?"

Mr. Yu appeared startled but addressed her question seriously. "Twenty thousand, I think. At ten thousand, you are getting a bargain."

"Mr. Yu," Caroline began, but Kimi steamrollered right over her.

"Where are you from? Taiwan? My father is Japanese, but he does a lot of business in Taiwan. I know, the Taiwanese don't have a good opinion of the Japanese because of World War II...."

I wondered if Caroline was as flummoxed by this cross-cultural history lesson as I was. She touched Mr. Yu's hand to get his attention and said to Kimi, "Excuse us, my assistant can help you now."

But Kimi wasn't done. "It was so nice talking to you," she said to Mr. Yu.

"Very nice talking to you, too," he said, and reached inside his jacket pocket. I noticed he no longer wore the fancy silver watch he'd had the first time he visited. He presented Kimi with his card, the same as he'd done with me when we'd met. I guessed he did it with all the young ladies.

Kimi took the card with both hands. "I've always wanted to visit Taiwan!" she exclaimed.

"You've always wanted to visit Taiwan," I said sardonically after Caroline led Mr. Yu back to her office.

Kimi ignored my comment. "So, was there a dedication on the painting?"

I shook my head.

"It's a fake, then."

"Maybe there's an explanation," I said. "Maybe Andrew Cantrell lied in the interview for *Artsbeat*. Maybe the dedication was removed from the back of the painting at some point, or it faded away. There isn't absolute proof."

Kimi gave me a strange look. "You don't need absolute proof. All you need is reasonable doubt that the painting is authentic. You have to tell Mr. Yu about this, right now."

"I can't. Not in front of my boss."

"Then later. Or you could alert someone in the media." Kimi had a gleeful glint in her eyes. "You could do an exposé! When else would you get such an opportunity to reveal how crazy the art world is? How insane the prices are?"

"I'm afraid there isn't anything here for you," I said loudly.

"What?" she asked.

"Nothing within your budget. Sorry!" I escorted Kimi to the door, and she pulled me outside with her.

"Where's your sense of right and wrong?" she demanded.

"Like you're one to talk."

"Okay, I deserved that. But at the very least, you can't let that man get on the plane with a forgery."

"Kimi," I said, "thanks for your help, but I really need you to leave now."

To my surprise, she did. I watched to make sure she had walked all the way down the street before I returned to the gallery. Having finalized the deal, I supposed, Caroline and Mr. Yu emerged from her office. A car arrived and the packers carried out the boxed painting and put it in the trunk. Then Caroline and I watched as the car with Mr. Yu and a two-million-dollar fake painting proceeded down the street and turned the corner.

A text was waiting for me on my phone when I returned to my desk. *Well?*

From Kimi.

*Am sending an e-mail,* I replied.

But all afternoon, I couldn't do it. I felt uncomfortable composing an e-mail implicating my boss in her own gallery, so I decided to do it when I got home.

"Molly." Caroline approached me before I could leave that day. "You were a great help today. All summer, actually. I hope you'll consider staying on through the fall. And to show my appreciation, I'd like to give you this."

She handed me a white envelope. At home, when I opened it, a check for a thousand dollars fluttered out. It felt like blood money.

Where *was* my sense of right and wrong? The trouble was that I couldn't tell what was the right thing to do. Caroline had taken me in as her assistant. Not because she especially needed or could afford one, but as a favor to my mother. She had been my mother's best friend in college; they were friends still. Exposing the truth about the painting would not only hurt Caroline, but my mother.

On the other hand, there was an innocent stranger, Mr. Yu. I imagined him arriving in the airport in Taiwan sometime the next day. Jet-lagged and exhausted, he'd collect his finely made luggage and the padded box with the painting. Everything would go in a car, and he'd bring *Elegy* to his home and hang it on his wall. I knew he was married; I imagined him showing the painting off to his wife. Maybe they had children. Someday those children would inherit a fake painting, and the lie would go on and on.

That decided it for me. I got out Mr. Yu's card, opened my laptop, and started to compose an e-mail.

# Chapter 8

When Harold opened the front door to his apartment early in the morning, he heard the patter of small feet. Adrian peered around the corner.

"What did you bring me this time, Daddy?" he asked.

Harold shook his head. So young and already so acquisitive. "I brought something back for all of us," he said. "You'll have to wait until your mother gets up, though."

He assumed at this hour that Vicki was still in bed. Adrian's nanny, a local young woman, appeared and they exchanged good-mornings before she carried Adrian away to get him ready for preschool. Harold wrestled the painting into the living room. The gallery owner's assistant had done a good job protecting it against the long-haul flight, but he might have dinged the corner bringing it into his own home.

Once inside, he rested it against the wall opposite the sofa and carefully began to remove the wrapping. He hadn't decided yet where to put it, or even if he wanted to display it at all. So much could go wrong: Adrian could accidentally damage it while playing; the humid weather, despite the climate-controlled settings in the apartment, could warp the frame. Putting the painting in storage was the safest option, but Harold felt compelled to see it every day.

"We're going now," the nanny announced, Adrian's hand in her own.

The boy broke away from her and ran up to the painting. "What's that?" he asked.

"Don't touch, Adrian," Harold cautioned. "It's very expensive."

Adrian continued to reach out toward the painting, and the nanny pulled him aside. "I'm sorry, sir," she said, picking the boy up. Adrian began to whine and kick as she hustled him out of the house.

"So what is it?" Vicki asked from the hallway, wrapped in her dressing gown. Harold suspected she had been standing there for a while, observing the nanny deal with their son.

"A painting."

"I can see that." She moved closer, first squinting against the morning light, then, as if remembering that it might cause wrinkles, shading her eyes instead.

"What do you think?" Harold hadn't realized his wife's opinion meant so much to him until that moment.

"How much did you pay for it?

"One point three million dollars." He didn't know why he had shaved off about a third of the price, but it wasn't as if Vicki would be able to find out the actual number, either, if she cared to.

Vicki tilted her head. "It must be quite special then. Who's the artist?"

Harold told her what he knew of Andrew Cantrell, including the gallery owner's comparison of him to Pollock, the fact that another one of his paintings hung in the Museum of Modern Art, but Vicki didn't seem impressed.

"It looks like someone used an eraser in the middle of the painting," she observed.

"It's really more of an investment," Harold amended.

"Then you'll put it in storage, right? Because you can't be thinking of hanging it in here."

"Why not?"

"It doesn't go with the living room."

Harold looked around the expansive space, the sofa upholstered in gray linen, the charcoal-colored cushions, the moss-green chairs. "What do you mean? Everything here goes with gray."

"I'm thinking of having it redecorated in brighter colors. Maybe turquoise and marigold."

"Okay, it won't go in here," he conceded. Then he was aware of how silent the apartment was, when usually there would be the sound of the housekeeper bustling in the kitchen. "Where's Maribel?"

"I fired her while you were away."

"Why?" Maribel had been with them for more than five years, since before Adrian was born.

"I believe she stole your watch."

"I told you, I lost the watch while I was in Shanghai."

"You didn't sound sure about it."

Harold opened his mouth, then closed it. He couldn't tell Vicki he'd given his watch away to a random bar girl.

"Anyway"—Vicki waved away the reason—"her food was always too salty. Don't worry, Serena has someone she can recommend." Vicki's friend Serena seemed to be taking over her life, just as her husband, Charlie, seemed to be taking over Harold's.

"I'm going in to the office soon," he told Vicki.

"Without breakfast? I'm sure Maribel left something behind."

"I ate something on the plane," Harold lied. He began to repack the painting as Vicki went into the kitchen to struggle with the espresso maker.

Half an hour later he was on his way into Taipei proper, into the Eastern District that contained the city's financial center. At this time of day the roads were clogged with vehicles, speedier mopeds weaving their way in and out among the cars. Harold's phone started to ring but he turned it off. He wanted these last few minutes of solace inside the car, protected from the world beyond.

He didn't know what kind of reaction he'd wanted from Vicki about the painting. Maybe an acknowledgment that he could appreciate an item for other than how much it cost? That he could still feel something?

When he got to work, a security guard helped him transport the painting through the lobby, up the elevator, and into his office. As Harold passed by her desk, his secretary called out, "Mr. Yu, you have a message—"

"I'll be back in a minute," he told her.

Harold's office commanded a breathtaking view of the skyline, including the vaguely pagoda-shaped Taipei 101, which used to be the world's tallest building. Often, when he'd gotten off of a difficult call, or felt unsure about a challenging decision, he'd stand in front of the window and gaze at the building for reassurance. After his last trip to New York, Taipei 101 reminded him of the Freedom Tower downtown, and its terrible legacy. Perhaps towers were no longer the signs of power they used to be.

After unwrapping it for the second time, Harold leaned the painting against the wall opposite his desk. Yes, that would do. He had just sent an e-mail to his secretary, asking her to arrange for someone to come and hang the painting, when Charlie Lin burst into his office.

"Didn't you get my calls? My messages to your secretary?" he demanded.

"I've been busy—"

Charlie glanced briefly at the painting. "Yeah, with interior decoration."

Ignoring him, Harold motioned Charlie to take the seat opposite his desk. "What's going on?"

"It's happened again."

"What are you talking about?"

"A second worker committed suicide at the Shanghai factory."

Harold was surprised, yet not truly, that this kind of tragedy had repeated itself. As Charlie filled him in, it seemed that the circumstances were different. Last time, it had been a young female worker who had taken rat poison supposedly over a breakup. This was a young male worker who'd thrown himself off the roof of the dormitory. He'd done it during an afternoon recess, when there were more than a hundred witnesses out in the yard. Harold imagined some of the boys playing basketball on the meager court, girls gathered in conversation, when the figure fell darkly from the sky behind them.

"What's worse," Charlie continued, "he left a note. A list of demands, or a manifesto, so to speak."

"What kind of demands?"

"That workers should be paid more for overtime and that the rent for their dormitory beds should not be raised, among other things."

"Workers pay rent for their beds?" Harold thought of the cramped girls' dormitory he'd seen on his recent trip to the factory.

"You didn't know that? Anyway, it's caused quite a stir among the workers and some of them are agreeing with the demands. No riots yet, but I wouldn't rule out the possibility."

Harold could believe that. With the female worker, the reason for her suicide had been fairly clear. It would be harder to spin this one.

"So what's the plan for damage control?" he asked.

"There's a press conference set for this afternoon, with local and foreign papers. You're expected to speak."

"Me?"

"As the head of the company, it can't be anyone else. You know that."

"I'll figure something out," Harold finally said. "In the meantime, find out where this worker who killed himself was from."

"Why?"

"We'll have to send his family some kind of compensation."

"A month's wages?"

"Something like that."

Until the conference was scheduled, Harold didn't leave his office. He attempted several times to write out what he would say, but it all sounded false. If he wanted to give excuses, he should have a company spokesperson do it. Charlie was right; in a situation like this, he had to be the person to speak. He just didn't know if he had the necessary confidence to pull it off.

When the appointed hour came, Harold went to the restroom. He rolled back his sleeves and doused his face with water. His shirt was wrinkled, and he regretted not thinking of sending back home for a proper suit. If he had and Vicki was around, though, she would suspect something had happened at work, and he couldn't talk about this with her.

He waited in there for fifteen minutes to give the press time to arrive and get settled before he entered the conference room. The atmosphere felt more like a trial than a public relations meeting. His every step was accompanied by the *click* of cameras, and all eyes followed him as if pulled by strings as he made his way to the head of the room. Harold spotted Charlie standing in the back, looking as if he'd rather be anywhere else.

"Thank you for coming," Harold said. "I'm sure you've all heard about the tragic event at Xingli Factory by now. At this company we give a great deal of oversight to what goes on there. In fact, my colleague Charles Lin and I visited just last month, where we personally inspected the work floor and the dormitories. While I'm not saying that the young man who so sadly took his own life had just cause for his grievances, it's also quite possible he was mentally unstable...."

This had been his strategy, to present the male worker as having non-work-related issues, as with the female worker who'd ingested the rat poison. But he could tell, looking at the faces of the reporters, that it was not going over so well.

"What about the other workers?" one journalist interrupted to say. "Is it true that they are planning to riot?"

Harold glanced at Charlie, whose earlier briefing was all the information he'd gotten on the matter, but Charlie shrugged.

"There are rumors of potential unrest, yes," he admitted, "but we are confident that the situation will be handled in the appropriate manner."

"How are you going to meet the workers' demands?" asked a young woman who looked like she could be a college student.

Harold continued to talk about improvements in the workers' conditions, finding himself citing Miss Hao's litany of amenities such as the basketball court, hair salon, Internet café, and other useless distractions, when he found his mind drifting off. It was as if he were standing in the audience, watching himself, this pathetic, middle-aged man in a wrinkled shirt, the hair at his temples growing shiny with sweat, talking about a situation he would never find himself in, because of where he lived and how he had grown up.

"And that is why," he heard himself saying, "our company is severing ties with Xingli Factory until it can be determined that their standards have been raised to acceptable, international levels. The worker who died will not have sacrificed himself in vain."

A buzz rose above the crowd and then dissolved into a hundred questions, all of which Harold ignored. As the security guard escorted him to the doorway, he passed by Charlie, who murmured, "What would your father have to say about this?" in his ear before fading into the background.

When Harold got back to his office, he noticed that his secretary had gotten someone in to hang the painting on his wall while he had been away. He got her on the phone, thanked her for her efficiency, and requested that all calls for him be put off until the next day. He was sure that the news was already spreading about his announcement, and the company's shareholders would be demanding answers.

As was his habit, he stood in front of the full-length window, gazing out at the tower of Taipei 101. Usually, looking down at the faraway street and the insectlike bustle of people below had a calming effect. It made him feel removed—even above—the rest of the world and its mundane problems. But this time he wondered what the male worker at Xingli Factory had thought the second before he'd stepped off the roof of the dormitory. Because of the list of demands, he'd had to have planned this act. But had the young man hesitated at the edge, wondered if his life was worth it? Harold knew he could never be so desperate, nor so brave.

Feeling as if the floor were falling away from him, he sat down at his desk and stared at the painting until the image began to blur. He stared at it until his mind felt like the white spot in the middle of the gray: a calm, blank space.

*What would your father have to say about this?* had been Charlie's last comment to him. Harold was sure his father would never admit he had done anything wrong. He'd never heard his father deliver an apology, or give an explanation for behavior anyone else would find questionable, especially to his son.

When Harold was in his last year at Taiwan National University, his mother had come down with a terminal illness. She spent her last few months at Kuang Tien General Hospital, attended by a twenty-four-hour nurse. Her mind became addled with the medication, and she stopped recognizing any of her visitors, including family members. Harold and his father never visited her at the same time, and soon Harold found out the reason for that.

One weekend, after a hospital visit, his father invited him out to lunch. Harold arrived first and sat at a table large enough for twice as many people as were expected, while around him entire generations of other families, from grandparents to restless children, swarmed at the other tables. Then his father came in with a woman he had never seen before. She introduced herself as "Auntie Mai," but Harold could never bring himself to call her that. He assumed she was his father's mistress.

Auntie Mai appeared to be around his father's age, and if Harold had met her under different circumstances, he might have found her facial features plain but pleasant. She was attentive to his father, cautioning him not to eat too much fatty meat because of his gout. As usual, his father ordered the most expensive dishes on the menu, including sliced abalone and shark fin soup, although Harold didn't know whom he was trying to impress. He could only be thankful that his mother was too far gone to know about this other woman.

After his mother's death, Harold's father continued to associate with Auntie Mai, who was euphemistically referred to by colleagues and friends as his father's "companion." Once, he tried to ask his father who exactly this woman was, but his father had curtly told him to mind his own business.

Having finished college, Harold began to see quite a lot of his father, as he was being groomed to take over the family business. The two of them never discussed their personal lives until Harold met Vicki and introduced her to his father, right after they had decided to get married. To his dismay, his father brought Auntie Mai, whom he hadn't seen in years, to the meeting. She and Vicki seemed to take to each other, talking about wedding venues and whether a hotel would be considered too much of a Western influence while a temple ritual was too Eastern.

"She liked my ring," Vicki pointed out afterward. "Your stepmother has good taste."

"She's not my stepmother."

"Whatever she is, she's very nice."

"You don't know her like I do."

"Really? How well do you know her? Do you even know how she and your father met?"

"Not really," Harold had to admit.

In later years, the gout and other consequences of extravagant living caught up with Harold's father. At his funeral, Harold walked in front of the procession, dressed in traditional white robes and hat, while the other mourners followed behind. Some of them carried banners, while professional musicians accompanied them with cymbals and clappers. Upon reaching the gravesite, he bowed and knelt several times, then lit the spirit money that would ensure his father was as wealthy in death as in life. The plot already contained his mother's remains, and there would be room for Harold and his wife, but none for any children they might have. There was definitely no room for Auntie Mai.

Out of the corner of his eye he saw Auntie Mai, standing apart from the rest of the procession. She was dressed in somber colors, but at least she didn't have the gall to wear white or black. Although he wanted to approach her, he managed to hold his feelings in check until the ceremonial rites were over and people started to leave.

"What are you doing here?" he asked her. The tightening of her lips indicated that he'd grasped her arm more tightly than he'd thought.

"I'm paying my respects," she replied evenly.

"Your presence is disrespectful to the memory of my mother."

She inclined her head. "I can see how you feel that way. But your father was an important part of my life, too. Surely I'm allowed to say good-bye?"

Harold was saved from answering with words that he might later regret as Vicki came up behind them. "I hope you are well, Auntie," she said.

Auntie Mai took her hands. "I'm so sorry for the loss of your father-in-law."

"And I'm sorry for your loss."

Harold couldn't listen to any more of this infuriatingly polite exchange. "Please," he said to Auntie Mai. "Leave my family in peace."

She nodded and walked away, and then Harold turned to Vicki. "What do you mean, 'your loss'? She's lost nothing but someone who paid for her lifestyle."

"What lifestyle? Auntie was hardly wearing the latest fashions."

"Stop calling her that! She's not anyone's 'auntie.'"

"Why are you so angry? I was just trying to be civil to your family." Vicki adjusted the veil on her hat. She had chosen to wear Western mourning clothes in black, and Harold hadn't had the will to fight her on it. But now that, combined with her reception of Auntie Mai, was too much.

"What makes you think you can decide who's part of the family or not?" he demanded. "When you're hardly part of the family yourself?"

Vicki's mouth quirked. "If you're not careful, Auntie Mai might be the only family you have left."

A month later came the reading of the will. Everything of his father's went to Harold, except for the apartment that had been set up for Auntie Mai. Harold took it upon himself to tell Auntie Mai this in person, thinking he'd finally get some satisfaction and a measure of revenge for his mother, to see her reaction that she hadn't been left anything else. He was sure that she was counting on a windfall that would allow her to live in luxury for the rest of her life.

But rather than the fashionable neighborhood he had expected, Auntie Mai's apartment was located in Wanhua, a working-class district that was one of the oldest in the city. The apartment was on the first floor of the aged building, prefaced by a small but well-tended courtyard of lush plants including *tan hua,* white flowers that bloomed one night a year before dying.

When Auntie Mai invited Harold in, he noticed that her living room, like the outside of the building, was shabby but clean. The white antimacassars on the backs of the sofa and chairs spoke of another generation, as did the heavy rosewood furniture. Her small television was set to one of the Taiwanese soap operas that Vicki liked to watch, or maybe it was a different soap opera; everyone looked the same when crying, so he couldn't tell the difference. Auntie Mai switched off the television and offered Harold tea and watermelon seeds, which he refused.

"I can't stay long," he told her. "I've just come to tell you about my father's will. He's left you this apartment but nothing else. No money. No assets." Harold searched Auntie Mai's face for some sign of disappointment, but she remained composed.

"That's very generous of him," she finally said. "I wasn't expecting anything else. From him or from you. You might be surprised," she added, "but I can take care of myself."

"What do you do?" This was the first personal information he'd asked of her.

"I'm an in-house nurse."

Harold remembered the various nurses who had been employed when his mother was sick. "Is that what you were doing when you met my father?"

Auntie Mai gave him a slight smile. "I met your father when we were children. I'm from Keelung Harbor."

This Harold found hard to believe; it sounded something out of a folktale. He could barely picture his father as a boy, running barefoot on the docks, before being taken in by his wealthy benefactors. "What was he like back then?"

"A very mischievous boy. He liked to tease the cats by dangling fish heads just out of their reach, and stowing away on fishermen's boats. He once boasted that he almost got halfway to Xiamen before he got caught. His spirit was attractive to the Leungs."

The Leungs were the couple who had taken Harold's father in, virtually adopted him, and given him a better life. "He especially liked Mrs. Leung. I did, too—she brought the children in Keelung Harbor toys and sweets. She even brought me new shoes once, which was special to me because I'd always had to wear my older brother's, these rough, ugly boys' shoes. The ones she brought me were delicate leather slippers, and I treasured them. I hoped the Leungs would take me away, but they chose your father instead. Of course, because he was a boy."

"This was when he was six years old?" Harold knew this much.

"Yes. One day they came to pick him up in a car," Auntie Mai continued. "Your father was waving to the rest of us kids from the backseat like he was in a parade. I don't know if he understood the Leungs were his new family now. I'm sure they paid your father's family a good sum for him. I never knew if he came back to visit, because my own family moved away from the harbor that year when my parents got jobs at the garment factories in Wanhua."

Harold looked around the room and its outdated furnishings. His eyes lighted on a framed black-and-white couple whom he assumed were Auntie Mai's parents. "So, when did you hear from my father next?"

"Not until after he started a successful business and married your mother. Of course I had heard about him. The newspapers were all about his financial deals. As the only single daughter out of my sisters, I lived with my parents and took care of them. In this very apartment, in fact. Then one year, the landlord raised the rent to beyond what I could pay on my nurse's salary. He threatened to evict us, and I couldn't think of anyone else to go to, other than your father. I sent him a note to his workplace, hardly expecting him to remember me. He gave me the money, and even offered to buy the apartment outright for me, but I refused. We didn't know each other well enough yet. That's how we met again."

Auntie Mai leaned forward, putting one hand over Harold's. He wanted to draw it away, but was afraid of offending her.

"By this time, your mother was sick. She knew about us, though. Your father didn't want to pretend. Your mother was able to express that she was glad your father had someone to take care of him. I'm not making this up to make myself look better, or to make you feel better. That's what she said, I swear it. We had your mother's blessing."

Harold looked down at the fraying rug beneath his feet. All at once his resentment of Auntie Mai over the years seemed petty and foolish, not to mention without reason. Instead of faulting her, he should have been grateful that there was someone to take care of his father in his last years. Certainly he and Vicki weren't going to do it.

"I'm sorry for how I acted toward you at the funeral," he said. "That was uncalled for."

"I understand," she replied. "You were grieving."

"Are you sure you won't accept anything other than this apartment?" He now felt obligated to provide as much as he could for Auntie Mai. But she shook her head.

"Knowing that you've accepted my place in your father's life is enough."

As Auntie Mai walked him through her courtyard, Harold noticed the heavy, cloying perfume of the *tan hua* in the air. Several of them were starting to bloom, spreading their narrow white petals in the evening dusk. Auntie Mai noticed him looking at the flowers.

"Let me give you a cutting for your wife," she said. "It'll be good luck for both of you."

She went back into the apartment before Harold could

refuse. He thought of how Vicki was trying to conceive—perhaps they needed this luck. Then he recalled another saying about *tan hua* that had a more negative connotation: *tan hua yi xian,* used to describe someone whose success was as fleeting as the flower's blooms.

Auntie Mai returned with a pair of shears, snipped off a part of the plant that had not started to blossom yet, and put it in a plastic bag. Harold bowed his head in thanks.

He didn't remember what happened to the cutting, but it was probably thrown out since Vicki had no interest in gardening. Aside from when she'd sent a polite note at Adrian's birth, Harold never heard from Auntie Mai again.

Harold waited until late in the evening before leaving the office, when he was sure the reporters had dispersed and Charlie was no longer around. When he got home, the apartment was dark, and he was sure that Adrian and Vicki were already in bed. Then he saw Vicki sitting in the dark, at the dining room table facing the French doors that led out to their balcony. He turned on the light, and she gave a start.

"I was watching the fireflies," she said defensively. "The last ones of the season."

He nodded, then noticed that the table was set for two for dinner. "Did you make this?" he asked.

"What, you don't think I can cook?" she teased. "I cooked for myself when I was studying abroad because of the terrible British food."

The food that Vicki had prepared was simple, just rice and eggs, but having skipped lunch, he gratefully devoured it. When he was done, he noticed the bowl in front of her remained untouched.

"Aren't you hungry?" he asked.

"I was waiting for you, but I lost my appetite." She paused. "How are you? It looks like you had a difficult day."

Harold couldn't remember the last time Vicki had asked

about his day. The words coming from her mouth seemed like they were coming from a different person: natural, unforced.

"Do you remember how I went with Charlie to inspect the factory in Shanghai last month? We wanted to check working conditions, especially after that female worker killed herself."

"And how were they?" Harold couldn't tell whether Vicki was feigning interest, but he continued.

"They weren't any different from the other factories in the area. Which is to say, not that good, but good enough." *For main-landers,* he anticipated Vicki adding, but she just nodded silently. "Then today, we were informed that another worker, a male this time, also killed himself, supposedly over these conditions."

"Oh, that's terrible."

Vicki looked properly sympathetic while he told her about the ensuing press conference, the impulsive decision he had made to cease operations at the Shanghai factory.

"Can you really do that?" she asked in wonderment.

"I have to. I made a promise."

Harold found his hands shaking. Reflexively, he pushed the dishes back from the edge of the table, as he'd do with Adrian. To his surprise, Vicki got up from her seat and went to him. She wove her hands through his hair, and he put his arms around her, pressed his face into her stomach, which he knew underneath her dress was smooth and slim and perfect except for the scar where Adrian had been lifted from her body.

He felt her stomach ripple with laughter. "What?"

"I'm just imagining Charlie's face when you announced your decision."

"He wasn't happy, that's for sure."

She drew away from him, placing both hands on the sides of his face. "Charlie is so full of himself."

"He may be that. But I'll need him on my side more than ever now with the shareholders."

Vicki kissed him on the forehead, her touch so light it was

like a whisper. "You can figure all that out tomorrow. For now, let's go to bed."

Harold reluctantly released his wife. "You go first. I should check to make sure my e-mails haven't overloaded the server at work."

After Vicki had left the room, Harold opened his laptop and scrolled through at least two hundred e-mails, most from reporters, interspersed with few apoplectic ones from Charlie. The shareholders were indeed upset and calling for an emergency meeting as soon as possible.

Harold deleted that e-mail. He was in the process of deleting the rest of them when he came across one from an anonymous sender. "Andrew Cantrell Painting," was the subject heading. The text below was direct and succinct.

> Dear Mr. Harold Yu,
>
> *Elegy,* the painting by Andrew Cantrell you purchased from Caroline Lowry of the Lowry Gallery, is a fake. It was painted recently and kept in Ms. Lowry's apartment, located upstairs from the gallery, until it was sold to you. I have seen it with my own eyes. You should not trust anything Ms. Lowry says. If I were you, I would demand my money back.
>
> Sincerely,
>
> A Concerned Artist

# Chapter 9

I should have known Kimi wouldn't be satisfied when I told her I was sending Mr. Yu an e-mail. She followed up every few days after that, asking me via text whether I'd heard from him. *No, I haven't,* I kept saying.

Then she changed tactics and asked if she could see the art project I was working on. Reluctantly, I invited her over to look at it one Saturday afternoon a couple of weeks later. She arrived at my apartment bearing a bottle of red wine, which I hoped didn't mean she intended to stay for dinner. Luckily, she suggested we open the bottle at once. Sam and I didn't have proper wine glasses, so we used empty jars.

"This is so Amberlin," Kimi commented when I handed her a jam jar; Amberlin's cafeteria was known for using their leftover canning and pickling jars for various purposes, even though with the tuition they were charging, they could have afforded water glasses. "Cheers." She raised her jar to mine and Sam's, and we clunked.

Sam only drank a little because he was going to be leaving the apartment soon for a conveniently scheduled dodgeball practice with his team from the urban farm. Their next opponent happened to be the team from Kimi's summer school program—I supposed there was some sort of nonprofit, do-gooder league—and she joked about joining it just so she could purposefully kick a ball into his face.

I wasn't sure whether I was more relieved that Sam wouldn't be there, or resentful that I would be left to entertain Kimi alone. I watched the two of them carefully when she arrived, and she just hugged him with overt enthusiasm in the same way she had me, but nothing more. Sam, on the other hand, appeared a little embarrassed, keeping one eye on me to gauge my reaction.

After he left, Kimi asked, "So why don't you think you've heard back from Mr. Yu?"

I concentrated on the level of wine in my jar. "Maybe his e-mail address doesn't work anymore. He could have left the company or something."

"Really," Kimi said. "Maybe I should try him, too, just in case."

"No!" I shouted. "I mean, please, Kimi, let me handle this." I tried to change the subject. "Sam seemed glad to see you."

"How *is* our boy doing?"

"He likes the kids at the urban farm," I said, ignoring her use of the plural possessive. "He's always telling me funny stuff they've said during the day." I repeated a few of them, and Kimi genuinely laughed at the *"vegans eaten by carnivores"* line.

"That's what I love about kids that age," she said. "They say things without being afraid that they're wrong."

"And then when you grow up, you become totally inhibited and expect to be judged," I added.

"Exactly. Speaking of judgment, let's take a look at your project." She said this in a teasing way, but my shoulders immediately tensed.

I couldn't tell by the look on Kimi's face as to whether she really was absorbed or not by the two finished paintings of my great-grandmother and grandmother. They were traditional portraits, as if they'd been done in the eighteenth century. Haltingly, I told Kimi the story behind the triptych, how I'd discovered the box of old photos in my parents' attic; and the meaning of the series itself, a representation of the female generations in my mother's family, as you might find in an ancient manor house in England, only this was in suburban America.

"So it's a commentary on how we honor our ancestors," Kimi remarked.

"Something like that."

She nodded slowly. "I can see the personal and the feminist angles being appealing to people. You just need to know how to sell it."

"And I need to finish it. I still have to do the third portrait, my mother."

"Once you've finished, get slides done," Kimi instructed. "My parents know a gallery owner in Williamsburg. Most of the art he likes is more conceptual than this, but maybe he'll go for the simplicity of the form and the idea."

"But I don't think I'm ready—"

"Stop that," Kimi interrupted. "From what I see, you're as ready as anyone who piles some rusted tin cans in the corner of a gallery and calls it art."

"I'm glad you feel my work is more meaningful than that," I replied dryly. "Anyway, I'll think about it."

"Don't think about it," Kimi advised. "Just finish your project."

I guess I could have dragged my feet, claimed I couldn't execute the third painting, said I'd gotten a mysterious illness, any number of things. But instead, every day for the next two weeks,

I came home from work, ate dinner, and went to my studio. I hardly interacted with Sam during this time.

The portrait of my mother was the easiest one out of the three. I had a million photos of her, all at various stages in her life. I'd chosen one that dated from college, of her in a pink sweater with a white headband holding back her hair. Next to her was her roommate, Caroline, who had long, curly brown hair and was wearing some kind of Indian-print top. Still, I could see a trace of her not only in the Caroline Lowry I knew today, but in the picture of her aunt Hazel. The two girls' arms were draped around each other in a relaxed, companionable way that I could never imagine being with Kimi.

The first person I told that I was done with the triptych was Kimi, via text. She immediately texted back a reminder for me to get slides done and send them to her. I did so, and then didn't hear from her for more than two weeks. Then, when I did, she texted, *Good news, the gallery owner wants to meet with you. Name is Solomon Finch.*

I looked up the website for Solomon Finch and saw that the gallery was located on Driggs Avenue in Williamsburg. Its mission was to "present the next generation of young artists to new and established collectors." I prepared for my meeting with the owner as I would for a job interview, which I could also count among my first, since I hadn't really had to interview for my job with Caroline Lowry; I'd just gone to lunch with her and my mother. Out came my one good black dress that I'd worn to Sandro Hess's opening in the beginning of summer, which now seemed like years ago. I'd thrown my heels away that night, so I had to wear flats. That and some inexpertly applied makeup, and I was ready.

That afternoon, I made my sweltering way to my appointment, envying every girl I passed who was wearing shorts and sandals. When I passed through the front door of the gallery, I stopped for a moment to soak in the air-conditioning. This space was considerably larger than the one I worked in, made for large sculptures and installations. The current installation was clichéd sayings rendered in cursive neon signs—like "Life Is a Bowl of Cherries" in red, "Let a Smile Be Your Umbrella" in yellow—except some of the words flashed on and off, like a broken hotel sign in Times Square. The effect was vaguely migraine-inducing.

Solomon Finch's assistant was situated at the far end of the room instead of the front, behind a white desk and a sleek silver laptop and nothing else, which made me appreciate Caroline's old-fashioned decree of fresh flowers every day. The young woman sitting there was my hipper doppelganger, with her short hair falling in an asymmetrical swoop over one eye, thick black-rimmed glasses, and an indeterminate amount of tattoos.

"I'm Molly Schaeffer," I said. "I'm here to see Solomon Finch at three?"

"Sure," the assistant said. "He's just about ready for you. But first, do you want some mineral water? Tea? Coffee? Beer?"

"Beer?"

She smirked. "Just kidding."

"Nothing, thanks," I said. "I'm fine."

The assistant shrugged and after a few minutes took me into a back office.

With his artfully tousled silver hair, Solomon Finch looked not that much younger than Caroline Lowry, although he wore flashy basketball shoes. Also, his desk and the shelves behind him were littered with collectible action figures.

"So, Molly," he said. "I hear you come highly recommended. You're a friend of the Kitanos?"

I nodded and tried to make polite conversation. "How do you know them?"

"Hugh Kitano and I were in marketing together. He stayed

and bought a town house in Brooklyn Heights, while I decided to go into art and live in a commune with four roommates. I've known Kimi since she was five, so when she says someone's good, I believe her."

I couldn't help blushing, which Solomon noted.

"Tell me more about yourself, Molly," he said. "Kimi told me that you work for Caroline Lowry?"

"Yes, I've been at her gallery since the beginning of the summer." I was surprised he had heard of my boss, but I guessed the art world wasn't that big.

"I'm surprised that place is still going. It was a big deal in the sixties, I think. Way before my time."

*Not that far,* I thought, looking at him.

"She showing anyone interesting these days?"

"Sandro Hess. A German-Argentine artist?"

Solomon gave a dismissive wave of his hand. "Never heard of him. In any case, it's good that you have some experience with the industry. So you know how important it is to make people believe there's a lot more under the surface of what you're seeing. What's the story behind your triptych?"

I gave him the same spiel that I'd given to Kimi when she'd visited, working in some of her observations, as well.

"And do you have a name for it?"

I said the first thing that came into my mind. *"The Three Graces.* My great-grandmother's name was Grace." It had actually been Hilda.

Solomon nodded. "Listen, I'm not denying that your work is different from a lot of what I exhibit. It's nonironic in a refreshing way. What you see is what you get." I felt like he could be commenting on my appearance, as well. "But at the same time, there's something appealing about it. Like folk art. Are you self-taught?"

"I've taken a few classes."

I must have sounded defensive, because he added, "There's nothing wrong with that. Outsider art can be very popular. Look at Henry Darger."

*And Grandma Moses,* I thought.

Solomon leaned forward. "I have a group show coming up in the fall for emerging Brooklyn artists under twenty-five. I'm guessing you're age-appropriate, given that you went to college with Kimi?"

"I'm twenty-two. But I live in Queens."

"We'll say Ridgewood. If you want to be part of the show, you can have a spot. You don't have to tell me your decision now. Just think about it and let me know by the end of the month. I'll need an artist's statement from you."

I think I stammered a thank-you to him before his assistant led me out. I walked down the street toward the subway stop, alternately feeling ecstatic and anxious. I guess you could say I was a human version of one of the on-again, off-again neon signs exhibited in the Solomon Finch gallery. In one moment I was beaming, and in another, I was missing something.

My phone buzzed in my pocket. A text from Kimi. *How did it go?* I turned my phone off.

Back home, I didn't tell Sam about my offer from Solomon Finch. He didn't even know about the connection with Kimi, unless she had told him. I had been given an opportunity that anyone my age and with my lack of experience would jump at, so why was I hesitating? Why did I feel like such a fake?

After days of trying to write an artist's statement and deciding everything came off as pretentious and implausible, I decided to ask Caroline for her advice. She had asked to take a look at my work and I'd chosen to show it to someone else first, but maybe she wouldn't hold it against me. So one afternoon, I tentatively approached her. Sandro Hess's failure of a show was in the middle of being taken down, leaving behind stark white walls. I didn't know if Caroline had anyone else scheduled.

"Sandro hasn't been calling lately," I observed. It was true that his once-daily calls had trickled off and he hadn't contacted the gallery in weeks.

"I think he's finally accepted the truth," Caroline replied. "It's too bad we didn't get any buyers, but at least he can add this to his CV."

"Why do you think no one bought anything?" She must have seen something in him. Or maybe it had been him and not his work.

"Honestly, I can't say. Maybe a lack of connection between the work and the audience. I might end up buying one of these pieces myself," she continued, looking at the painting that had been visible from the front window. "As a consolation prize."

"Can I talk to you about something?" I asked.

Caroline turned and seemed to sense my nervousness. "Certainly. Let's go into my office."

After we both sat down, I hesitated a moment before telling her about how my old college roommate had arranged a meeting for me with a Williamsburg gallery owner, and I had been given an offer to be part of a group show.

If Caroline was disappointed I hadn't asked her to take a look at my work first, she didn't let on. "Solomon Finch," she mused. "Not sure if I recognize the name."

"He'd heard of you," I said. "He had a lot of respect for the Lowry Gallery and its legacy."

If that pleased Caroline, she didn't show it. "So, what's your question?"

"I don't know if I should be part of the show."

"You don't think you're good enough. That you belong there."

"No," I admitted.

"Do you have images of your work that I can take a look at?"

I'd stored digital copies of the slides online, so I was able to quickly pull them up on her computer. Together we looked at them, and I noticed Caroline's eyes brighten when she saw the one of my mother.

"I used a photograph of the two of you from college for inspiration for that one," I remarked.

She nodded. "These are very well done, Molly. I can see why Solomon Finch would be interested in your work."

"You don't think they're too simplistic?"

"It doesn't matter. What matters is that they're true to you."

"What about the show?"

"That's for you to decide. But let me tell you a story about one particular artist. When he was a young artist, he made up a story about his background. Based on some truth about his parents, but stretching it about himself. He maintained this persona for years. He said his first show was based on memories of his childhood. Without them, the paintings would have been competent, but he gave them stories, context. Later in life, he ran out of stories—or rather, his stories caught up to him."

Belatedly, I realized Caroline must be talking about Sandro Hess. But I wasn't sure what I was supposed to get out of this cautionary tale.

"All I'm trying to say," she finished, "is that what you decide now could affect the way you handle the rest of your career. Or it could not. You're still young."

I left work that day no closer to making a decision than before. Was this what being an adult was all about, making your own choices, and living with the consequences? How did you know you'd made the right choice? I was beginning to suspect that you never knew. All you could do was forge ahead with what you felt was best, and hope that you hurt as few people around you as possible.

\* \* \*

I asked Kimi to meet me, and we decided on a café in Ridge-wood, on the border of Brooklyn and Queens, about equidistant from where we both lived. On the way there I passed by a gallery and a sign advertising artists' spaces. Remembering what Solomon Finch had said about the neighborhood, I guessed that maybe by the time I was ready to show my work, it would be here instead of Chelsea or Williamsburg.

"How did the meeting with Solomon Finch go?" Kimi asked after we collected our drinks from the bearded barista and sat down.

"It was great," I replied. "I appreciate your setting it up."

"He's such a cool guy, right? For an old person?"

"He offered me a place in an upcoming show for young artists."

"And?"

"I'm saying no. I'm going back to school instead."

Kimi stared at me. "Tell me you're taking extension courses at the New School or something, not that you're going back to Amberlin."

"I need to finish what I started there."

Kimi was silent for a while. "Okay, I get that. But why not be in the show, too? It isn't an either-or situation. Come down on the weekends to prepare for the opening."

"I just don't feel ready. I haven't really figured out what the triptych is about."

"Make something up. You'll believe it by the time the show opens."

I shook my head. "I can't."

Kimi gave an exasperated sigh.

"I'm sorry if I've disappointed you, after all you've done for me in setting up the appointment," I said, a little archly.

"It's not that. It's just that if I knew Solomon Finch was doing a group show of young artists, I should have come up with my own project for him." Kimi paused. "What does Sam think about your decision to go back to Amberlin?"

"I haven't told him yet," I said. "But it's not like we're engaged or anything. I don't need his permission."

"You'd better watch out while you're gone," Kimi teased. "One of his coworkers at the urban farm could steal him away."

I laughed that off, but also knew that I needed to tell Sam about my decision before he heard it from Kimi herself. When I did tell him that night, after dinner, his immediate response was not to convince me otherwise, or ask about the state of our relationship, but "What am I going to do about the rent?"

A little hurt by his practicality, I said, "I need to find out from Dr. Renfeld what I should do to enroll for this coming semester. If I haven't missed the deadline, I'm willing to pay up to a month after I leave so that you have time to find a new roommate." Or rather, my parents would be paying for it, but I was sure they'd be so relieved I was going back to school that they wouldn't mind.

"Should I sublet or find someone more permanent?"

What he was really asking was whether I was intending to come back to the city, or whether we were breaking up. Funny how so much of this conversation was revolving around housing when it actually had to do with something much larger.

"Let's say sublet. But if you find someone who fits well but wants a longer lease, you should go for it."

I could see the trajectory of our relationship already. In the first couple of months, I'd travel down every other weekend to see him, then decide that the trip took too long. We'd make arrangements to spend the holidays with each other, but couldn't decide with whose family. Then, around New Year's, when I had gotten my degree, I would tell him I didn't want to live in New York. Maybe I'd live in Boston. Maybe I'd go overseas.

I could tell Sam was thinking this, too. "You know," I said gently, "I don't mind if you and Kimi hang out after I leave."

He almost looked offended. "Why would I do that?"

"You seem to have a lot in common...you both like teaching kids."

He gave me a sheepish smile. "You'll be the first to know if that happens."

Later that evening, I composed an e-mail to Dr. Renfeld telling her I was ready to go back to school. After I sent it, I clicked open an e-mail that had been sitting in my drafts folder for the past couple of weeks. It was addressed to Harold Yu, telling him that the Andrew Cantrell painting he had bought was a fake. I thought of my conversation with Caroline earlier, how delighted she had been when she recognized the portrait of my mother.

I deleted the e-mail.

Dr. Renfeld e-mailed me back with instructions on how to enroll for the fall semester. Apparently I would be considered on probation for the rest of the time I was there, but I would be allowed to graduate if my record was clean. I was also required to redo my thesis. Maybe I'd choose a more challenging topic this time.

I'd thanked Solomon Finch for his offer to show my work, but told him I needed to finish school first. "Do what you need to do," was his indifferent, single-line response. Now all I had left to do was give Caroline my two weeks' notice, but I figured my mother would have contacted her already.

I had an errand to run downtown in the East Village. While I was walking down St. Marks Place and its combination of tattoo parlors, souvenir shops, and Japanese eateries, I spotted Sandro Hess coming toward me. Quickly, I ducked behind a rack of novelty hats. After he passed by, I watched as he continued down the street and stopped at the corner. He took the hand of the little boy next to him, as did the pretty, dark-haired woman on the boy's other side. I assumed they were his son and ex-wife—perhaps not ex-wife anymore, the way she looked at him.

They waited for the light to change and then the three of them crossed the street together.

# Chapter 10

"Who are you?" Harold had responded to the mysterious e-mailer about the Andrew Cantrell painting, but he received a bounce back in reply.

Who could it be? Caroline Lowry's assistant? Her art historian friend? If either, then why sign the message as "A Concerned Artist"? Was that to throw him off the scent? While the e-mail had not sounded malicious, Harold suspected there was a degree of personal revenge involved. He went so far as to ask an IT person at work to trace the IP address, but all that could be found was that the server was located in New York City.

Still, the seed of doubt had been planted. Now, when Harold looked at *Elegy* in his office across from his desk, he wondered about its authenticity. All he could go on was Caroline Lowry's word and the art historian's subjective analysis. The art historian himself had told him that the three things necessary to determine whether a painting was real were provenance, connoisseurship, and forensics. Caroline had provided the first two. Harold had forgone forensic authentication, figuring it would only place the painting's materials in the right time frame. Now he wondered if he had subconsciously not wanted to know the truth.

The more time Harold spent in the same room with *Elegy*, scrutinizing and thinking about it, the more uncertain he became. But it was a welcome distraction from what was happening at work. The day after the press conference, the papers had breathlessly published his statement about severing ties with the Shanghai factory, ranging from calling him a champion of workers' rights to setting a dangerous precedent for Chinese-Taiwanese relations. He knew there had been a shareholders' meeting without him that Charlie Lin had been privy to, although Charlie would not reveal to him what had happened. Harold felt like he was a prisoner on trial, awaiting his sentence.

Then late one Saturday afternoon, Charlie paid him a visit at his home. First, Charlie greeted Vicki and Adrian, kissing Harold's wife on the cheek and tickling the little boy, who clung to him like a vine.

"Leave Uncle Charlie alone," Vicki admonished, then turned to their visitor. "How is Serena?" she asked, even though Harold was sure she'd seen Serena within the past couple of days.

"You'd probably know better than me," Charlie said. "I've been busy cleaning up the mess your husband's made." Although he made it sound like a joke, Harold could sense the underlying truth beneath his statement.

"Well," Vicki said in the awkward silence that followed, "I'll leave you two alone," and she headed into the interior of the house with Adrian.

"Let's go outside," Harold suggested, motioning for Charlie to precede him through the French doors onto the deck.

"This is a great view," Charlie said, indicating the green curtain of trees that immediately fell before them, providing a veil for the mountains of Yangmingshan National Park beyond. It gave a sense that they were isolated in a forest, even though the neighbors were located just a few yards away. Charlie and Serena, Harold knew, lived in a luxury apartment complex in town—still very nice, but privacy in a city of two million people was hard to come by.

"You didn't come here to compliment my view," Harold prompted.

Charlie shook his head. "You must be wondering what went on in the shareholders' meeting."

"That I wasn't invited to, yes."

"I don't know how to put it any other way. The shareholders are insisting that you step down from your position. You can't be surprised," Charlie added. "What you said at the press conference caused the company's stocks to plummet to the lowest they've ever been. They still haven't recovered."

"So what are the shareholders suggesting?"

Charlie said softly, "They aren't suggesting, they're ordering. You'll be taking on a consultative role."

"And who do they want to take my place?" Charlie was quiet, which told Harold everything. "You?" He gave a shout of laughter. "Did you make the great sacrifice and offer yourself up?"

Charlie spread his hands. "I'm in the same situation as you, my friend. I have to do what I'm told."

"Why don't you take my house and wife while you're at it?" Harold demanded, in the moment before he understood it was already happening.

Charlie refused to look at him. "You know Vicki and I have a history."

It was true that many years back, when Charlie had introduced Vicki to Harold, he had referred to her as an "old friend," which he'd admitted after a night of drinking too much meant she'd actually been his old girlfriend. But how many times had Harold and Vicki joked about Charlie, his "little third" in Shanghai, the way he treated Serena? Harold couldn't believe she had been putting on an act the entire time.

Even Charlie seemed to realize he had gone too far. "I'll leave now. Let me know when you want to talk."

"About what?" Harold asked pointedly.

"The shareholders' decision. I'll let Vicki handle the... other thing. In the meantime, I'll see myself out." Charlie paused, his hand raised as if meaning to pat Harold on the back, then thought better of it. Harold was glad he had; otherwise he would have been tempted to try to push Charlie off the deck.

After Charlie had left, Harold stepped closer to the edge of the deck, his hands unconsciously gripping the railing. Ironically, he thought that even if he were the kind of person who would throw themselves off a building in despair, the deck wasn't high enough to do much damage.

He heard a tentative step behind him. "Harold?" Vicki asked, and he knew Charlie had updated her before he'd left.

"How long has it been going on?" he heard himself say.

"Not long."

"During my trips to New York?"

"Yes."

He turned to Vicki, expecting her to be ashamed, pleading, close to tears, but she appeared resigned. "You know he has a mistress in Shanghai," he said, purposefully trying to hurt her. "I've met this woman. She's gorgeous. He'll never let her go."

"As long as he never brings her to this side of the Taiwan Straits, I can live with it. After all, Serena did."

"Does Serena know?"

Vicki nodded. "She doesn't care. She's given up Charlie a long time ago. 'You're welcome to him,' she says. She's moved on."

"And you'll be okay with people talking about you behind your back, the same way they talk about Serena?"

"I can take care of myself when it comes to gossip."

Harold couldn't keep the bitterness from his voice. "It sounds like you've got it all figured out."

"Charlie and I—we have a connection," Vicki said. "We always have. You and I—we've given each other as much as we can possibly give. Charlie wants to start over, he wants more children...."

Harold knew there must have been a pragmatic reason for her turning to Charlie. He cringed inwardly at thinking about how his wife must have confided in Charlie about their marital problems, but that was the least of the indignities he would have to suffer at the hands of his so-called friend.

"What about Adrian?" he asked.

"You've seen how well Charlie gets along with him. Of course, he could never take your place. You'll be able to see him anytime you want."

His wife had thought through her new future with Charlie much more thoroughly than Harold had anticipated. Perhaps as long as she and Harold had been unhappy together, which had been at least a year. This wasn't Vicki having an affair with an old boyfriend because she needed a distraction, which was what Harold had initially hoped. This was Vicki wanting to get out of their marriage, and Charlie being the most convenient way to do it.

He couldn't fight Vicki on this. There was nothing to fight. She had made up her mind long ago, and her decision did not involve him. Just like the decision the shareholders had made about his role in the company his father had founded. He could put up a protest, but in the end, it wouldn't matter.

"You can have the house," he told Vicki. "Starting from now on. I'll go to a hotel."

Vicki seemed taken aback by his easy surrender but didn't try to stop him when he left the room. After Harold had finished packing a bag, he stopped by Adrian's playroom to say good-bye to his son. The playroom was stocked with enough toys for a day-care center, and it took a while for him to get Adrian's attention.

"Daddy's going away for a little while," Harold told him.

"Bring me back a present?" Adrian asked. "Bigger than the

ferry?" Harold noticed the Staten Island Ferry replica lying in the jumble of other toys.

"Of course."

Where should he go? Harold had told Vicki he'd go to a hotel, which was the most logical place, but that just seemed to emphasize his failure. He had no reliable friends whom he could stay with, and he didn't want to have to explain or make up an excuse. You did not invite pity from other people. Then he thought of one other person, someone whom he was not connected to either by blood or friendship, whom he didn't need to impress, who would accept him as he was.

When he reached Auntie Mai on the phone and asked if he could stay with her, rather than asking him why or acting surprised that she hadn't heard from him for so long, she agreed. Instead of taking a car, Harold walked to the closest bus stop, which was only used by housekeepers, gardeners, nannies, and other invisible people who came into the district for the day. Settling into his seat, Harold wished he truly were invisible.

The next morning, when Harold awoke, it took him a few seconds to realize where he was: lying in a single bed swathed in a pink mosquito net, in a small, dim room with no other furniture but an old armoire. He would have thought he was dreaming until he saw his bag lying on the floor. Then he remembered everything that had happened the day before, when he'd lost both his job and his family in one afternoon.

He could hear the movements of someone else bustling around in the apartment. The evening before, when he'd arrived, Auntie Mai hadn't asked him any questions but led him to his room. After he'd gone to bed, he could hear her settling into her living room, the television volume turned down on a soap opera. He was sure that if he told her what was going on between him and Vicki, it would rival any soap opera plot.

When he emerged from his room, the table had been set with

a simple but hearty breakfast of rice congee, boiled peanuts, and pickled vegetables.

"Did you sleep well?" Auntie Mai asked, and Harold assured her that the television had not kept him up, that the bed was comfortable, that he hadn't gotten bitten by mosquitoes.

Then he said, "I was thinking of going to Yangmingshan Number One Public Cemetery today to see my father's grave. Would you come with me?"

"I have one patient I need to see today," she said. "Otherwise I have the afternoon free."

Harold and Auntie Mai took a bus from the Wanhua District past the grand white edifice of the Chiang Kai-shek Memorial Hall and the cool greenery of Da'an Forest Park, in which he had often sought refuge as a student at nearby Taiwan National University. Their destination was a condominium complex on the edge of the park. Auntie Mai's patient must be quite well off.

A middle-aged woman met them at the door, her anxious face relaxing a shade when she saw Auntie Mai. She led them into a spacious bedroom—with an expansive view of the park below—where a hospital bed had been set up. Upon it lay an elderly man—possibly the oldest person Harold had ever seen—hooked up to a ventilator. With the deep wrinkles coursing down his face and his frail, twisted body, he looked less like a human and more like a tortoise. He remembered when Vicki was pregnant with Adrian and he had seen an early sonogram. While Vicki had been overcome with emotion, Harold had merely thought the embryo that would turn into his son looked indistinguishable from the images he had seen of amphibian, reptilian, and mammalian embryos. Perhaps all life was meant to look the same at the beginning and the end of it.

"He just turned one hundred years old," the woman who had let them in confided to Harold. "Two weeks ago he was still eating out at his favorite restaurants every night." By her attitude, he guessed she was not a younger second wife but the patient's daughter.

Watching Auntie Mai tend to the old man, Harold thought about his mother's last days in the hospital, the beepings of monitors and machines, the flurry of interchangeable nurses. Being at home seemed like a preferable way to go, for both the patient and their family. Why hadn't his father chosen this option? He certainly could have afforded it. Harold wondered whether his father had established Auntie Mai in his household by then and had wanted to keep the two halves of his life separate.

A student at the time, Harold had gone to see his mother at the hospital whenever he could, sometimes skipping classes. Early on, when she was still lucid and discovered what he was doing, she'd scold him.

"Don't waste the tuition your father is paying," she said.

"It doesn't matter," he replied. "We all know I'm going to go work for him after graduation."

"You might not want to. You might want to do something on your own."

Not as long as his father had any say in it, Harold had thought. Sometimes he wondered whether his father purposefully kept his son dependent on him, so that he could control what happened to him.

"When was the last time he came to see you?" he asked his mother. "I've never seen him here."

"He comes when he can. You know how much your father doesn't like hospitals."

His mother's deterioration was gradual but unmistakable, until one time when Harold visited, she did not recognize him at all. He might as well have been one of the nurses or doctors; there were so many of them, he had trouble keeping them straight, too. When, alarmed, he asked a nurse what was going on, she just indicated the morphine drip hooked up by his mother's side.

In her delirium, his mother talked about her childhood in Nanjing during the Japanese Invasion; how her family had fled inland twice, once during World War II and then ten years later during the civil war with the communists. She and her mother and siblings had moved to Taiwan after the defeat of the Nationalists, while her father, a government servant under Chiang Kai-shek, had gone missing for two years. Of course, Harold had heard versions of this history from his mother before, but not as she was telling it now, as a wide-eyed girl listening to the Japanese bombs dropping in the fields beyond; and as a teenager on a boat crossing the Taiwan Straits, not knowing the whereabouts of her father, and full of fear about the future ahead.

All he could do was listen and bear witness to her passing, as the one-hundred-year-old man's daughter was now doing. At the end of the caretaking session, she thanked Auntie Mai and handed her an envelope with what Harold assumed was her payment. It didn't surprise him that Auntie Mai seemed to be operating a private nursing business. He felt a little better about imposing upon her, knowing that she was probably making a decent wage.

"How long do you think he has to live?" he asked her about her patient as they took the elevator down.

"A week at the most. That will be enough time for the rest of the family to arrive from where they live in America." Auntie Mai shook her head over the children's lack of filial piety.

"At least he has a daughter who takes care of him."

"She's the oldest and unmarried. Perhaps she'll be able to have her own life once her father dies. One hundred years old is far too old to be alive," she added.

Once outside the building, Harold offered to pay for a taxi to Yangmingshan Number One Public Cemetery, but Auntie

Mai thriftily insisted on taking public transportation. So they took the MRT to the Beitou District, slightly northwest of the direction Harold had come from the day before, and boarded a bus with a number of other families heading to the cemetery and farther into the park. A few foreign tourists were scattered among the passengers, and Harold remembered that the cemetery also held the graves of some famous people, including the American advisor to Sun Yat-Sen, the father of modern China. They disembarked at the cemetery's entrance and proceeded through its grounds, well-kept save for roving bands of stray dogs of every size and breed, who appeared indifferent to people unless they carried food.

The last time Harold had been to his father's grave had been on April fifth, for Qingming Festival, or Tomb Sweeping Day, which was a national holiday since it was also the day of Chiang Kai-shek's death. Vicki and Adrian had come with him, and Adrian had run around the tombs, ranging from simple headstones to near mausoleums, as Vicki had helped him clear his parents' graves of weeds. She'd been reluctant to go on this trip, and about bringing Adrian, as she considered it too morbid for a child of three to be playing in a cemetery.

"This is his heritage," Harold had told her.

"Then why not take him to the Chiang Kai-shek Memorial Hall?" she suggested. "He has relatives on both sides who worked for the government."

While this was true, Harold felt the connection was too tenuous. And perhaps there was some guilt on his part that he only visited his father's grave once a year on Tomb Sweeping Day. As a compromise, he had bought Adrian a kite, and after cleaning, burning incense, and bowing in front of the grave, the three of them went to a clearing to fly it. They weren't the only families who were doing this, as kite-flying was a common activity during the holiday. Some said the kites were able to bring messages to the dead, while others contended that the kites represented departed souls from this earth. Harold had grown up with the first tradition; in order to convey the message, you had to let the kite go free.

Adrian's yellow butterfly joined the colorful spread of kites jostling for position in the sky. Whenever Harold tried to guide his son's hands with his own, Adrian pushed them out of the way, wanting to fly the kite by himself. That made Harold think, rather sadly, of all the things that Adrian would no longer need him for someday—already was starting not to need him for.

When they were ready to go home, Harold told Adrian he should let the kite go.

"No!" Adrian insisted. "It's mine!"

"If you don't let the kite go," Harold tried to explain, "you can't send a message to your grandfather."

Adrian had never met his paternal grandfather, and on that day he had barely made the connection between the tomb they were visiting and a person he was related to, but Harold still hoped to be able to uphold this part of the kite-flying tradition.

He looked at Vicki for help. She sighed and said, "Adrian, if you do what your father says, he'll buy you an ice cream."

The promise of the treat convinced him.

"Think of something you want to say to *Ye Ye*," Harold instructed.

Adrian tilted his head and looked quizzically at his father.

"Maybe that you miss him?"

"Harold," Vicki said, putting her hands on Adrian's shoulders. "That's enough. If you want to take part in this ridiculous custom, go ahead, but don't force your son into doing it for you."

Harold didn't think he had been pressuring Adrian, but he fell silent. He placed his hands over Adrian's, and for once, the boy let him. Then, on the count of three, they released the kite. It floated over the others and out into the empty blue beyond.

"Ice cream!" Adrian bellowed.

They headed toward the entrance of the park, where they'd

spotted a line of vendors when they'd first arrived on the bus. Adrian sat on a bench with a chocolate ice cream cone while Vicki crouched next to him, a handful of napkins ready. A few feet away sat a trio of stray dogs, hungrily watching every lick.

Halfway through, Adrian announced, "I'm done," and before either of his parents could take the remainder of the cone from him and throw it in the trash, he made as if to toss it on the ground. Before he could do so, one of the dogs leapt up and grabbed the cone. Sharp teeth closed around Adrian's hand. At Vicki's scream, all three dogs ran away. After a second of shock, Adrian started to howl in pain. Harold knelt on trembling knees to examine his son's injury. To his relief, the dog's teeth had barely broken the skin. Harold took the napkins from Vicki and pressed them against the wound.

"He'll be okay." He tried to calm her down.

Vicki clutched Adrian to her. "What you mean? That dog could have rabies. We need to take him to the hospital as soon as possible."

"Of course." Harold kept from pointing out that her panic was probably making Adrian more upset.

A small crowd had gathered around them now, including a man who drove a taxi and offered to take them back into the city. He dropped them off at the closest hospital, which was Chen Hsin General. Carrying Adrian, Vicki rushed into the emergency room while Harold paid the driver, then hurried in after his family. Luckily there weren't many patients this holiday afternoon, and a young female doctor was able to see them within minutes.

Harold leaned against the wall opposite the examination table while the doctor gave Adrian a tetanus shot and bandaged his hand. Vicki stood by their son's side, murmuring what a brave little boy he was and promising him all kinds of treats.

"Don't worry," the doctor said. "The bite might leave a small scar, but your son will be fine."

Vicki looked horrified, as if she were being told that Adrian might lose a limb.

Back at home, Harold took over and bathed and put Adrian to bed, the boy's right hand wrapped up in white gauze as if he was holding a baseball mitt. Harold held Adrian's other hand until his son fell asleep.

When Harold came out into the living room, he found Vicki sitting in the dark.

"How is he?" she asked.

"Asleep. It was quite a day for him. For all of us." He moved closer to his wife to comfort her, but the grim expression on her face made him pause.

"I blame you, you know," she said.

"What?"

"For getting him that ice cream."

"It was your idea."

"To make up for the fact that you were going to take away his kite! And for what? Some silly belief that kites bring messages to the dead? You didn't even seem that concerned when that dog bit him."

"Vicki," Harold said. "I may not show it in the way you do, but I was concerned. I *am* concerned. But you heard the doctor. Adrian's going to be fine."

"If you consider a scar to be fine." Vicki stood up. "I know you didn't have the best relationship with your father, but that doesn't mean you have to have the same with your son."

Harold had no chance to say anything in his defense before she left the room.

Now he and Auntie Mai approached his father's tomb, a modest edifice of pink marble compared to some of the elaborate memorials nearby. To his surprise, the grave was relatively clear of weeds and debris.

He looked sideways at Auntie Mai, and before he could ask, she said, "I come here sometimes. I hope you don't mind."

Shamefaced, Harold again recalled his rude reaction to her appearance at his father's funeral, how he had thought it an insult to his mother's memory. "I don't mind at all. I only come here once a year myself, during Qingming Festival. I know in order to be a filial son I should come more often."

"It must be hard for you," Auntie Mai said. "You're a busy man with a family." She paused, gauging his reaction. "How are your wife and son?"

Harold supposed there was no way he could avoid explaining why he needed to stay with Auntie Mai instead of his own home. "They're fine, but Vicki and I...we're going through some difficulties in our marriage." It took him a great deal to admit this, but somehow it was easier with a relative stranger like Auntie Mai than with someone he knew well.

"You can get help," Auntie Mai offered gently.

"I don't think so."

As modern and Westernized as Vicki liked to think herself, Harold knew she would never consent to go to a marriage counselor. He himself thought marriage counselors were mostly for expats, or Taiwanese married to non-Taiwanese. Family problems needed to be kept within the family—that's what his father had taught him. Otherwise why had he carried on with Auntie Mai while Harold's mother was still alive?

Harold looked at the pink slab of marble where his father's name in Chinese characters was etched in gold. "I don't think he would care as long as I had a son to carry on his name and his legacy. Although I'm not so sure about the second anymore."

"I read about your company in the newspaper," Auntie Mai said, saving him from having to reveal the other source of his recent disgrace. "I think you were right to say what you did. Something should be done about the way those workers are treated."

Auntie Mai must have been reading one of the less-conservative newspapers. Harold would never have pegged her as a proponent of labor reform. "Well, it doesn't matter now."

Auntie Mai was silent for a moment. Then she said, "When you were away doing your military service, your father asked me whether I thought he should turn the company over to you. It wasn't that he didn't think you were up to it. He just wasn't sure whether it was what you wanted to do."

"And what did you tell him?

"I said, 'Let him choose for himself.' He agreed."

"I didn't know I had a choice," Harold said.

"You do now," Auntie Mai replied.

It certainly hadn't seemed Harold had options when he'd come back from his year of military service on the southern tip of the Taiwan island. Neither had the military service been a choice. Many of Harold's classmates, including Charlie Lin, had come up with ways to get out of it. Some of them feigned mental illnesses; others made themselves physically sick by not eating. Those who had the means to travel abroad left every few months so as to escape conscription. Charlie had been exempted for a heart murmur. Harold still wasn't sure whether it was true or if Charlie's family had paid a doctor to say so.

"Who's the enemy here? China?" Charlie would ask, always forward thinking. "In a few years we should be so lucky as to do business with China."

Harold knew he had no choice when it came to military service. His father would want him to serve just as he had; as would his mother, dead for two years. In his day, his father's training had been for the navy and his service had lasted for three years. He felt it had given him the discipline and perseverance for building his company. Young people now, he maintained, were too weak.

To please his father, Harold chose boot camp when he could have transferred to an office job or done translation work because of his facility with English. He was duly hazed, and in turn helped haze new recruits. His body ached in places he never knew existed, and muscles he never knew he had hardened into knots. Then he gradually became used to the routine and found comfort in the physicality of it, that it did not require him to think about the future, what plans his father had for him after that year, and whether he'd have a girlfriend when he came back.

Charlie had introduced Harold to Vicki before he'd left. They'd gone on several group dates, which didn't count, and then one date by themselves before he was scheduled to depart for the south. Vicki was planning to spend the year studying overseas in England, so they would have been separated anyway. Some of his fellow conscripts talked about their girlfriends or fiancées, and while Harold would have liked to boast that he had gone on a date with the first runner-up to Miss Taipei, he wasn't sure where his relationship with Vicki stood. All he knew was that the committee that crowned Miss Taipei had made a huge mistake, and that he hoped Vicki wouldn't fall in love with an ambitious Taiwanese or foreigner while she was away.

His year away seemed to solidify what his future would hold. When he returned to Taipei, his father began teaching him the business of running his company. Vicki was also back and introduced him to her parents, who were impressed with his commitment to the nation. Looking back, it all seemed so archaic. Harold was sure that by the time Adrian was old enough, military service would be voluntary. And as Charlie Lin had so eloquently declared when they were fresh out of college, China was no longer the enemy.

Harold and Auntie Mai spent the rest of the afternoon in silence while cleaning the tombs of Harold's father and mother. As he had the day of his father's funeral, Harold thought about how someday he'd lie in this burial plot, as well. In the past Vicki would have joined him, but he wasn't so sure now. Perhaps Auntie Mai would be on the other side of his father. He shook his head to clear it of such thoughts.

The sun was starting to go down when he and Auntie Mai headed for the entrance of the park. The packs of stray dogs were still lounging around the vendors, looking for a handout. Harold mentioned to Auntie Mai the incident last Tomb Sweeping Day when Adrian had gotten bitten by a dog, though not that Vicki had blamed him for it.

"Is he okay now?"

"There isn't a trace of a scar." Nearly six months later, Harold wondered whether Adrian could even remember what had happened, even if it was seared into his mother's memory.

Auntie Mai said, "I hope you and your wife will work things out, but if not, you are welcome to stay with me as long as you need to."

"I don't want to inconvenience you."

"Your father purchased this apartment for me, so it really belongs to you."

"He wanted you to have it," Harold corrected. "But I appreciate it all the same. It will only be for a couple more nights, at the most."

He would need to find his own apartment soon, move his things from his house. And his office would likely move, as well, to somewhere else in the building, according to his new status. Later, there would be lawyers, for both the marriage and the company. But for now, he was choosing to let go of everything that had been expected of him.

From the view from his new apartment in central Taipei, overlooking Da'an Forest Park, Harold could just see the row of palm trees flanking the front of Taiwan National University. Fleetingly, he thought of Auntie Mai's one-hundred-year-old patient; that had been over a month ago, so the man had likely passed away by now. If Harold himself lived until that age, he still had nearly two-thirds of his life left. Two-thirds of a life that he would dictate himself.

While he was still working for the company started by his father, it was in a truncated role. No longer feeling any obligation to his job, he imagined he'd eventually leave and work for another company. Since that one afternoon, he hadn't seen Charlie Lin. Neither did Vicki talk about him, and Harold preferred to keep it that way. When he saw Vicki nowadays, when she handed off Adrian to him, she seemed happier than she used to be. Or maybe she was pretending for his sake.

What Harold looked forward to most during the week was seeing his son. Vicki let him take Adrian for Saturday and Sunday, and he'd set up the second bedroom in his new apartment as Adrian's room, albeit with half the amount of toys from back home. He'd take Adrian to the park, or the harbor, or the market, sometimes in the company of Auntie Mai, who treated the child as if he were her own grandson.

Perhaps in reaction to the chilly interior of his former house, which Vicki had decorated, Harold's new apartment contained bright, primary colors. The only spot of gray was *Elegy* hanging on the wall by itself across from the plush sofa. There was no other place Harold could put it, and he also found it strangely comforting. He looked at it as often as he looked at the view outside his living room window. After the divorce settlement, it would be the only item of monetary value he owned. Or maybe not even that, if it truly was a fake.

Harold had never received another message from the person who had e-mailed him about the forgery. At this point, he supposed it didn't matter. He wasn't planning to sell the painting, and would probably never need to. Someday, he hoped to pass *Elegy* on to his son.

# Chapter 11

Caroline was coming down the stairs of her building one morning when she ran into her oldest neighbor, Mrs. Greeley, who lived with her husband in the apartment below hers. As a young couple, the Greeleys had raised their two children in a space no bigger than Caroline's current apartment. They'd known Hazel since she'd moved in and were now in their eighties but healthy, still navigating the stairs of the walk-up building. Sometimes, when Caroline encountered one of them with their shopping cart, she offered to help them carry their things upstairs. Mrs. Greeley usually acquiesced, while Mr. Greeley refused any help. Caroline would ascend the stairs slowly, keeping an eye on him until he reached his front door.

Ever since their landlord, Adam Alexiou, the son of the original landlord who had rented to Hazel and the Greeleys, had let them know the building was turning co-op, Caroline had often discussed the matter with her oldest neighbors in passing. Today, she felt comfortable enough in having funds from the sale of the Andrew Cantrell painting to confide in Mrs. Greeley that she intended to buy the gallery space downstairs.

Mrs. Greeley paused, holding on to the banister with a bird-like hand. "My dear, didn't you hear?"

"Hear what?"

"The co-op deal is off. Mr. Alexiou intends to sell the building to a real estate developer...."

Caroline had stopped listening beyond the first sentence. "So there isn't even a possibility that we can buy in to the building anymore?"

"Maybe after they're done turning it into glass condos. But they'll probably be bought by foreign businesspeople who won't live here for most of the year. Not that Henry and I would be able to afford buying in to the co-op anyway."

Caroline turned her attention to the old woman. "What will you and Henry do now?"

"Our daughter has already made plans to move us into a retirement community in Riverdale. We've gone to see it. It's quite nice. Not as nice as having our own place, of course."

"I'm sure you'll be quite comfortable there."

"It's just that Henry and I have only lived here for most of our lives. Our children grew up here. We fully expected to be carried out feetfirst. Well"—Mrs. Greeley patted Caroline's hand—"at least Hazel didn't have to see her gallery destroyed because of one man's greed. She'd likely padlock herself to the doors when the construction workers come, like those people who chain themselves around trees. I read an article about them once, how they'll literally stop bulldozers...."

Caroline wasn't quite sure how they'd gotten on the topic of ecological activists. "Thank you, Alice, for telling me," she said firmly. "Best of luck to you and Henry."

Downstairs in the gallery, Caroline gazed at the empty white walls. Sandro Hess's paintings were still leaning against them, packed up; he was scheduled to come take them away later this week. It was early enough that Molly wasn't in yet, so Caroline felt free to use the phone at the front desk. She called Adam

Alexiou at his office, banking on the fact that he was someone who got to work before everyone else.

"I just heard from Alice Greeley that you're planning to sell the building to real estate developers," she said after they exchanged perfunctory greetings, trying to keep her voice from trembling—with anger or fear, she wasn't sure. "Is that true?"

"I was going to send an e-mail this week," her landlord said. "Alice Greeley happened to find out first because her daughter called about scheduling their move."

Now the tremble in her voice was definitely due to anger. "Don't you think we're owed more than an e-mail? How about an explanation in person? Especially those of us who've lived here for decades?"

"Caroline, I understand why you're upset. But the truth is, no tenant was going to buy in to the co-op. The Greeleys' daughter is using this as an excuse to get her parents into a retirement home, the Singhs are having another baby and need more room, and the two girls on the second floor are splitting up."

It occurred to Caroline that he didn't remember the two female roommates' names, although she didn't, either. "I was going to buy in," she pointed out.

If Adam Alexiou was surprised that she had the funds to do so, he didn't show it. "You have to admit you've gotten a great deal since your aunt died. But all good things must come to an end."

"If my aunt Hazel were here, she'd say you ought to be ashamed of yourself," Caroline spat. "She'd say you're not half the man your father was."

She breathlessly hung up the phone, a little taken aback at where her venom had come from, when she heard Molly say from behind her, "Is everything okay?"

Caroline manufactured a smile. "Yes, I was just talking to a vendor."

Molly didn't look convinced, but she didn't press further as she got settled at her desk. Caroline moved deeper into the gallery out of sight from her assistant, pretending to double-check the padding around the Sandro Hess paintings. Within the space of a half hour, her plans had turned into dust. All of the subterfuge, the risk she'd taken in forging the Andrew Cantrell painting—it was for nothing. She was just sitting on a pile of money that she couldn't use to buy what she most wanted. She had failed Hazel and, most of all, she had failed herself.

Where could she go? Even with what was left of two million dollars after taxes couldn't buy her a corner of a gallery in this neighborhood anymore. She could decamp to Brooklyn like so many others, including Solomon Finch, whom Molly had told her about. But that would mean starting over, and Caroline wasn't sure she had it in her to do it. She didn't know who the hip, young artists were, how to get people interested in them. She only knew what Hazel had passed down to her, and that wasn't enough. Perhaps it was time for her to get out of the business altogether, when her biggest success was selling a forgery to an unsuspecting buyer.

For the next few days, Caroline ruminated on what to do. Her landlord duly sent an e-mail informing his tenants of the impending sale of the building and a date later in the fall by which everyone was required to vacate the premises. That morning she also received an e-mail from Sandro Hess informing her that he'd be stopping by on the weekend to pick up his paintings. Ordinarily, the end of a show—even one that had produced no sales, as Sandro's had—would be a source of renewed energy for Caroline. She'd usually have another artist lined up or be well on the hunt for one. But now, if she was going to be closing in about a month's time, there was no point in finding someone else. For better or for worse, Sandro Hess was the last artist to be exhibited at the Lowry Gallery.

Caroline was a little irritated that Sandro couldn't make it with his van during the week to pick up his paintings, but at least if he came on Saturday, Molly wouldn't be around to hear their final exchange. She anticipated Sandro would have some choice words for her, fault her for the lack of sales. But he seemed somber, resigned almost, on Saturday morning as they transported the paintings into the van.

"Couldn't you have hired someone to help you?" Caroline asked.

"Where would I get the money?" Sandro pointed out, and Caroline subsided.

Finally, when there was one painting left, the large Mickey Mouse kaleidoscope that had hung in the front window of the gallery, she said, "Wait."

"We'll probably need another person to help with that one," he agreed.

"Come on into my office," Caroline said.

Sandro raised an eyebrow but did as she directed. She handed him a check for ten thousand dollars.

"What's this?" he asked.

"I'm buying that last painting."

Sandro stared at her for a moment, then laughed. "You must be kidding."

For a moment Caroline was tempted to snatch the check back and tear it up. "This was the painting that first caught my eye when I went to your studio. I want this for my own. I think it'll be a good investment."

Sandro still looked dubious. "You feel sorry for me."

"Maybe a little of that, too," she admitted.

"That's okay. You never promised me big sales."

"That's not all that I'm sorry for." She held his eyes for a moment, long enough for him to realize what she was saying.

He slowly nodded and pocketed the check; she knew he wouldn't be too proud to accept it. Then he removed from his other pocket a set of keys, which he handed to her. Confused, she looked up at him.

"I thought you gave these back to me." She could picture her spare apartment keys now, hanging on a hook by her front door.

"I made a copy and gave you back the originals."

A chill rippled through her, thinking Sandro could have entered her apartment at any time. "Why would you do that?"

"I guess I wanted to show that I had power over you somehow, even if I didn't have it any other way."

"Did you take anything?"

"Of course not. But I did notice you had a painting by Andrew Cantrell for a few days in your apartment. A fake Andrew Cantrell painting."

She immediately grew defensive. "What makes you think it's a fake?"

"You don't cover your paper trail at home very well, Caroline. Receipts, a business card. Who is this Liu Qingwu?"

"Someone I met on the street. A Chinese artist."

"Ah, they make the best copiers. You know about Ely Sakhai?"

Caroline faintly recalled hearing the story of the famous New York City art collector whose scam involved selling forgeries of Impressionist and post-Impressionist paintings to Asian businessmen, only to also sell the originals some time later. He supposedly kept a team of Chinese immigrants in the attic of his gallery producing these paintings, like some kind of sweatshop. After spending more than three years in jail for fraud, he was said to have opened an art and antiques store on Long Island.

"How much did you pay him?" Sandro asked.

"Three thousand dollars."

Sandro shook his head. "Poor man. Sounds like you fleeced him well, considering you sold it for more than six hundred times that."

"All right," Caroline said, reaching for her checkbook again. "How much do you want to keep silent?"

Hand over his heart, Sandro acted offended. "Do you really think I would blackmail you?" He patted his pocket where he'd put the check she'd given him for his painting. "This is enough. Besides, I've already e-mailed the buyer. Harold Yu, correct? Anonymously, of course."

Caroline felt the bottom beginning to fall out of her world again. "What did you tell him?"

"That you sold him a fake. He hasn't gotten in touch with you, has he?"

"No. Did he e-mail you back?"

"I shut down the account after I sent the e-mail. I figured I had done enough."

*You sure have,* Caroline thought. She was beginning to feel more positive again. If Harold Yu had never gotten in touch with her, it was likely he hadn't read Sandro's e-mail. A busy man like that must get hundreds of e-mails a day; it could have even gone into his spam folder. Or maybe he had read it and thought it was a prank. "*The desire to believe is a powerful thing,*" she remembered Peter saying.

"Let's call it even," Caroline told Sandro. "You have your check, I have your painting. And that other thing...we don't have to speak of it ever again. Or the fact that you broke into my apartment."

"Sounds fair to me," Sandro said lazily.

After he left, Caroline looked at the painting of his that she'd purchased. She wasn't sure if she wanted to have it in plain sight, as it would forever remind her of the useless crime she'd committed. But she would put it in storage, just in case it became valuable someday.

At first, Caroline didn't mention to anyone that the gallery would be closing—not Peter, and not even Molly, even though she supposed she should, given that the girl would be out of a job soon. Then Rose Schaeffer, Molly's mother, called her one evening.

"Has Molly told you her news yet?" Rose asked.

"That she's been offered a place in a group show?"

"I didn't hear about that. She's going back to school in the fall. I'm so relieved."

As was Caroline, since now it would be easier to tell her assistant that she no longer had a place to work. "That's great news."

"I told Caleb that if we didn't interfere, she'd eventually come around and do the right thing. Whereas if we did what he wanted, which was to completely cut her off, she'd probably never speak to us again."

"I don't think that would happen. From what I've heard her say about you and her father, you have a pretty good relationship."

"I'm glad you think that." Rose paused. "I just wanted to thank you, Caro, for taking her in at such a confusing time in her life. I know you didn't want to, but having this job has given her such stability. She's lucky to have you, and I am, too."

If only her friend knew what had really been going on at the gallery that summer. Caroline tried to divert attention from herself. "Molly seems like a levelheaded girl, and a talented artist. You should be proud of her."

"You know, I've never seen her work. Maybe I'll ask her to show it to me before she leaves to go back to school."

Before they said good-bye, Caroline added, "Oh, what did you think of the squirrel vase?"

"What squirrel vase? Oh...yes."

"Molly and I thought you would really like it," Caroline couldn't resist saying.

"It's certainly unusual, isn't it?"

Caroline let several seconds pass before she said, "Who are we kidding? It's ridiculous!" and both of them laughed.

The next morning, when Molly came into work, Caroline said, "Your mother called to say you're going back to school."

"I meant to tell you—"

"That's fine. I should have told you earlier that the Lowry Gallery is closing down next month. The landlord is planning to sell the building to a real estate developer."

An odd look crossed Molly's face, so quickly that Caroline wondered if she had registered it properly. "I'm sorry to hear that. What are you going to do?"

Caroline threw her hands up in the air. "What is there to do? I knew this was going to happen at some point, that the market value of the space would be more than I could pay. I was just postponing the inevitable."

"You could start the gallery somewhere else."

"Like Williamsburg?"

"Or Ridgewood, in Queens. I met a friend there recently, and it looked like several galleries were opening."

Caroline shook her head. "I appreciate your suggestions, Molly, but I think it's time for me to get out of the game. At least here in the city. Speaking of Williamsburg, though, did you decide whether you were going to participate in that group show?"

"I turned the offer down."

"Because you're going back to school."

Molly looked down. "Because I realized I wasn't ready. You helped me make that that decision, actually."

Caroline couldn't remember what she had said to Molly, and hoped she hadn't steered her on the wrong path. But if the girl felt she wasn't ready to show her work, she wasn't ready.

Next, she called Peter and told him the gallery was closing.

"I'm so sorry to hear that," he said. "But don't blame yourself. You did everything you could—and more—to save it."

"I feel like I've failed Hazel."

"You kept the Lowry Gallery running for thirty years, against all odds. That's more than anyone expected you to do. Do you think that if Hazel were still alive, she'd still have her gallery? Too much has changed in the art world since then."

Caroline considered Peter's scenario. If Hazel had lived, she'd be around seventy-five, way past retirement, although Caroline could imagine her still living in her walk-up apartment like the Greeleys. As for where Caroline would be, she didn't know. Maybe she'd have gone back to San Francisco, tried to rekindle things with Bob. She did know she would not have gotten involved in the art business.

Caroline knew Peter would spread the word and soon condolences started to trickle in, from artists and art dealers, framers and gallery owners she hadn't heard from in years. Those who were old enough to remember Hazel mentioned her, while others lamented the rising property costs and confided to her their own real estate woes. Not many people asked her what she planned to do next, and she realized they already considered her out of the picture.

Then one afternoon, Caroline picked up the phone to hear an elderly woman's quavering voice. "Is this Caroline Lowry?"

"Yes," Caroline replied. "How may I help you?"

"This is Naomi Cantrell." The woman paused to let the words sink in. Caroline recalled the elegantly dressed woman who showed up at Hazel's memorial at the Lowry Gallery. Naomi Cantrell had been a few years older than her husband, so she must be in her mideighties by now.

"What can I do for you, Naomi?" Caroline asked politely.

"I heard you were closing your gallery and wanted to have you over for tea. I know you must be quite busy," Naomi continued in her measured, gravelly voice, prompting Caroline to get over her momentary surprise.

"Of course I'd be happy to have tea with you."

After they settled on a date, Naomi gave Caroline directions to her apartment on Park Avenue, and they hung up. Afterward, Caroline wondered if the old woman just wanted to reminisce about the past, or did she have another motivation? So many years had gone by, so many people gone. Naomi couldn't possibly harbor any bitterness toward Hazel anymore, or Caroline as her aunt's proxy.

Feeling that she still represented her aunt and the gallery, Caroline dressed carefully for her lunch date with Naomi. When she arrived at the building off of Park Avenue, she was ushered by the doorman into the elevator, which opened directly into a foyer. There a maid led her through several expansive rooms furnished with what appeared to be eighteenth-century French furniture, shrouded in near darkness from the drawn curtains, and into a sitting room that had the aura of a mausoleum.

The figure on the sofa was half-hidden in shadows, but when the maid announced Caroline's presence, she leaned forward and Caroline saw that it was indeed Naomi Cantrell, whom she hadn't seen since Hazel's funeral. The years had diminished her height, turned her hair pure white, her skin as fine and translucent as paper, but jewels still winked at her earlobes and flashed on her hand as she gestured for Caroline to sit diagonally from her. The same maid brought in a tray of tea for the table in between them, served it, and then receded into the background.

"How did you hear the gallery was closing?" Caroline asked.

"It might surprise you, but I've been following your gallery for years. Since you took over for Hazel, actually. You've had some impressive shows."

"And some not-so-impressive shows, especially lately," Caroline interjected.

"I won't pretend I know anything about the art business," Naomi continued. "I simply know what I like." With a nod of her head she indicated the paintings on the walls around them.

Now that her eyes had adjusted to the semidarkness, Caroline was able to see some of the paintings, which seemed to be mostly from the 1960s, Andrew Cantrell's contemporaries, at distinct odds with the furniture. One of them appeared somewhat familiar, a white canvas with a red circle migrating to the top right-hand corner like a wayward sun. Then she recognized it as the Mark Finnegan painting she'd discovered in the basement of Hazel's building not long after Hazel had died, which at Peter's suggestion she'd put up for auction. It had unexpectedly fetched 1.2 million dollars from an anonymous buyer, and had allowed Caroline to keep the gallery open.

Caroline set down her teacup so as not to spill anything. "It was you. You were the one who bought the Mark Finnegan painting at the auction."

Naomi inclined her head in acknowledgment. "A very good investment that was, too. It's now worth at least twice that. But it happens to be a painting that I like, so I'll never sell it."

She would never need to sell it, Caroline thought. But that couldn't be the whole story, that Naomi had bought the painting simply because she'd liked it. "Did you know I needed the money to fund the gallery?" she asked.

"You're asking if I had another motivation aside from my own whims?"

"There must be."

"In order to explain," Naomi said, "you must understand what Andrew's and my marriage was like. From the moment we met, people accused him of going after my fortune. Members of my own family said that. But we lived quite frugally, first in the city in a modest apartment in the East Village, then later in my family's farmhouse in East Hampton."

"Hazel mentioned the place, that it wasn't your typical summer home."

"No, it wasn't. My mother would take me there during the summers when I was young, and I played with local children who lived year-round in similar houses—only theirs belonged to working farms. It was a lovely, quaint place, and that's why I wanted Andrew and I to move out there—not because, as the tabloids suggested, I wanted more distance between him and his mistress. I knew I couldn't keep him from going to the city, and I couldn't keep him from seeing or communicating with Hazel. And then the fire occurred."

"Hazel said you were away at a charity function that night?"

"For the New York Public Library, I think. Or the City Opera. In any case, I was in the city when all that happened. Later, from the police, I learned that Hazel had been with him that night, although according to her testimony she left hours before the blaze started. She swore she had nothing to do with it."

"Do you think that's true?"

"I don't think we'll ever know what happened that night. I prefer to think that she wasn't involved, although after it happened, I was looking for someone to blame. You have to remember, I went out to the farmhouse early the next morning, as soon as I'd heard. I saw the ruins of the studio, the bits of charred canvas. Andrew's body was burned beyond recognition. He had to be identified by his medical records. Imagine, I wasn't even able to identify my own husband. I swore I would never forgive Hazel for that."

"But you did forgive her."

"Many years later, after she died. I realized at her death, aside from her gallery, she was completely alone." Naomi corrected herself. "She had you, of course. But I mean that with Andrew's death, someone was taken away from her, too. Growing up as an only child, with the kind of family I was born into, I was never expected to share. And I couldn't share Andrew with anyone while he was alive, not with another woman. I didn't want to acknowledge that he and Hazel had a relationship just as real as ours, if not more so." Naomi gave a short laugh. "You know, Andrew never dedicated any of his paintings to me. But he dedicated one to *her*. Wrote it on the back of the painting, plain as day."

Caroline's hands grew cold. "Which painting?" she asked, even though she already knew the answer.

"*Elegy*. Hazel inspired that painting in many different ways. I thought I could never forgive her for that. But after many years, in death, I could finally do it."

"So, is that why you came to Hazel's memorial? Why you bought the Mark Finnegan painting?"

"Yes. By that time I'd regretted the way I'd treated Hazel and wanted to make amends. I saw that the Lowry Gallery was putting a Mark Finnegan painting up for auction—an artist whom Andrew knew and was friends with, by the way—and it just made sense to buy it. From an investment, aesthetic, and cathartic standpoint."

Caroline could see that. "Well," she said, "I want to thank you for doing that. Without those initial funds, the Lowry Gallery would have had to close after Hazel passed."

"And you've kept it going since then. She would be proud of you."

They finished their tea, and Caroline said good-bye to Naomi. She waited until she was outside of Naomi's building before she allowed herself to think about what she'd just learned about *Elegy* and its very visible mark of authenticity. Who other than Naomi knew about the dedication? She had to lean against the side of the building, breathing deeply to keep her mind from racing away from her.

She'd already dodged a bullet in that Harold Yu had never responded to Sandro's e-mail. But she'd thought that even if Mr. Yu decided to question the authenticity of the painting, the painting's materials, Peter's analysis, and the provenance she had provided would stand the test. If Mr. Yu found out the original painting had a dedication on the back, there was nothing she could to do explain its absence on the painting she had sold him.

Caroline would never know what Mr. Yu thought about the painting. But one thing was certain: She would never feel safe again for the rest of her life.

*   *   *

With the Lowry Gallery officially closed, Caroline started to look for a new apartment. It was, she thought ironically, what she had been intending to do more than thirty years ago when she'd moved to New York after her divorce, before she found out Hazel was sick and moved in with her.

She ended up in an apartment in Long Island City, on the second floor of a yellow vinyl-sided house. The rest of the street contained warehouses and buildings advertising artists' lofts. While she didn't think she was going to get involved in the art business again, she liked the thought of being close to people who were creating art. In the evenings she'd walk down to Gantry Park, amid the young couples and families who lived in the luxury waterfront buildings nearby, and gaze at the midtown Manhattan skyline across the East River. On one of those walks she thought about Mr. Liu and how she'd paid him a pittance compared to what his painting of *Elegy* had sold for. Maybe it was too late to give him what he had earned, but she had some money left over. She could try to make up for her various deceits.

Now more familiar with this borough's subway lines, she wasn't as confused as she'd been before in taking the train to Elmhurst. She rang the bell for his first-floor apartment. No one answered. After spending a few minutes ringing the bell and knocking, she walked around to the back, where she saw that the gate to the fence around the small backyard and garage was open. She remembered he used the garage as a studio, so she slipped in. The windows were still partially covered with black trash bags, but she was able to glimpse inside. The space was empty, cleared of any paintings or artist paraphernalia.

"Hey!" someone called from the back door.

Caroline whirled around, feeling like a thief. A man stood on the cracked concrete step, possibly the same one she'd disturbed the first time she'd come to Mr. Liu's studio.

"You want something, lady?" he asked.

Caroline gathered herself. "I'm looking for Mr. Liu."

"Don't know where he is. He moved out without paying rent. Landlord's looking for him."

"How long ago?

The man scratched his head. "Two weeks?"

"I don't suppose he left a forwarding address?"

"A what address?"

"Never mind. Do you have any idea where he went?"

The man shrugged. "Maybe he went back to his own country."

If Caroline remembered correctly, Liu had told her he had been in America for thirty years, so she didn't think he'd pack up and go back to China now. But if he was in need of money and couldn't pay his rent, maybe he had left the city. She thought of the check in her purse, written out to him for thirty thousand dollars. It was too little, too late.

"Okay," she said. "Thanks for your help."

The man swept his arm toward the gate with exaggerated politeness for her to leave, and Caroline quickly did so. She didn't suppose Liu was about to come back, or there was any way to locate him. But at least she had tried.

At the end of the block, she went down into the subway station, heading back to her new home. Maybe now she'd find out who she could be, as she'd intended to do thirty years ago when she'd arrived in New York City, standing in front of her aunt Hazel's building.

# Chapter 12

After the painting was taken away from me, I tried to immerse myself in my work—my classes, my sidewalk sales—all of which were growing more hollow by the day. I hadn't realized how much I'd depended on working on the painting to distract myself from Jin's absence. Without that, I had to focus all my attention on finding out where she'd gone. I had been operating too long on the principle that if she wanted to come back, she knew where I was—a solid enough reasoning if you've lost your dog, but not your wife. With your wife, I knew now, you needed to go after her.

Jin's sister, Hong, was the most likely person to know where she was. I had never met her in person before, but I knew she had come to America more than ten years before Jin had. I believe they were actually half sisters, sharing the same father, who had married Jin's mother after his first wife had died. Their family lived in Guangzhou in the south of China, and in the intervening years between the sisters' births, you could tell the direction of the country. Hong's name meant "red," the color of communism; Jin's name meant "gold," the commodity that supplanted patriotism.

Hong had married the owner of a shoe repair shop in the Sunset Park neighborhood of Brooklyn, and by the time they'd sponsored Jin to come over, they'd had two daughters, ages seven and nine. When she first arrived in America, Jin had shared her nieces' bedroom. She often commented to me about the state of their Americanness, from their names (Sophie and Olivia) to their interests (princesses and horses). "They're growing up just like American children," she said, with equal amounts of wonderment and disdain.

After she moved in with me, Jin continued to visit her sister's family almost every week, bringing them Ecuadorian pastries and Peruvian roast chicken, even though those things were also readily available in their neighborhood. The Chinese population of Sunset Park was mostly Fujianese, like an extension of East Broadway in Manhattan's Chinatown. They'd settled along Eighth Avenue, while Fifth Avenue remained mostly Hispanic.

I never went on these visits, citing the weekend classes I had to teach and that I wanted to take advantage of the afternoon when Jin wasn't there to do some of my own work. Also, from comments relayed by Jin, I felt Hong disapproved of me. Jin told me her sister had said she should have married a hard worker like her shoe-repair husband rather than an older itinerant artist like myself. "Does he do anything that justifies his existence?" Jin reported her sister as saying, whenever we were having a fight. Sometimes I wondered that myself.

I wasn't surprised when Hong had not been forthcoming about how much she knew concerning her sister's disappearance. It was clear over the phone that she had been expecting me to call her and had been coached as to what to say. No, Jin had not been in touch with her recently. No, Jin didn't have any friends to stay with. No, she didn't know where Jin had gone. I knew Hong was lying but couldn't very well say it.

So, that Saturday I boarded the train for the hour-plus ride from Elmhurst to Sunset Park, which wound its way through

Manhattan. Slowly the passengers changed from mostly Hispanic and Asian to white, then back to Hispanic and Asian again. I stepped into the bright sunlight, momentarily disoriented by the combination of takeout restaurants, cheap electronics stores, and bodegas that also characterized my neighborhood.

Hong's apartment couldn't be far away. I located the correct, postwar brick building, and rang the buzzer. A woman's voice answered, and I wavered. Should I act like I was there on some sort of pretense, like delivering a package, and risk being turned away, or just be myself and risk the same? I chose the latter.

"It's Liu Qingwu. I've come to talk to you about Jin."

There was such a long silence afterward I wondered whether she had been able to hear me over the staticky connection. Then the front door buzzed and I pushed my way through.

Three flights up, Hong was waiting for me. When I entered her cluttered but homey apartment, I saw Jin's nieces playing with a board game on the coffee table. I didn't know which was Sophie and which was Olivia, and it didn't help that both of them had bangs and shoulder-length hair, making one look like a slightly smaller version of the other.

"Say hello to your aunt Jin's husband, girls," Hong said in English. I was heartened that she acknowledged my relationship to them, rather than treating me as if I were a stranger.

"Hello," they chorused without looking up from their game.

"Girls, go to your bedroom while we have a chat."

"But we just started," the larger of them (Sophie?) complained.

"Now, please."

At the sharpness in Hong's voice, both girls jumped up, leaving their game on the table.

"I am sorry about that," Hong said to me. "Would you like some tea?"

I declined, and we both sat down on the sofa, awkwardly

angled toward each other. From this proximity, I could sense the physical similarities between Hong and Jin—their delicate noses, the round set of their chins—features that must have been inherited from their shared father. An unexpected sense of longing rose in me, and I looked at the pattern of the rug beneath my feet for a moment to compose myself before speaking.

"I know you're hiding something about Jin," I said. "I have a right to know—I'm her husband. What if you disappeared?" I tried to remember her husband, the shoe-repair owner's name, but failed to recall it. "Your husband would want to know, too."

Hong sighed. "That's true. But I have to honor Jin's wishes. She told me under no circumstances to tell you where she's gone."

"But why? Did she say something about our fighting?" I held up my hands. "I never touched her, I swear. I'd never hurt her."

Hong seemed to take pity on me. "I know you wouldn't. Jin is one to keep secrets. From me, even."

"Is it about her past? Before she came to America? Did she have money or boyfriend problems back home in Guangzhou?"

Something in Hong's face when I'd said "Guangzhou" suggested I'd hit upon something. "She's not in New York anymore," I stated. "She's not even in America. She's gone back to China."

Hong's silence afterward indicated I was correct. So the question of where Jin had gone was answered. But why? If it was to get away from me, China was a safe bet, because there was no way I had enough money to be able to afford a plane ticket, and it wasn't clear whether I'd be allowed back into the States if I left. The same was true for Jin, too, that she would not be able to reenter this country. She'd effectively cut me off and ensured I would never see her again by what she'd done. Could she hate me that much?

I decided to play the sympathy card. In my most dejected voice I said, "Jin must really detest me if she decided to go so far away. I don't know what I did to deserve it."

"You didn't do anything," Hong blurted out. "It's because of something else."

Something, not someone, else. I let hope creep into my voice. "Like what?"

"All right." Hong leaned forward. "I can tell that you're a sincere man, Liu Qingwu. I had my doubts at first, but I do believe that you care about my sister, even if you weren't able to give her the kind of life here she deserved."

"If she came back, I would give her anything she wanted," I declared. "I'd stop being an artist. I'd find a steady job. We'd try to have a child." Until then I hadn't considered these possibilities, but once I'd voiced them, I knew they were true. I'd do anything for Jin if she came back to me.

Hong shook her head sadly. "I'm afraid it's too late for that. Especially that last part."

"What do you mean?"

As Hong turned her large, dark eyes on me, I belatedly recognized she also shared that physical trait with Jin, or it could be that my eyes were playing tricks on me. "Jin is very sick. It's doubtful she could come back even if she wanted to. The last I heard, she was living with her parents in Guangzhou. They're looking for a miracle cure."

The familiar features started falling away—the nose, the chin, the eyes—leaving a void beneath. I caught my breath. When I was able to speak again, I said, "What does she have?"

"Ovarian cancer."

I recalled how Jin had fainted one day at the salon, and how she'd thought she might be pregnant. Instead, the truth was the opposite—instead of harboring life within her, she was harboring a darkness. "That's why she left the salon," I said.

Hong nodded. "She didn't feel like she could work there anymore. She was convinced that something in the chemicals she used had made her sick."

I thought of the women who came in to the salon to get their hair dyed, the poor ventilation, how the smell of the substances made me want to retch every time I went in there. Jin had been a hairdresser in Guangzhou, too, so the exposure must have started years ago. "Did she tell Old Guo this?"

"She tried to but he wouldn't listen to her. Said she couldn't prove it and if she didn't want to work at the salon, she could leave. So she did."

I couldn't believe that Jin had done all this behind my back. When had she gone to the doctor? How could she have lived with this secret without informing me, her husband? Had she thought me so ineffectual, so incapable of comforting her?

"I wish she had told me," I said.

"I wish she did, too," Hong agreed. "I told her you should know. But she didn't want you to suffer with her, and she didn't think you could do anything about it. No one could. First she went to an American doctor, who told her about the treatments available, all very expensive. Then she went to a Chinese doctor, who told her to take medicine to compensate for her *yang* as opposed to *yin* deficiency, also very expensive."

"So, why go back to China?" I asked. "The best medicine is here."

"The best *Western* medicine. In the village where our father grew up, before he went to Guangzhou, lives a healer who has cured everything from liver cancer to mental illness. When Jin told our father she was sick, he said she should come home and he would take her to this man, who could treat her."

"Do you really think he can cure her?"

"She has to have some hope," Hong said gently.

In a daze, I thanked Hong for her help, and emerged onto the streets of Sunset Park more confused than when I had arrived earlier that day. Jin was sick but didn't want my help, and I couldn't blame her. I had done nothing in our marriage to indicate that I could be of any use.

Many times in the ensuing days I started writing Jin a letter—Hong had given me her parents' address in Guangzhou—but always ended up putting down the pen. Was she getting better? Or was her illness progressing? Did she miss me? Every time I wrote something, it ended up coming back to myself. I understood even more why Jin hadn't told me anything about her condition. I was unable to think about anyone outside of me, of my painting, that damn mountain in my mind. I was useless to her—even more so now, separated by an ocean and continent.

I did what I usually did, which was to ask Wang for advice. He looked gravely at me as I talked about going to Jin's sister and discovering Jin's illness.

"I should have tried harder to find out what was troubling her," I said. "Even before she left, I knew something was wrong."

"It's too late for that now," Wang replied reasonably. "The question is, what will you do now? And I think there is only one answer."

I mournfully lifted my face from my hands. "What is that?"

"You must go to her."

"In China? But you know my situation. I could never come back here."

"We are all in that situation. But really"—he gestured at the walls of my small apartment—"what is left for you here?"

He had a point. I had no family, no real friends besides him, and no artist career to speak of in New York. This had been true for most of my thirty years here. I also now had the money from the forged painting. I could afford a plane ticket.

"You're right," I said. "Wang Muping, you've been a good friend to me all these years."

Wang clapped me briefly on the shoulder. "So have you."

In the next couple of weeks I got rid of nearly everything I owned. None of it was valuable, especially the furniture. For so many years I had not paid attention to what I slept on, sat on, ate meals from. I had not accumulated any possessions worth saving. I could see how a woman like Jin might find this fact infuriating. More regretfully, I discarded the small items she had bought to try to make our apartment livelier: the colorful dishes, the cheery knickknacks. When she had first bought them, I had ignored them. If only I had known.

When it came to my studio, I was indecisive. Here were the paintings I had labored over, that were distinctive to me even if an outsider might say they all looked the same. But ultimately, I was ruthless. After dipping a rag in turpentine, I wiped the surface of one canvas. The top of the mountain was instantly erased, as if hidden by a cloud. Another wipe, and its eastern side was gone as if obliterated in an earthquake. I found this strangely cathartic, as if by physically removing the mountain from the painting, I was also removing it from my psyche.

What I had left after a day's work was a pile of blank canvases, still streaked here and there with green where my paint removal had been less successful. I suppose a more appropriate disposal for them would be to burn them in the backyard, but mindful of my neighbors, I just piled them into the already overflowing trash bins.

I told my landlord I was leaving and paid up any outstanding rent. I also told the Chinese Baptist Church senior center that I would no longer be teaching classes; I think the only person who would regret my absence was the flirty widow. The framework for my stall I left to a neighboring vendor. No one there would notice my absence; another poor artist from another country would soon take my place.

As summer had turned into fall, so had the category of

tourists changed from overseas visitors to groups of students. As a treat, I spent a weekday afternoon at the museum like a regular tourist. I hadn't stepped inside its massive halls for years, ever since I was a student myself, even though I'd worked so many days just outside its entrance. I spent most of my time looking at the Greek and Roman sculpture and Islamic art, which had not been on display the last time I'd been there. The paintings, including the Impressionist and post-Impressionist rooms, I skipped entirely.

This was quite the opposite of my first visit to the museum, thirty years ago, just a few weeks after arriving from China. I went with Wang, he with his long hair and me with my buzz cut, two twenty-year-olds working their way through the Old Masters. With our sketchbooks we camped in front of paintings that we had only seen in textbooks in China, works by Rembrandt and Velásquez and Vermeer, just inches away from our awestruck faces. We stayed so long that the guards had to ask us to leave.

Now I was leaving America in an almost identical way that I had come to it, plane ticket in one hand, duffel bag with a few essential items and clothes in the other. Grayer and wiser, I liked to think, although maybe only that first part was true.

The last thing I did was to pay Old Guo, Jin's former boss, a visit.

When I entered the hair salon, he looked up from the front desk and said, "What, you want to borrow a hair dryer again?"

I ignored him and walked up to the counter so that we were eye to eye. Loudly enough for the hairdressers and their customers to hear, I demanded, "Why didn't you tell me about your last conversation with Jin?"

He feigned ignorance. "What conversation?"

"She told you she was sick. That it was caused by working with chemicals here."

"Nonsense. Our working conditions here are fine. Look." He pointed toward several framed notices on the wall behind him: beauty salon credentials from China, a minimum-wage poster, and some other ordinances I didn't understand. "Besides," he added, "what makes her think it was working here that got her sick? She's only been here for five years. The rest of the time she was working in China. Their conditions are much worse. That's where you should put your blame instead of a man's honest business. Now, get out."

I looked around and saw that the people in the salon, hairdressers and customers alike, were hanging on our every word. Perhaps that was enough revenge. I turned around and walked out the door. I was ready to leave now.

Optimistically, I had thought that going back to China would feel like a kind of homecoming. That my senses would instantly adjust, despite the intervening decades. Nothing could be further from the truth, from the Cantonese language that assaulted my ears to the thick layer of pollution that engulfed me when I exited Baiyun Airport in Guangzhou. My eyes and lungs burning, I hailed a taxi and handed over a piece of paper that contained the address of Jin's parents.

The driver eyed my scant luggage, then gave my appearance a quick scan. "You just come over on the flight from America?" he asked in Mandarin Chinese.

"Yes, New York," I said, too tired to wonder what had given me away. Maybe my physical reaction to the pollution.

"*Niu Yue!*" he exclaimed. "What's life like there?"

"Difficult," I replied, hoping my clipped answers would stem any further conversation.

"How long were you over there?"

"Thirty years."

"That's a long time! Welcome back, brother."

Unexpectedly, I found his word encouraging as I gazed out

the window at the street scenes beyond. I had never been to Guangzhou before, and of course I knew that in the past thirty years China had rapidly modernized—was still in the process of modernization, judging by all the half-finished skyscrapers and construction sites and cranes we drove by—but this was like an alternate universe. Despite it being around nine o'clock at night, couples strolled on the sidewalks, neon signs for restaurants and bars blared through the muggy haze, and traffic clogged every street artery. As the taxi inched forward, and I kept glancing at the meter, I wondered if it was a good idea to go straight to Jin's parents' house this late. Perhaps I should have found a cheap hotel in which to rest and clean up so I could properly present myself the next morning. But I was wide awake from jet lag, and mindful of my dwindling funds.

About an hour later, the taxi pulled up in front of an apartment block. I handed the driver the correct fare, and then, when he looked disappointed—he obviously expected more from a compatriot returned from America—added a tip. He thanked me and drove off in a cloud of exhaust, leaving me in the street. I climbed the concrete stairs, each step more difficult than the last, despite the fact I was only carrying a light bag.

When I reached the front door, which was behind a metal gate, I hesitated. The sound of a television came from within the apartment, as well as a crack of light from the bottom of the door. Then I knocked firmly, once, twice. A stirring came from inside, as well as the sound of slippers approaching across a linoleum floor.

An elderly woman's voice—not Jin's—called out something in muffled Cantonese. Then, when I didn't answer, she asked in Mandarin Chinese, "*Ni yao shui?*" Who do you want?

I gave Jin's name, then waited a few minutes before locks rattled on the other side of the door and it opened, revealing not an old crone, but my wife. We gazed at each other through the metal gate. Even though she was backlit, Jin's face was dearly familiar. She looked the same as when she'd left, healthy even, and for a moment I thought she wasn't really sick, it was something she had just told her sister to get away from me.

"It's you," she finally said in English.

"Yes, it's me," was my lame reply.

Another voice, this time that of an elderly man, asked a question, and Jin opened the gate to allow me to enter. Inside, within a small living room dominated by a huge television set, sat Jin's parents. Her mother appeared to be in her sixties, and her father in his seventies, both frailer than I expected. It was almost as if Jin had returned to take care of them instead of the other way around. Again, a spark of hope kindled in my heart.

Jin spoke in Mandarin Chinese for my benefit. "This is Liu Qingwu from New York. He is my...husband."

At her hesitation, I realized that Jin had never told her parents she had gotten married. To their credit, her parents seemed to readily accept this news. Perhaps they didn't think getting married in America was legitimate. I should have brought them presents like a proper son-in-law, like cigarettes from a bodega for her father, perfume from a discount store for her mother. But Jin would have taken one look at these items and known what cheap places they had come from.

Her father said something in Cantonese, and Jin told me, "He insists you stay here as our guest."

I noticed Jin herself was not insisting on anything. She spoke to her parents, then suggested to me that we go take a walk outside, for privacy. As she closed the front door behind her, I heard the door of the apartment opposite hastily *click* shut behind its metal gate. The neighbors were listening in. I had no doubt rumors would be spreading in the building the next day about who Jin's late-night visitor was.

The street outside the apartment building was relatively quiet, but once we rounded the corner, late-night food stalls and vendors selling electronics and cheap clothing sprung up in droves. Jin and I were just another one of the couples weaving among them, enjoying the relative coolness of the night air.

"I'm guessing my sister told you where I was," Jin finally said.

"Don't blame her, she held out for a long time. I had to go to her house in person to get her to talk." I paused. "How are you feeling?" I half-hoped she would reveal to me that her illness was a lie.

She sighed. "I have some good days, some bad days."

"You look the same." But even as I said that, watching her sideways as we walked, I could see a slowness in the way she moved, a new hollowness in the bones of her face. "Are you seeing a doctor?"

"I go to a doctor in my father's village every weekend. He prescribes me some herbs for the week, and my mother brews them. It tastes awful, of course. But maybe it does something."

"Why didn't you tell me you were sick?"

She gave me a half smile. "What good would it do? We didn't have the money for any kind of treatment, Western or Eastern."

"I could have found a better job—"

Jin stilled me with a hand on my arm. "You are fifty years old. How can you start over? Who would hire you?"

"I'd think of something. I am your husband—"

"That has nothing to do with whether you can take care of me. I have to take care of myself. Do you understand that?" She turned her luminous eyes to me, and I had to nod. "Now," she said briskly, indicating that we were not going to talk about her illness any more, "tell me about Hong. How is she doing? How are my nieces?"

When we got back to the apartment, Jin's parents had gone to bed. Jin slept in a small, separate bedroom of her childhood, and I was to sleep on the fake leather couch in the shadow of the enormous television. Jin quickly and efficiently made up the bed, and showed me the concrete-lined bathroom located off the living room. We formally wished each other good night, and I lay in the dark, unable to go to sleep, distracted by the strange sounds of a Chinese city instead of a Queens neighborhood coming through the open windows.

The following day was a Saturday, and Jin's scheduled visit to the village healer. I asked if I could go with her and her father, and she agreed. Her father collected and sold used electronic parts that he transported in his van. He and Jin sat up front in the vehicle, while I clung to the rickety backseat surrounded by broken-down computers, refrigerators, and other appliances I couldn't identify. This was Jin's father's job in retirement; before that he had owned a nearby electronics store. Although I wasn't able to communicate with him directly, given our language barrier, my impression was that he was a practical, hardworking man, the kind a family could depend on.

We drove about two hours from Guangzhou to the outskirts of Taishan, a coastal city in Guangdong Province best known for being where most Cantonese-speaking immigrants in the world come from. Then, instead of entering the city itself, we turned onto a road that wound among palms and banana trees, rice paddies and ponds that reflected the green mountains in the distance. Gradually the road diminished into a muddy track, and we had to park and proceed the rest of the way on foot, picking through pools of water left by a recent storm.

Jin's father's ancestral village was like stepping back two hundred years or more. The gray stone houses with their dark-tiled roofs were virtually deserted, many crumbling into the reddish earth. More than a few had trees growing unchecked in the front yards, or through the walls and roofs. Peering through broken or missing front doors, I could see chickens wandering through the empty rooms.

Once we got closer to what seemed to be the village center, the infrastructure seemed to improve, with electrical wires crisscrossing the path overhead and a few shops selling vegetables.

Motorbikes were parked along the street; apparently they were able to navigate the washed-out roads more easily than cars. It being close to the middle of the day, almost no one was outside in the sunny, humid weather, although I spotted through an open door several people gathered around a television, watching a soccer match.

Through Jin, I asked her father where everyone was.

"It's *xiuxi* time," she replied. Siesta.

"I mean, where are the people who live in this village?"

"Most of them have immigrated to other countries or to larger cities like Guangzhou. Anyone still here is too old or poor to leave."

The healer whom Jin had been seeing ever since she'd arrived seemed to fall into the first type of person. He looked to be about the age of Jin's father, and the two knew each other well. When I was introduced as a family friend, the healer smiled and nodded at me and pumped my hand.

He said something in the local dialect, and Jin unexpectedly laughed.

"What?" I asked.

"He says you're looking somewhat listless and could use one of his tonics."

I was about to retort that I had just flown over half the continent, but desisted. It was nice to hear Jin's laugh again, even if it was at my expense.

Jin's father excused himself to wait outside, or perhaps down the street with the men watching soccer. Jin allowed me to go into the examination room with her, if it could be called that. It was simply a small alcove with a twin bed surrounded by a mosquito net, now drawn back, that she sat on. She waited patiently as the healer felt the sides of her neck, moved her head and limbs this way and that.

"He says everything is the same as last week," she reported. "That's good news."

I did not want to bring down her spirits so I said nothing. But although I knew nothing about medicine, this hardly seemed like a legitimate examination to me.

Jin's father reappeared, and the healer handed him—not Jin, I noticed—a plastic bag filled with what looked like herbs and bark. In return, Jin's father handed him a few crumpled bills—no more than three hundred *yuan*, I guessed, or fifty dollars, but still a lot to pay for what was likely useless. But it was not my place to protest.

"We will have lunch now," Jin told me.

*Where?* I wondered. Not only was it still nap time, but I hadn't seen any place that remotely resembled a restaurant. But Jin's father took us to a sundries store, where an old woman carried out a round folding table and three camp stools and set them up underneath the awning. Within ten minutes she brought out three bowls of dumplings that I had to admit were better than any I'd tasted in Chinatown. The three of us did not say anything to each other but simply slurped away. Then Jin's father leaned back, belched, and said something to Jin.

"He is going to visit the family altar now," she said. "He'll meet us there. Let's go take a walk in the meantime."

"You don't want to pay your respects?"

She shrugged. "I'll be joining them soon enough."

I closed my eyes and swallowed at her macabre comment. When I looked up, I saw her noting my response with sly amusement. I didn't know how she could maintain a sense of humor about her condition. Maybe it was all she could do.

Before we left, her father again pulled out some bills. I wondered if I should offer to pay for lunch, but it seemed pointless compared to what had been spent on Jin's medication.

Her father went in one direction and Jin and I went in another, heading out of town. The path wound through fields in which water buffalo grazed, tails idly switching. Although the heat was oppressive, the green surrounding us gave the illusion of coolness. We crested a hill and faced a landscape dominated in the distance by a mountain that appeared oddly familiar to me. Then I identified it. Although we were several hundred miles south, this was the mountain from my childhood, the mountain from my mind. Here it was, all this time.

Jin searched my face as I stood still, but I was unable to explain my vision to her. I had never thought when, or if, I saw that mountain again, it would be in the company of someone I loved and whom I was about to lose.

"How long are you planning to stay?" she asked, in her usual, blunt way. "I need to let my parents know."

It was only my second day in China, and she was already pushing me away. I had to be honest. "As long as I have the money."

"Where did you get it?"

I told her about Caroline Lowry, how she'd approached me one afternoon at my stall in front of the Metropolitan Museum of Art, how I'd thought she was interested in my work when she was really looking for someone to forge a painting for her.

"She asked you to commit a crime?"

"Well." I hesitated. "I didn't know what she was going to do with the painting. She never told me she was intending to sell it as the real thing, just that she was selling it to a client from Taiwan."

"But what do you think she did?"

"She probably sold it as the actual painting," I admitted.

"You should have asked for more money."

"I wasn't sure if I could do the job."

Jin made an impatient sound. "You've always underestimated yourself. What happens when your money runs out here? What will you do?"

"I'll teach art classes, English classes. I'll help your father with his scrap collection."

The ghost of a smile hovered around her mouth. "He'd like that. But *why* do you want to stay?"

There was no artifice between us anymore. "Because you are here. Because if I can't help you in the way you don't want to be helped, I just want to be here with you. Until the end."

Jin shaded her eyes, looking off into the distance. "It won't be easy."

"I know."

She didn't say anything, just slipped her hand into mine. Turning our backs on the mountain and the landscape beyond, we walked back to her father's village.

# Chapter 13

Although he doesn't like to admit it, Andrew Cantrell is glad he moved from the city out to East Hampton. He especially likes the sympathy he receives from his artist friends, who believe his wife, Naomi, made them set up residence at her family's summer home to get him away from Hazel Lowry. Only he and Hazel know their relationship ended years before, even though they continued to attend gallery openings and other events together. For him, it was good for publicity and kept Naomi on her toes. What Hazel got out of it, he wasn't too sure.

Hazel called him on Friday when he was in the city, staying at the home of his friend Mark Finnegan. She said she wanted to see him out in East Hampton.

*Why not here?* he asked.

*I need somewhere private to speak to you,* was all she said.

He didn't think she needed to go all the way out to the tip of Long Island for privacy, but she insisted that she wanted to get away for the weekend, so he agreed to meet up with her that Saturday night, when he knew Naomi was going to be at a charity event in the city.

He doesn't blame Hazel for wanting to leave the city, as in the summer it's intolerable; the very concrete seems to seep with sweat and other unmentionable fluids. Driving down Sunrise Highway late Saturday afternoon, he wonders how he thrived on it, the long, sticky nights, whether he was in the company of someone else or alone working. He turns off onto a side road, past houses that increase in size and opulence until, almost at the ocean, he pulls into a small lane that leads to a modest farmhouse weathered gray by the salt and wind.

Almost everyone who comes to visit him and Naomi is surprised that this is her family's summer home, left over from the days when it was surrounded by farmland. He remembers the first time he laid eyes on the place, when he was courting Naomi. That is, as much courting as he was able to do with his lack of funds, which Naomi didn't seem to mind. She considered herself a cultured person and him as her entrée into a world where her kind was regarded with suspicion. Later, when they were settled in their quiet, domestic country life, it occurred to him that Naomi looked upon him as her family looked upon their summer home—a bit run-down but worth preserving, if just for the badge of authenticity it bestowed.

Naomi lured him there with the promise of turning the barn, just down the hill from the farmhouse, into a studio. He thought he'd do his greatest work within those walls, but once he ensconced himself there, he found himself uninspired. For most of his career, he'd been extraordinarily lucky, especially compared to some of his friends—like Mark Finnegan, who couldn't convince his dentist to take a painting in lieu of payment for a root canal. By the age of thirty-five Cantrell had a piece in the Museum of Modern Art. Then a few years later he painted *Elegy*, for which a private collector—a woman who'd made her fortune in Texas oil—had offered two million dollars.

Naomi made the connection through her family, and he would have seriously considered the offer, except Hazel wouldn't let him. His refusal to sell had been a humiliation of sorts for Naomi, but he couldn't explain to his wife the real reason he had to listen to Hazel, that Hazel had told him *under no circumstances* could he sell this painting.

Instead, he told the private collector that his work was worth more than two million dollars, and the art world took notice. The media attention culminated in a splashy photo spread for *Life* magazine, which impressed Naomi and did much to alleviate her resentment toward him. She spent days preparing for the photographer, rearranging the furniture at proper angles, accentuating the rustic charms of the place with carefully chosen antiques. She unearthed a tea set from somewhere, and he had to laugh at the resultant photo of her carrying it while wearing an apron, as if she were an ordinary housewife. Which was, he suspected, exactly the image she wanted to present—the wife of an artist who had once painted a work someone thought was worth two million dollars, even though she herself was worth much more than that in family money, and without her he was worth nothing.

Naomi had known about Hazel from the beginning. She orchestrated overly theatrical moves like hiring a private detective or barging in on him and Hazel at a restaurant and slapping Hazel in the face. Privately, he thought Naomi loved the drama; this was part of what she had signed up for by marrying so beneath her. Hazel, too, made the best of the negative attention and turned it into publicity for her gallery and his work.

Then, on a rainy day about a month before he painted *Elegy*, Hazel confronted him in his studio, which was located around the block from his and Naomi's apartment in the East Village. The humidity had turned her red hair into a frizzy aureole around her face, reminding him of a painting by Gustav Klimt, the one entitled *Hope*. He was admiring the effect of her silhouette against the light when Hazel told him she was pregnant.

*Well?* she asked, and he realized he was taking too long to answer.

*Please, sit down.* He hastened to clear a chair for her.

*Do I look like I need to sit down? I'm not that pregnant yet,* she snapped.

*So what are you going to do?* he asked, at a loss for what to say.

*It depends on Naomi.* Hazel wavered for a moment, as if she was going to take the chair he'd offered her, but then she straightened her spine. *I want you to leave her.*

*I can't do that.* It was an automatic response, and she knew it.

*You've never tried. In all these years I've never asked you for anything, but I'm asking you now.* The look on her face was almost stern, and he knew this was the closest she would come to pleading with him.

*I'll speak to her,* was all he could say.

After she left, he turned his attention back to the painting he was working on, but his concentration was shot. Instead he looked out the grimy window of his studio to the uninspiring view of an air shaft through which dim sunlight and the faint cooing of pigeons streamed. What would a life with Hazel be like? Would they run the gallery together, would he be free to pursue his work? And there would be a child. He had almost forgotten that part.

In the end, Naomi made the decision very easy for him. *You leave me for that woman,* she said, *and my family will hire the best lawyer in town to make sure you don't get a cent. Furthermore, your work will never be shown in New York City again.*

Except at the Lowry Gallery, he wanted to point out, but one gallery wouldn't be enough to sustain his career. Naomi was right. If he left her, doors would be closed and he'd end up like so many of his friends: unappreciated, uncompensated, and unremembered.

When he told Hazel his decision, something in her eyes shut

down and shut him out forever. He didn't ask her what she planned to do about the pregnancy, and forced himself not to think about it until one night at the dinner table Naomi casually informed him that her private investigator had spotted Hazel at a certain doctor's office in New Jersey, a doctor known for performing illegal operations. That was almost enough to make him walk out on her, but he swallowed his anger along with his meal.

Later, he left the apartment and went around the corner to his studio, where he began to paint *Elegy*. The gray background reminiscent of the sky just before the rain started falling, back home in Iowa. The white blur in the center the sun shining through. On the back, in the bottom right hand corner, almost hidden where the canvas overlapped, he wrote a dedication: "For H.L." By this time Hazel was refusing to talk to him, so he showed the dedication to a young female reporter from a downtown magazine called *Artsbeat*. Predictably, the reporter, who seemed more interested in his relationship with Hazel than the painting itself, gushed about the dedication in her article. He knew Hazel read everything that was written about him.

Of course, Hazel wasn't the only person who knew about the dedication. Naomi found out, as well, and arranged for the sale of the painting. When she found out he had refused the offer, as if relenting, Hazel invited him to exhibit *Elegy* at her gallery. The night of the opening, no one could tell their relationship was over. Eventually, they stopped going around together, their names were no longer coupled in the tabloids, and after a few years no one in the art world or outside of it seemed to care. It didn't help that he was unable to come up with any new work, and that the more desperate he was to produce something, the less able he was to paint. He felt cursed by Hazel, by Naomi, by every choice that had led him to this salt-stained place.

\* \* \*

When he enters the barn that is his studio, Hazel is already there.

*How did you get in?* he demands. He usually keeps his studio locked, less out of fear that anything would get stolen, but that someone would be able to see he hasn't produced a work of value since he's been there. Even Naomi isn't allowed to enter; she just places the tray with his lunch outside the door every day, and he waits until her footsteps fade away before opening the door.

*Locked doors are easy to open if you know how,* Hazel replies with a lazy smile that he's never seen before. Indeed, he keeps a spare key underneath a loose flagstone by the studio's front door, so she's either been lucky at guessing the hiding place or she knows how to pick locks—he wouldn't put the second past her.

*What do you want?* he asks, more curtly than he intends. *What's so important that you couldn't tell me in the city but had to come way out here?*

*Where's Naomi?* She neatly sidesteps the question.

*She's at a charity dinner for the City Opera. She won't be back home tonight.*

*Good.* Hazel says it in a way that some would take as suggestive, but he knows better. He isn't sure she's thought that way about him in years. Ever since...

Maybe Naomi's private investigator was wrong. Maybe it wasn't Hazel who was spotted at the doctor's office in New Jersey. Or Hazel went there, but she changed her mind. Their son would be five years old now (of course, he thought it was a boy). He almost expects her to be hiding the child somewhere in the studio, behind the blank canvases that she's walking toward now.

An unaccustomed hope surges in him, only to subside when Hazel stops in front of *Elegy,* which he should have put in storage for safekeeping but instead keeps in his studio.

*That was your last great work,* she observes.

*How do you know?*

She gestures at the space around her, evidence of paintings he's started and failed to finish, or failed to start at all.

*You're right,* he admits, thinking to elicit a confession from her in return. *I haven't been able to work since we came out here.*

*Don't expect me to feel sorry for you.*

Hazel puts a hand out to *Elegy,* traces the surface of the painting as if she's trying to remember the way something felt.

*I want you to give me this painting. You dedicated it to me. I deserve it, after what you took from me,* she says, and the last glimmer that there is still a child after all is extinguished.

*Are you going to try to sell it?* he asks. *Do you need the money? Is the gallery in trouble? Because I can get you the money.*

*You mean, you can get it from Naomi,* she sneers. *It isn't about the money. I just want what's due me.*

True, she was part of the inspiration for the painting, but he bristles at the idea that she has any ownership over it, as if it's akin to ownership of him.

*You can't have it,* he says. *As you said yourself, this is my last great work.* He tries to lighten his words, for his sake as well as her own. *I can will it to you after my death, if that makes any difference.*

She fixes him with an exasperated look. *That's the best you can do?*

He figures he should do his old friend a favor. *If you want to invest in something, invest in Mark Finnegan's work. He'll be worth something someday.*

Hazel nods, in acceptance of his advice or his decision not to give her the painting, he doesn't know. Just as she did when she visited him in his East Village studio nearly six years before, she doesn't beg. But this time her tone has more rancor.

*Keep it. You'll need the money yourself when Naomi leaves you, after she realizes what a fraud you are. An artist who can't paint anymore. That is, if you find someone who'll buy it.*

*Hazel,* he says gently. *I think you should go now.*

After she leaves, the sound of her car's motor disappearing down the driveway, he tries to forget her final words to him. He wants to chalk them up to the bitterness of an aging woman who has lost so much in choosing to be with him—a husband, a child—but he knows that's a cliché. Hazel is more complicated than that. And there is some truth to what she said. What good is an artist who lacks the ability to create something original? Hell, at this point he'd settle for creating a reproduction.

Maybe he should go back to the basics and copy one of the Old Masters, like Rembrandt, who painted by candlelight. He assembles the necessary materials, pours himself a strong drink, and extinguishes the overhead lamps. He looks at the blank canvas in front of him. The light from the single candle makes a perfect oblong in its center, flickering with possibilities. But it isn't long before his head starts to droop from fatigue and alcohol, and he begins to dream.

In his dream, he's meeting Hazel for the first time at her gallery. He's walking up behind her, this vision in a white-and-gold dress. He can't resist reaching out to touch the curve of her back, even with the knowledge that he's only been married for a month, and that an affair might very well destroy him. Still he reaches out, and there's a brief moment when she turns around, and he basks in the glow of her smile, before it bursts into flames.

# Acknowledgments

I'd like to thank the following people:

Esi Sogah, Karen Auerbach, and the entire team at Kensington, for their hard work.

Deborah Schneider, for her support.

Kay Kim, Zoraya Nambi, and Harpreet Kaur Sandhu, for their friendship.

James Lee, Claire Lee, and Lydia Lee, for being part of my family.

Neil Gladstone, for making me laugh every day.

And Spencer Lee Gladstone, for making me a better person.

# THE ART OF CONFIDENCE

## Wendy Lee

## ABOUT THIS GUIDE

The suggested questions are included
to enhance your group's reading of
Wendy Lee's *The Art of Confidence*.

# DISCUSSION QUESTIONS

1. What are the reasons Liu decides to forge *Elegy*, even if he suspects he's committing a crime? How has his life in America not turned out the way he expected it to be?

2. In what ways does Caroline take on aspects of her aunt Hazel's life? What has been lacking in her own life that makes her want to emulate Hazel?

3. Why does Molly help her roommate, Kimi, in breaching school policy? How much is she responsible for Kimi's actions?

4. How has Harold's life been determined for him by his family upbringing and the culture in which he lives? Has he been able to make any decisions for himself?

5. Molly turns down a group art show because she doesn't feel like she's ready. Do you think she made the right decision? What would you have done in her place?

6. Why does Harold decide to keep the painting, even though he knows it's a fake? What meaning does it have for him?

7. Do you find Caroline a sympathetic character? Do you feel she deserves to lose her aunt's gallery, or for her forgery scheme to be exposed? Why or why not?

8. Why is Liu obsessed with painting a certain mountain from his memory? What does he learn about life from his wife's fate?

9. Hazel asks Andrew to give her *Elegy* because she feels he owes it to her. Does a work of art ever belong in part to the person who inspired it? Or does it solely belong to the creator?

10. What and who determines the worth of art? Why do you think people are willing to pay hundreds of millions of dollars for one painting? If you could afford it, is there a painting you would be willing to pay millions of dollars for? Which one, and why?